Film Crews
and
Rendezvous

Film Crews and Rendezvous

A
JULES KEENE
GLAMPING MYSTERY

Heather Weidner

To Stan,
thanks for all the love and support and for joining me on this writing journey!

Praise for the Jules Keene Glamping Mysteries

"In *Vintage Trailers and Blackmailers*, the calm of Jules Keene's Blue Ridge Mountain camper resort is disturbed when a man's lifeless body is found in the woods. What follows is a cozy mystery full of blackmail, secrets, mysterious strangers—and handsome security guy, Jake Evans. Jules and her loyal pup Bijou are in for a suspense-filled adventure. I love the warm and friendly characters and the twists and turns in this new down-home, mutt-loving series."—Susan Van Kirk, Author of The Endurance Mysteries and *A Death at Tippitt Pond*

"Jules Keene is focused on her vintage trailer camping resort, but when a dead guest is discovered in the woods and her aunt is questioned, Jules decides to help catch the killer. She must stop the culprit, keep her guests satisfied, grow her business, run for president of the town's business council, and stay alive when the bad guys come after her. This book is a joy to read."—Jackie Layton, Author of the Low Country Dog Walker Mysteries

"Packed with action and filled with "Oh, man, I didn't see THAT coming" moments, this first installment in the Jules Keene Glamping Mysteries series will not disappoint. And Weidner made glamping sound so glamorous that I think I'll take my husband up on his suggestion to go camping…but only if it's Fern Valley Camping Resort style!"—Jayne Ormerod, Author of *Goin' Coastal*

"Smart and persistent businesswoman Jules Keene puts on her amateur sleuth hat to track down murderers at the upscale Fern Valley Camping Resort, set in the beautiful Blue Ridge mountains. The bad guys have met their match in this fast-paced mystery."—Frances Aylor, Author of *Money Grab*

"Heather Weidner's *Vintage Trailers and Blackmailers* is an exciting addition to this year's cozy mystery line-up. Fern Valley Camping Resort, with its refurbished vintage trailers and tiny houses, is as enjoyable as can be, but don't be fooled, this book is all excitement. I don't know how she combines charm with a fast-paced story but I'm so glad she did."—Lane Stone, Author of the Pet Palace Mysteries and the Tiara Investigations Mysteries

"I love the premise of this well-written and light-hearted whodunit where we meet Jules Keene, who owns a camping resort where murder does not mix with vintage trailers...From the introduction of the characters to the small-town atmosphere to the vintage trailer camp to the victim to the events leading up to his death and the killer's identity and apprehension, the author did a great job in presenting this well-crafted mystery that kept me immersed in all aspects...I look forward to more adventures with Jules and her friend in this delightfully entertaining series."—Dru Ann Love, Dru's Book Musings

Chapter One

Monday

Jules Keene's phone buzzed as she clipped the leash on Bijou, her Jack Russell Terrier. Another text from someone in town who just had to be an extra for the filming at her resort. Ignoring the latest request, she headed across the grassy area to the office.

Hollywood had arrived in Fern Valley, and Jules wasn't sure the one-stoplight town would be the same. She had had to keep all the location scouting a secret, and that was difficult with the town's active gossip grapevine. Now, everyone seemed to be plotting ways to get close to the action.

Jules enjoyed the calm walk across the resort before her day started. With all the arrivals this week, the peacefulness would not last long. Normally, the Fern Valley Luxury Camping Resort was a place for visitors looking for solitude in refurbished, vintage trailers stocked with posh amenities. Recently, the resort had been a hive of activity as crews turned it into ground zero for the on-location filming in the Blue Ridge Mountains of Virginia.

Bijou took off after a butterfly, and when she got bored with the insect, she checked out all the new smells since the day before. The terrier bounded up the wooden steps, where she waited patiently for Jules to open the screen door to the resort's office and store.

The summer season had ended Labor Day weekend, but this year, the film crew for *Fatal Impressions*, a cult classic for streaming TV fans, had rented the resort for two months to do location shots in a small town. Jules, excited to have the opportunity to extend the season, had been inundated daily with requests from friends and townsfolk who knew they had talents that the casting director had to see.

A screeching voice echoed through the resort's store, interrupting Jules's quiet morning. "I thought I told you I didn't want to be disturbed before ten. What kind of place is this?" Sorbonne, the show's head writer, pounded her fist on the counter and shook her head.

Bijou hurdled into the store with an overabundance of energy.

Sorbonne, an overly thin woman with a jet-black bob, whipped around. The jagged points of hair on each side of her face sprang forward. She pointed her blood-red fingernail at Bijou and screamed, "What is that?" When Bijou darted forward for a pat, Sorbonne's face turned the same color as her nails, and the vein on the side of her sinewy neck bulged.

Jules tugged lightly on the leash, and Bijou sat. Neither were sure what to make of the woman who waved her arms and ranted.

"Who allows animals in a place of business?" Sorbonne pointed at the dog and then at Jules's aunt, Roxanne Mallory, who leaned one elbow on the front counter.

Surprised that her aunt had not responded with her usual sassiness, Jules said, "That's Bijou. She works here." She led the Jack Russell Terrier to her office, unclicked her leash, and closed the bottom portion of the Dutch door to keep Bijou out of the fray.

"First all the noise and now this. I'm going to have to be moved to other accommodations if this keeps up. Rod is going to hear about this. I have to be able to work. I am critical to this production." She spun on her four-inch stilettos and stomped toward the door.

"Ms., uh," Jules said to her back.

"It's Sorbonne. Just Sorbonne. And I want this rectified now. I want quiet or new accommodations. And I'm still going to let Rod, the producer, know. He'll be interested in how I was treated at this place." She looked down her pointed nose and made a face like she had licked a lemon.

"What disturbed you? Our goal is for you to enjoy your stay in Fern Valley,"

Jules said.

"She'll tell you." Sorbonne wagged her daggered fingernail at Roxanne. "And it better not happen again." The show's writer stormed out the door, slamming it hard enough to make it rattle for several seconds in her wake.

A pained look crossed Roxanne's face. "Sorbet blew in here complaining of excessive noise in the early hours of the morning. She's in the Beatrix Potter tiny house. It seems Jake stopped by to do some work on the new house going up next to it, and it woke her up. At ten-thirty."

Last summer, Jules added tiny houses to the resort's offering with the help of her maintenance/security guy, Jake Evans. Each tiny space was themed for a different author and came with a cozy reading nook. The houses ranged from about four hundred square feet to larger, modular models with lofts and upstairs. These let guests try out tiny house living and also served as model homes for Jake's side business.

Roxanne rolled her eyes. "I thought these movie folks started work early. I saw a lot of activity when I got here at eight."

Jules tried to stifle a grin. "She must keep different hours than the crew. I'll talk to Jake."

"About what?" Jake Evans asked as he came in through the back door. He picked up Bijou, carried her into the store, and kissed her on the head.

"It seems you woke up one of our fussy guests." Roxanne added an extended pause between each word and returned to straightening the flyers on the front counter.

"I waited until ten. It just needed a few touch-ups. My buddies helped me move the Baum tiny house in place yesterday at dinner time." Jake made a beeline for the coffee maker.

"I love the ruby red door on that one," Roxanne yelled behind him.

"All I have left to do is the hookups and install the lattice work around the bottom to cover up the crawlspace and the cement trailer pad. I didn't think I made any noise. I was trying to get it ready in case you needed the extra space," Jake said from the back room.

"It wasn't you, Jake. She's a temperamental writer if you ask me," Roxanne said. "That's the third time she's been in here since she checked in. The first time she was appalled that we didn't have room-darkening shades in the Potter house. Then she wanted to know where she could get a case of her designer mineral water since no stores in town stocked it. Oh, and I forgot her request for lightbulbs that give off Vitamin D. It seems our regular bulbs are substandard."

"We need to be patient. They're bringing a lot of business to the valley and lots of media attention. Let's be as helpful as we can," Jules added.

Roxanne put on a half-smile and did a fake clutch of her pearl necklace in her best southern drawl. "Customer service is my middle name." She winked at her niece and busied herself at the reservation desk.

"I'm going to check on things and leave Bijou in the back if you're going to be here for a little while," Jules said.

"She'll be fine. I'll sic her on Ms. Sauvignon if she comes back. Some people." Roxanne shrugged her shoulder and flipped through a magazine at the front counter. "And don't forget to wear your lanyard with your credentials. I hear their security teams are working hard to keep the riffraff off the property. Lester got stopped over near the barn this morning."

Jules held up her lanyard with the show's logo on it. She cut through her office and headed to the golf cart parked under the carport at the back of the store. Hopefully, Lester and the rest of her team could do their work without bumping into the film crew.

Jake followed his boss. He shut the door and touched her shoulder as she descended the steps.

"I'll figure out a way to finish the Baum house during daylight hours. It shouldn't take me that long."

Jules turned and faced him. "I appreciate it. Sorbonne seems to be easily disturbed."

"It must be a Left Coast thing," he said, drawing her closer and kissing her. He folded her in his arms.

She returned the kiss and pulled away, staring into his jade-green eyes. "I thought we agreed to keep this under the radar," she whispered.

"Embarrassed?" Jake pushed his longish brown bangs out of his face.

"You know that's not it, but I'm a little concerned about how an employer-employee relationship looks."

"Then I quit. Problem solved."

Jules's jaw dropped. She could feel the flush cross her cheeks.

"I know. You need me. I wouldn't let you down." Jake grinned.

"Dinner tonight?" she asked, smiling back and giving him a quick peck on his lightly stubbled cheek.

"You cooking?"

"Spaghetti okay? I need to catch up on the earlier seasons of *Fatal Impressions*. I think I'm the only one in Fern Valley who hasn't seen all of the first three seasons."

Jake rushed down the steps. "See you around six."

"Wanna lift?" Jules slid into the golf cart's front seat.

"Wouldn't want folks to talk." Jake winked and trotted off toward the barn.

Jules put the cart in gear and drove toward the lodge, the resort's social hall. Jules's mother-daughter team of Mel and Crystal Carson usually served guests breakfast, but the film crew had brought their own caterers to provide craft services for all meals and snacks. For the duration of the filming, they handled the cleaning and turn-down services.

She drove past the red barn and waved to her groundskeeper, Lester Branch. Tinkering with the tractor, he saluted in return and held up his lanyard. Lester had been part of the resort's crew since she was in elementary school. He, like Jake, lived in one of the tiny cabins near the barn.

Jules's parents had bought the campground, west of Charlottesville, Virginia, in the seventies, and she and her father spent the last few years of his life refurbishing and upcycling the vintage trailers at the beginning of the glamping craze. The vintage trailers were a hit with folks looking for an interesting getaway, and the tiny houses offered more choices.

Jules ducked into the cut-through from the woods to the meadow, the open area reserved for tents and camper hookups. The film crew had parked buses, small vans, catering trucks, and tractor-trailers in the meadow. One of the large trucks, a vehicle carrier, housed cars, and other big things to be used as props in the show. Not seeing anything unusual, she headed back and drove around the vintage campers. By the end of the week, all the trailers would be filled.

She made a loop and headed to the village of tiny houses, the newest addition to the resort. The previous summer, Jules and Jake had formed a partnership to explore interest in cozy accommodations loaded with luxurious amenities and a variety of books. So far, the demand had been good. She used her degree in interior design to decorate the small spaces with lots of surprises, like reading nooks and a revolving bookcase for her guests. Two were available for use, and the third would be open for business if he could finish it without offending Sorbonne.

The film crew had taken over about every square foot of the resort. The grassy field near the tiny homes, which was normally used as space for camper hookups, was now a parking spot for the support trailers for costumes, props, makeup, and anything else they needed for the production. It was nice to have a guaranteed full house for several months.

All quiet on this side. As Jules turned the cart to leave, Kat Mason exited Sorbonne's tiny house with a black leather case and an oversized nylon bag.

"Hey, Jules." Kat waved and sauntered over to the cart. The slender woman's height was accentuated by her long, black coat and leather boots with spiked heels.

"How are you? Getting settled in?" Jules asked.

"I love it here. It's like we have a three-sixty view of the mountains from anywhere at your resort. I bet it's gorgeous here when the leaves turn." Kat flipped her long, highlighted curls with a flick of her wrist.

"Autumn puts on a great show here in the mountains. It should start soon and last until October."

"Oh, good. We should get to see autumn in the mountains." Kat slung what looked like a gym bag over her shoulder.

"Need a ride?"

"No, thanks. I'm heading back to the makeup trailer. Sorbonne had a hair emergency."

Jules raised her eyebrows almost to her bangs.

"She likes her bob to have distinct lines, and the sides were a little too long for her taste. I usually do touch-ups for her once a week."

Jules nodded.

Kat angled her head, studying Jules. "Your red hair is gorgeous, you know. So many women would kill for such long curls. It's quiet now that filming hasn't started. Stop by the trailer tomorrow, and I'll help you pick out the best makeup for your complexion."

"Sounds fun. Thank you," Jules said.

"Plus, it'll give us time to chat. I want to know all about Fern Valley. I like the quaintness. I'm sure there are some cool must-see spots in the area," Kat said.

"I'll pop by tomorrow morning."

"See you then." Kat waved and headed toward the oversized RVs parked in neat rows in the grassy area behind the vintage trailers.

Jules did one more lap around the vintage trailers before heading back to the office to check emails and return messages. If she could wade through all the requests about the filming and casting calls for extras, maybe she could get some resort work done.

Chapter Two

Tuesday

Jules punched in the security code at the back door as Bijou danced at her feet. She barely got the door open before the dog scrambled up the steps in search of Roxanne and her desk drawer full of treats.

A squeal echoed from the store. Jules unleashed Bijou and stepped through the doorway to the office, pulling the door shut behind her.

Emily Owens, a diminutive teen who worked part-time at the resort, held her phone up for Roxanne to see and squealed again. "I can't believe it. I just can't believe it. I think I'm going to pass out." She waved her phone in front of her and did a happy jig. "This is too amazing!"

"Are you okay?" Jules asked, looking at Emily and then her aunt.

"It's better than okay. This is the best day of my life. Everything is awesome! You'll never guess who came in the store." Emily beamed.

Before Jules could respond, the teen blurted, "Chavis Ratner. And I sold him some gum. He said spearmint was his favorite." She sank onto the stool behind the counter and stared at her phone. "He has the deepest blue eyes. He touched my hand. And he told me to keep the change." Emily looked at her hand and back at her phone. "My life is never going to be the same."

"He took selfies with both of us." Roxanne held up her phone for Jules to see. It was clearly her aunt, decked out in an aqua cardigan, pearls, and black leggings, hugging the blond actor. Chavis Ratner reminded Jules of a young Val Kilmer.

"My friends are going to die when I tell them," Emily said, not looking up from her phone. "I'll remember this day forever. Oh, Jules, I swapped out the dollar in the cash drawer because I wanted to keep the one he handed me."

Jules smiled. The star-sightings had begun.

Roxanne chimed in. "We've had fifty-two requests for accommodations this week from all over the country. People must have found out that they're filming here. Too bad we're booked solid. Maybe afterward, you could market our little resort as the location where the filming took place. You know, like one of those movie-location tour thingies. I went on one in Savannah one time for *Midnight in the Garden of Good and Evil*," Roxanne said as she posted her picture with Chavis on Instagram.

Jules headed toward the coffee machine to kickstart her workday. Her lips turned up in a grin. It was going to be an interesting autumn with everyone in town, and now even her staff, starstruck.

No sooner had Jules settled in at her desk than she heard the screen door slam.

"Okay, I've had it with this back-water, podunk place. There is no Wi-Fi in my house. What year is this? I don't know how I'm supposed to work in this environment. I've got edits to do for Rod, and this is unacceptable. I have to be connected. This is like a third-world country," Sorbonne yelled. "I expect you to rectify this now!"

Jules stepped through the doorway. "There's internet and cable in the Potter house. Is the power out?"

Wearing her designer jeans and a clingy wrap-around red blouse, Sorbonne tapped her matching stilettos on the wooden floor. "Well? What are you going to do about it?" She glared at Jules.

"The password is on a card on the counter. Did you select the network?" Jules asked as the woman continued to tap her foot to a beat that sounded like a metronome.

The woman stared daggers at Jules. "I must have missed it," the writer said, turning her head. "Oh, and before I forget. Tell that old geezer to stop weed-whacking near my room so early in the morning. The noise was unbearable. He woke me up today. Who wants to hear that constant buzzing?"

Jules glanced at her Fitbit. Ten-thirty. "I'll be sure to let Lester know to alter his morning routine."

Sorbonne turned on her heels and stomped out, slamming the door. The hinge rattle echoed through the store.

Roxanne straightened the pamphlets on the counter. "It seems Cinnabon is hard to please. I'll tell the guys not to breathe around her tiny house until after lunch."

Jules stifled a giggle. "I keep reminding myself this is good for the resort and the town. If she's the worst part of it, we'll be fine. I'm going to go see Kat and find out how things are going in the RVs. I'll be back before Bijou notices I'm gone."

"We'll be fine," Roxanne said. "I'm having lunch with Matt in town, so I'll be heading out in a little while, too. Emily will be here, though."

"Tell Sheriff Hobbs I said hello." Jules smiled. Her aunt had been dating the sheriff since they'd found one of the resort's long-term guests dead in the nearby woods. Sheriff Hobbs had spent a lot of time investigating at the resort, and while they had known each other for years, something had clicked for them last summer. Jules was happy for Roxanne. She'd been single since her husband's death almost twenty-five years ago.

Jules stepped out onto the wooden front porch to soak in the view of the mountains. Autumn was her favorite time in the valley. The trees put on a fantastic show that drew people from all over the East Coast. She walked across the field past the vintage trailers and her cabin to where the RVs and trucks sat in the field. She wandered up and down several rows before she spotted Kat and a man sitting in lawn chairs outside of a tan and brown RV.

"Hey, Jules," Kat waved. "It's good to see you. This is Jayden Diamond. He's one of our makeup artists extraordinaire."

"It's nice to meet you. I hope y'all are all settled in," Jules said.

"It's great here. When we get some time off this weekend, I'm going to hike up to the waterfall," he said. "I love that there are so many places to explore."

"Enjoy. We're supposed to have good weather through the weekend. If you all are around in the evening, we have fire pits for campfires and s'mores."

"Sounds adorable," Kat said. "Why don't you come in."

"She's got great hair," Jayden said. "I'd do soft curls everywhere with a lot of pinks and browns in her makeup."

"You can play dress-up with her tomorrow. We girls are going to have a chat. Ciao," Kat said with a wink.

Jayden lit a cigarette as the women climbed the metal stairs to the RV. Inside looked like a beauty salon with pedestal chairs, three wash stations, and a wall of mirrors. Brushes and makeup kits covered every available flat space on the top of the black cabinets.

"Sit here." Kat patted the black chair. She plugged in a curling iron with an oversized barrel. "How long have you lived here?"

"All my life. My parents bought the campground before I was born. I went away to college, got married, but I moved back after my divorce from the Idiot. Best thing that could have happened to me. I missed the mountains. This has always been home."

"It's pretty here." Kat curled Jules's hair and bangs and used a thin comb to fluff the top.

"Rod said that folks would be arriving at different times this week, but everyone should be here by Thursday," Jules said.

"Most of the crew and the folks in charge are here now. The actors are trickling in as usual. Chavis Ratner is here. Kayleigh Bell and Derek Stone are flying in tomorrow. I haven't heard anything about Ashe Lyons or Zoe Marshall."

"So, how long have you been involved with *Fatal Impressions?*" Jules stole a peek at her big hair in the wall of mirrors that lined the front and back of the trailer.

"This is the fourth season. I've been here since the beginning. They typically film a new season about every two years. All of the characters from the beginning are still around except for Betsy Taylor. They killed her off at the end of the first episode of the first season. We always joke about how unfair that was for her residuals. She wasn't even on the scene when the show became such a hit."

"So, what do you do between shoots?" Jules asked as Kat twirled the chair around.

"Close your eyes. I'm going to use the airbrush for your foundation. You'll feel a light spray. Just close your eyes and mouth. It won't take long."

Jules tried to sit still while Kat applied the foundation. The cool mist tickled.

"Okay, all done. You can open your eyes." She rummaged through a drawer for an eyeliner. She outlined Jules's eyes with a kohl pencil. "Look up. I work on other productions when we're on hiatus from the show. I did a couple of soap operas through the years. And my friend Dayvon has a studio in Los Angeles, and he lets me work there if I'm between gigs."

"Who was the most interesting person you ever worked on?"

"Sean Connery."

"You did James Bond's makeup?" Jules's eyes widened.

"Several times. He was as lovely in person as he was on the silver screen," Kat said, applying eye shadow and blending the colors. "I'm almost done. Hold your mouth still. I want to outline your lips."

"What do you like about these location gigs?"

"It's fun to see the country. I was gonna say that I liked working with new groups, but I've been on this assignment with this team so long that I know everyone and their quirks. Plus, I'm like a bartender. People tell me everything when they're in my chair."

"I've met Rod, the producer, and Paul. He's the director, right?" Kat nodded, and Jules continued, "Chavis Ratner came by the office today, much to the delight of my staff. I've met some of the crew, you, and Sorbonne."

"Ah, yes, Sorbonne. She's the head writer, but if you ask her, she's in charge of this entire production and everyone in it. She has an opinion about everything."

"She seemed annoyed today," Jules said as Kat created a blush storm with an oversized brush.

"That's a nice way of saying it. She's usually a holy terror. We all think she has some kind of dirt on Rod, Paul, or Eric Renfield, our executive producer. There has to be a reason they keep bringing her back season after season. I do her hair to stay in her good graces and to get an idea of what she happens to be railing about at the particular moment. She has Rod's ear or something," Kat said with a wink. "I don't need her bad-mouthing me…Looking good, Jules. I hope you have someone to call for a date tonight. You're ready for a night on the town."

Jules smiled. "Sounds like a plan."

"Take a look. What do you think?" The stylist whirled the chair around, and Jules stared at the finished product.

She leaned closer, inspecting herself. "Wow." She hadn't been this dolled up since her wedding day. Maybe Jake would like to head into town tonight. She'd have to swing by the barn to see if he noticed her new look. "Thanks so much. I need you here every day."

"You look like a million bucks."

"Stop by the office if I can help with anything." Jules stepped outside and blinked as her eyes adjusted to the bright sunshine. The perfect autumn weather tugged at her to stay outside, but she needed to check on things at the office.

At the office's back door, she reached for her phone. Not finding it, she checked all her pockets. She turned and jogged back to Kat's work trailer.

She climbed the metal steps. Jules heard voices and paused. The low tones stopped. Jules waited. When she didn't hear anything, she tapped on the door.

A male voice said, "Come in if you dare."

"Kat, hey Kat. Did I leave my phone?" Jules asked, sticking her head inside.

Kat pulled away from an embrace and tapped the guy on the shoulder. She turned her head and stared at Jules. "What?"

"I didn't mean to interrupt. I can't find my phone, and I wanted to see if it was here."

Chavis Ratner turned. "I don't see it. Sorry. And as you can see, I'm working here."

Jules hoped her face didn't reveal her surprise. "Sorry to bother you."

"Shut the door behind you, would you?" Chavis asked as he turned toward

Kat and pulled her closer to him.

That was interesting. Kat neglected to mention a thing with Chavis Ratner. Maybe it's one of the perks of this job.

Jules walked back to the office. When she traipsed through the store, her aunt let out a low whistle. "Look at you. Gotta hot date or a photo shoot?"

"Something like that. You're still here? I thought you had a lunch date."

"Had is the operative word. Sheriff Matt got called out on a case. Marshall Pierce's car was stolen early this morning, and he had to walk all the way home from Red's Honky-tonk. It seems he woke up and remembered to call the police about his car. Matt and I'll catch up later when he's not on duty."

Jules nodded. "You haven't seen my phone, have you?"

"You left it on the counter. I put it on your desk."

"Whew. I panicked when I couldn't find it. Anything I should know about before I head home for an early lunch?"

"Nope. Everything is under control here. I haven't heard from Cinnabon anymore, so I guess she settled down and decided to do some work."

Jules cracked a smile. "Good to hear. Bijou and I'll be back later. Call me if you need me."

"I've got it covered. And I can handle Sorbonne if I need to," her aunt rolled her eyes and flexed her arm muscles.

"I know you can, but we want the crew to have a wonderful time and spend money in town. Let's do our best to make their stay memorable. I was hoping this would be a profitable occasion for the business council members."

"Uh-huh." Roxanne picked up a magazine. "It'll be a big draw for our town this fall. Probably higher than we imagined with the show's fan base."

Jules and Bijou slipped out the back door. On the way to the barn, Bijou wanted to sniff every blade of grass. The dog's ears perked up when she heard whistling. The terrier transformed into a bundle of excitement and tugged on her lead.

"Hey, there," Jake said, bending down to pet Bijou, who licked his face. "What brings you out to the barn?" He stood up and looked at Jules, and let out a wolf whistle. "Hey there to you, too. You're looking mighty fine this morning. Got a date?"

"I hope so. Dinner in town? My treat."

"Sure. If my boss lets me off in time." Jake's grin showed his dimples.

"I think I can convince her. How about Pop's Diner? I could go for a burger."

"Perfect. I'll come and get you around six," he said.

Jules winked and walked outside toward her cabin. "Deal."

After burgers and onion rings in a quiet corner of Pop's Diner, a 1950s-style restaurant that had been a fixture in Fern Valley for decades, Jake pulled up in front of Jules's cabin. One goodnight kiss turned into another and another. Then after making sure she made it safely inside, he roared off in his Mustang to the other side of the barn.

Bijou greeted Jules at the door like she had not seen her in ages.

"Come on, puppy. Let's go for a walk." Jules clicked the dog's leash in place, and the terrier dashed outside, ready for an evening adventure. The pair walked around the cabin near the fence that bordered the area between the tiny houses and the pop-up RV lot. Bijou was in no hurry to go home. Yellow lights glowed from some of the trailers' windows. No one except Jules and Bijou moved around outside in the crisp autumn air.

The Jack Russell led the way to the neighborhood of tiny houses. Only the Beatrix Potter one had the porch and interior lights on. Jules tugged on Bijou's leash to get her to head back toward the cabin when she noticed movement in the front room of Sorbonne's house. Bijou sniffed the grass at her feet. Two people appeared in the front room, and Jules's breath caught in her throat. Sorbonne, wearing a bright orange kimono, was wrapped in an embrace with the much younger Chavis Ratner. And not in a casual, friendly embrace. No, it was a rumpled-clothes kind of hug.

The pair groped and kissed for a few moments. As Jules turned around to pick up Bijou for a quiet exit, Chavis tossed open the door and jogged down the three steps. Jules stepped back into the shadows. He ran his fingers through his blond hair to fluff it back to its normal hipster style. Chavis crossed the grassy area and disappeared down one of the rows of

RVs. Sorbonne watched from the front window for a few moments and then disappeared inside her tiny house.

Jules walked home with Bijou by her side. "Lots of action and drama in Fern Valley and the filming hadn't even started yet," she whispered to the dog.

Chapter Three

Wednesday

Jules woke up to a buzzing that would not stop. She shook off the fuzziness left over from a deep sleep and grabbed her phone. 1:30. Phone calls at this hour were never good.

"Hey, Boss. Sorry to wake you up. I found something you really need to see right now at the Baum house. We're going to need the sheriff," Jake said.

Jules's pulse raced, and she bolted out of bed. "Do we need an ambulance?"

"No, no rush. Just get here when you can," he said, slightly out of breath.

"Okay, be there in a few," she said, disconnecting. She found a sweatshirt and jeans, stepped into a pair of work boots, and pulled her hair in a scrunchie.

"Be back in a minute," Jules said to Bijou, who did not bother to get up from her warm bed in the corner.

Jules hurried over to the tiny houses. Lights still shone in the upstairs window and from the porch of the Beatrix Potter house. Everything else around it was dark and quiet. She shivered in the early morning coolness. A golf cart sat alone in the grass near the fence. She looked around. Jake stood near the Baum house, which sat on a cement pad, the crawlspace visible on all sides.

"What's up?" Jules whispered as she approached Jake, who faced the side of the house.

"I think you need to call the sheriff," he said grimly, shining his flashlight on the base of the structure.

Jules stepped closer for a better look, hoping it wasn't a coyote or some other wild animal that wandered into the resort. Jake illuminated the space under the house, and Jules jumped back. Two Christian Louboutin stilettos, with their trademark soles, jutted out at different angles. Jules gasped. Only one woman wore stilettos like that. When she went to speak, only a squeak came out. Jules cleared her throat, "Did you check for a pulse?"

"There's none. The skin's cold, too."

Jake's flashlight caught something metallic. They both stepped closer. The beam glinted off a shiny pair of multicolored scissors that jutted out of Sorbonne's neck. Jules gasped again. Blood stained the collar and the front of the writer's kimono.

Jules recoiled, taking several steps backward. She breathed deeply to ward off the queasiness that welled up in her stomach.

Jake jolted her back to reality. "Jules, you okay?" He put his arm around her and pulled her closer.

She snuggled in to shake off the shivers. It felt warm and safe, and she didn't want to think about the chaos this was going to unleash.

Not again. Thoughts of last summer flashed through Jules's head. Two of her birdwatchers found a guest dead in the woods. Memories of that murder investigation and the creepy stalker gave her goosebumps.

Pulling herself away, she apologized. "Sorry. I had a flashback to last summer and Ira Perkins." Jules pushed off the eerie feeling. "I'll make the call," she said, tapping her phone. "Hi, this is Jules Keene at the Fern Valley Luxury Camping Resort. I need you to send a deputy. We found a body on the property."

"Are you or anyone else in danger?" the dispatcher asked.

"No. The body has been here awhile. There's no pulse."

"Where are you?"

"On the grounds of the Fern Valley Luxury Camping Resort. We're by the tiny houses on the right side as you come in the main gate."

"Police and EMTs are on their way."

"Thank you." Jules disconnected. She looked at Jake and then at the lifeless body of Sorbonne with her red-soled, designer shoes.

Within fifteen minutes, two cruisers and an ambulance arrived with no sirens. Jules said a silent thank you that there wasn't much fanfare. There would be enough drama when word of Sorbonne's death got out. The red and blue lights bounced off the houses and the wood's dark canopy. Sheriff Hobbs asked one of his deputies to cordon off the area with yellow tape and move everyone back as more investigators arrived.

Jules sat next to Jake in the front seat of the golf cart. She leaned her head on his shoulder and waited as the forensic team brought in portable lights, a generator, and bags of equipment.

"Who's staying in the Rowling house?" Jake asked.

"Rod Avery, the producer."

"I don't see any lights on. And surprisingly, all this noise hasn't stirred up curious onlookers."

"Sorbonne was the only one in the Potter house unless she had a guest." Jules crossed her arms and wiggled her fingers to fend off the morning chill.

Sheriff Hobbs walked up and leaned an arm on the roof of the golf cart. "I'm gonna need to get your statements. Jules, do you mind if I borrow your office?"

"No problem. Hop in, and we'll give you a lift. I can also offer you warm coffee."

He slid in the back seat of the cart, and Jake put it in gear for a hasty ride across the field.

As Jules started the coffee machine, the sheriff poured his tall frame into her office chair. Jake grabbed Roxanne's chair and moved it closer.

"Who found the body?" Sheriff Hobbs asked, flipping his notebook open and pulling a pen from his shirt pocket.

"I did," Jake said.

"What caused you to look for it? It wasn't in plain sight."

"I was doing my rounds, and I saw the lights blazing at one of the tiny houses, so I did a drive-by. I haven't finished the third house. That one's empty. Something caught my eye, and I drove over for a closer look. I shone my light around, and that's when I noticed a shoe sticking out from under the house. When I checked it out, I could see she wasn't moving, and there was blood."

"You said the house was new. Did it somehow fall?" Sheriff Hobbs looked up from his notes.

"No. It was secure. The electrical and water had already been hooked up. I got that finished today. It's missing the decorative lattice at the bottom to cover up the crawl space. They're built to sit above the cement trailer pads."

"Did you move anything?" Sheriff Hobbs asked.

Jake shook his head. "I touched her wrist to see if there was a pulse."

Jules put a mug of black coffee down for the sheriff. "Her name is Sorbonne. I don't know her last name, but she was staying in the house with all the lights on. She's one of the writers for the show."

"When's the last time you saw her?" Sheriff Hobbs asked.

"I've only seen her walking around the property," Jake said. "I don't think we've ever talked."

"She came in the office yesterday to complain," Jules said. "She came in or called when something didn't meet her standards. Ask Roxanne, Sorbonne was quite vocal."

The sheriff nodded and continued to jot notes.

Jules returned to the counter to get Jake's coffee. "I saw her last night, too." Jules hesitated about revealing that she had been watching through the window.

The sheriff leaned back in the chair, waiting.

"I guess it was after nine or nine-thirty. Bijou needed to go out, so we walked from my cabin to the tiny houses. All the lights were on in Sorbonne's house. It was kinda hard to miss. While I was trying to coax Bijou back home, I spotted Sorbonne and a guy kissing. I could see them through the front window. Nobody had bothered to pull the drapes. The guy left a few minutes later and headed back to the RVs."

The sheriff raised an eyebrow. "And."

"And that's it."

"Who was the guy?"

She paused. "Chavis Ratner, one of the show's actors."

"I know who he is." Sheriff Hobbs scribbled more notes. "Anything else?"

"No. Not really." Jules waited for the coffee machine to finish, and she stirred in French vanilla creamer.

"Where can I find who's in charge of the filming?" The sheriff shifted in his seat, and his leather gun belt creaked.

"Rod Avery is the producer. He's staying in the other tiny house. The one with no lights. Paul Bishop is the director. He's staying in one of the show's mega RVs."

"I'll start with Avery. We're going to be here a while. I'll call you if I have any more questions. Thanks for the coffee." The sheriff rose and strode out the back door.

Jules plopped down in her desk chair, her head in her hands. Another death, another murder would give J. P. Gross, her archrival on the business council, new ammunition to go after her. He already used every opportunity to point out that her business brought the wrong kind of people to Fern Valley. She groaned out loud. "Not another murder."

Jake stood and rubbed her shoulders. "It'll be okay. The murder last summer didn't destroy your business. This one will probably create a bigger buzz because of the filming."

"Thanks for the vote of confidence, but what if we are bringing crime and big city woes to the valley? That's not what I want. I was trying to create business opportunities."

"And you're doing a good job," he said. "Stuff happens. You didn't cause this. This town was worse off when I left for the army. Most of downtown was boarded up or abandoned. If we hadn't had revitalization efforts, we'd have no jobs, and there would be more problems with crime and opioids."

She stood and hugged him, soaking in the warmth from his arms. Pulling away, she said, "There's no sense for both of us to stay up all night. I can stay here in case the sheriff needs anything."

"I'm already awake. I'm going to check out what's going on. I'll be back as soon as I can." Jake kissed her, and Jules wished that the moment would've lasted longer.

"I'd open up the lodge for them for food, but Crystal and Mel don't do breakfast since the film company brought in their craft caterers and supplies. When you come back, maybe you and I could whip up coffee and something for them."

"Sounds like a plan." Jake headed out the back door.

Jules turned on her laptop and skimmed her social media sites. She checked all of the resort's camera feeds, but nothing stood out as nefarious. Not many people walking around the resort in the pre-dawn hours. She made a copy for Sheriff Hobbs. Maybe he would spot something she missed. Finding it hard to concentrate, she cruised the internet and clicked through a series of funny dog videos.

Stomping noises on the back steps interrupted her from her mindless web surfing. Jake closed the door behind him.

Jules rubbed her eyes. "What's going on over there?"

"The forensic team is combing through the area. Bubba showed up with another deputy, and there are three techs taking samples and photographing everything. Some of the film crew is hanging around the perimeter."

"It's going to be a long morning and probably afternoon. Should we take coffee over now?" Jules shut down her laptop.

"I asked the sheriff. He said they don't need anything yet. Why don't you go home and get a few hours of sleep? I can hold the fort down here."

"We don't need to stay here. I'm going to go home and get a shower and Bijou. You haven't had any sleep either."

"I may try to get a couple of hours. I feel it when I do all-nighters these days." Jake grinned.

Her heart skipped a beat. He still looked good, even after being up all night. The rumpled hair and stubbled chin looked cool on him. Jules was sure the exhaustion was giving her dark circles and baggy eyes. Hopefully, a shower and a shot or two of espresso would provide enough energy to plow through the rest of the day.

When the sun started to turn the sky an orangey-pink, Jules and Bijou headed back to the office. No dilly-dallying. The brisk morning air kept them both walking at a good clip.

Police had cordoned off the tiny house, and officers milled around the perimeter. A news truck from Charlottesville pulled in next to the split-rail fence.

Jules sighed and opened the back door. She busied herself with turning on lights and computers while Bijou found her puffy pink bed to continue her sleep time. At least one of them could relax.

She made two to-go cups of extra-strong coffee and stepped out the back door to get a closer look at the investigation. More news crews gathered near the parking lot.

Now, yellow police tape outlined the entire perimeter around the three tiny houses. Deputy Charles Dempsey, who went by Bubba when he and Jules were in school, stood about thirty yards away, making sure that the cast and crew stayed behind the tape. He checked his phone every few minutes. The sheriff and Rod Avery stood nearer to where they had found Sorbonne. Forensic techs moved methodically around the area, collecting samples, taking measurements, and photographing the scene.

A tall Virginia State Trooper, who looked like the Laurel to Bubba's Hardy, strode up to the scene, ducked under the tape, and headed for Sheriff Hobbs. The three chatted for a while, and then the men split into two groups. The two law enforcement officers walked toward the Baum house, and the film producer headed toward the RVs.

About the time that Jules was tired of standing behind the yellow tape, the sheriff walked toward her.

"How's it going, Sheriff?" She held up a to-go cup as part of her greeting.

"I've had better mornings." He put his black notebook and pen in his shirt pocket.

"I brought coffee, but it's probably lukewarm by now."

"That's fine. Caffeine is always appreciated." He took the cup and gulped several swigs. "We'll be wrapping up here in a few hours. I talked with the director. He's going to have a staff meeting to talk to his people. Though it's probably on the news by now." Sheriff Hobbs glanced over his shoulder at the news vehicles in the parking lot. "Filming will probably go on as scheduled."

Jules nodded. "I'm curious. Did the show's producer Rod say where he was last night? I'm surprised he didn't hear anything if he was in the Rowling house at the time."

The sheriff grimaced. After a pause, he replied, "He stayed in another trailer last night."

When it looked like he was not going to offer any additional information, Jules added, "Okay. I'm headed back to the office. I'll probably pull up with my staff first thing today, too. I want to make sure nobody talks to the media. Holler if you need me."

"Sounds like a plan," he said. "Tell Roxanne I'll call her later when I get some time."

"Will do. She should be in soon. I gave you a copy of last night's camera feeds."

"Thanks, I was going to ask you about that," he said.

Jules walked across the grassy area back to the office. A Channel 29 TV truck pulled up to the entrance. She picked up her pace. It was time to pull her team together before they started getting questions about what happened.

She found a bottle of water in the fridge and texted her crew about a nine o'clock meeting. By the time she finished her drink and checked the reservation emails, most of her staff had assembled in the back office. Hungry for news, they appeared in record time.

"Hey, y'all, thanks for coming. I know we've had a lot of excitement around here. But I have some sad news. One of the show's writers was found dead under the Baum house. Sheriff Hobbs and the police are investigating. That's about all I know. The media is already here. Let's refer everything to the sheriff's office and try not to answer any questions. Our main concern is the safety of our guests. I'm not sure they've had time to notify next of kin yet."

"I heard it on the scanner this morning," Lester said. "From the chatter, it sounded like the house fell on her."

"The house didn't fall," Roxanne added, looking at Jake. "Someone put her there."

"The police are investigating it as a homicide." Jules studied the room.

Everyone on her team looked bright and refreshed, and she felt like death warmed over. "I'm not sure what this will do to the filming schedule. Just go about your normal routines. We'll roll with whatever the film crew decides to do. Any questions or concerns?"

Jules looked from face to face. They were unusually subdued. "Okay. Let me know what you guys need."

Snoring emanated from next to her desk, and the humans chuckled at the snoozing dog. "Well, on that note, I guess we're done."

The staff headed out to other parts of the resort as Bijou continued her nap.

Roxanne reapplied her crimson lipstick.

"Sheriff said he'd call you later. He's up to his elbows in alligators," Jules said.

"He texted a minute ago. I'm sorry that she was killed. No one deserves to die that way, but you have to recognize the irony."

Jules furrowed her brow.

"You know it was all Baum-related. Just missing a broom and the flying monkeys," her aunt added.

Jules stifled a snicker and busied herself with checking what the news sites were posting.

About an hour later, stomping interrupted Jules from scanning the resort's Facebook site. She walked to the front of the building as Sheriff Hobbs came through the screen door.

"Would you like some coffee?" Jules asked.

"'Preciate it." The sheriff removed his Smokey Bear hat and followed her to the counter.

She started the machine as he dropped in one of the vinyl chairs at the table in the kitchenette.

"Any leads?" Jules asked over her shoulder.

"They're collecting prints and DNA, especially on the scissors. They're the high-end professional kind. Do you have a spare key to the house?"

Jules nodded and went to retrieve the resort's key. "Do you think I'm going to need to do heavy-duty cleaning in there?" she asked when she returned.

"Uh, probably, but not because it was the scene of the crime. We're not sure where she was attacked. It looks like she had been dragged under that other house."

Now Jules was curious about where the murder took place. She hoped all the stylists had good alibis. Her thoughts flicked to Kat. Both Kat and Sorbonne seemed to have something going with Chavis. *Did they know about each other?*

"Thanks. I'll have someone bring it back later." The sheriff took one last swig from his mug and rose.

"Let me know what you want us to do with her belongings when you're done," Jules said.

"Will do. We still have a bunch of movie folks to talk to. It's going to be a long week." He tipped his hat at her. "Roxanne, I'll call you when I can." He strode out front, and the sound of the door closing echoed through the store.

By four-thirty, the office had emptied. Jules was glad to stop fielding calls about what was going on. She turned on the night answering service and whistled for Bijou. "Come on, baby. Let's go take a walk and then see what's for dinner."

They strolled across the grass where the police worked around the growing neighborhood of tiny houses. She and Bijou edged closer to the crime scene tape.

Sheriff Hobbs spotted her and ambled over. "Here's your key. The team will lock the door behind them. They're almost finished."

"Do I need to get the cleaning crew in there now?" Jules scowled.

"It'll probably need a once over, but it's not urgent. They dusted for prints, and there's a lot of garbage. It's not a hazmat situation if that's what you're asking."

Jules pocketed the key to the Potter house. "What should I do with her stuff?"

"The producer said he'd coordinate with you to get it boxed up."

Jules looked down at Bijou, who had taken up residence in a patch of clover.

"We'll be wrapping this up soon. Then everything goes to the lab in Richmond," Sheriff Hobbs said, looking past Jules at something in the parking lot. "See you later."

So far, the investigation was not as exciting as the ones portrayed on television. There was a lot of waiting. She was curious to find out where the murder happened. Hopefully, the sheriff would have some answers soon.

Jules pulled on the leash. The terrier followed her over to where the crew's RVs were parked. Kat, in her long burgundy cardigan, skinny jeans, and tan suede boots that laced up to her knees, sat in a folding chair on the patio under the awning. She pushed a handful of hair out of her face and stared at her phone until Jules approached.

"Hi. Are you okay?" Jules asked.

Before Kat could answer, a shriek pierced the quiet. Kat jumped up and threw open the door. Jules and Bijou stuck their heads in behind Kat.

Jayden, dressed all in black and sporting a pink pompadour hairdo, let out a string of obscenities.

"What is wrong with you?" Kat demanded.

"My stuff. My stuff is missing. They're going to think I did it." The thin man slid down to a seated position on the floor. He buried his head in his arms.

"What stuff? The police searched everything. I'm sure it's only been moved. Calm down. Just breathe," Kat said.

"I don't need this negativity right now." Jayden didn't lift his head, and his fuzzy sweater muffled his voice.

"What are you looking for?" Kat moved closer to him.

"I had a black folding bag with two complete sets of Matsui shears in it. You know my signature rose gold snips and the rainbow ones that I use for special clients. One pair from the rainbow set is missing."

Kat moved things on the counter as she searched for the missing scissors. "Here's your case. Oh, there is one missing. Right there at the bottom."

The young man sniffed. "I told you. And I'm gonna get blamed for this.

Sorbonne and I hated each other. Everyone knew it."

"That doesn't mean you killed her," Jules said.

"Did you?" Kat glared at him.

"No, of course not." Jayden sobbed harder. "How am I going to explain this? I already have a record. I'll be an easy target. That officer said that Sorbonne had been stabbed. I'll be the number one suspect."

Jules frowned. "You've got to tell the sheriff. It'll be worse if it comes out later."

"I don't see how it could look worse. They found her dead with my scissors stuck…well, you know…." His voice trailed off.

"We all have pasts. It can't be that bad." Kat moved gear on the counter. When no one said anything, she asked, "What did you get arrested for?"

Jayden hesitated. "For stabbing someone," he said softly. "With stylist scissors. But he didn't die. He got what was coming to him." Jayden lifted his head and looked at both women. "It was justified."

Chapter Four

Thursday

A steady stream of people drifted into the office to inquire about lodging or opportunities to watch the filming of *Fatal Impressions*. Between the walk-ins and calls, Jules and Roxanne hadn't had a break all morning. Sorbonne's demise didn't dampen any of the enthusiasm around the filming. It felt like everyone in town had contacted her at least once about the show.

In a lull between phone calls, Jules asked, "Do you think you'll be okay here by yourself? I want to check on things and make sure the amphitheater is ready for this evening's memorial service."

"I'll be fine. If it gets crazy, I'll call Lester or Jake to come up and help me," Roxanne said.

"Help with what?" Jake asked, stepping through the Dutch door. He picked up Bijou and patted her on the head.

"Rod asked if they could use the amphitheater tonight for those who wanted to say a few words about Sorbonne." Jules pushed a stray curl out of her face. "Roxanne is holding down the fort. She said she'd call you if she got swamped."

"Not a problem. I can hang out here with these gals." Jake snuggled the dog, who was putty in his hands.

"What time is the thing? I'm going to let the sheriff know," Roxanne said.

"About four o'clock before their dinner line starts." Jules picked up her phone and slid out the front door while Bijou was occupied with Jake.

A cool breeze ruffled the leaves and made for the perfect autumn day. Cotton ball clouds dotted the blue sky. The days were getting shorter and the nights chillier. It was a matter of weeks before the leaves were in full color, and the mountains would be inundated with day tourists and leaf peepers.

Deciding against walking, she looped around the building to get the golf cart. Rounding the corner, she stopped in her tracks. Chavis Ratner was leaning against the store's back wall with a girl that Jules didn't recognize. Neither interrupted the kiss to acknowledge Jules. She had to walk by them to get to the golf cart.

When she passed the preoccupied couple, she said, "Hi there. How are you doing?"

Chavis waved her away with one hand, not stopping to speak.

Jules shrugged her shoulder and jumped in the cart. She backed up close to the couple and threw the cart in gear. Chavis and his friend did not miss a beat or try to move out of the way.

Chavis had a different partner every day. He didn't seem too broken up over Sorbonne. Jules wondered if all Hollywood folks were like him.

She cruised by the tiny houses. Nothing looked amiss except the yellow police tape that fluttered in the breeze. Thoughts of Sorbonne popped in her head. Jules needed to talk to Rod Avery about what to do with the writer's things.

Jules shook off the melancholic feeling about the dead writer and tooled over to the RV village. A few people milled about. Spotting Jayden in a patio chair smoking, she parked nearby.

"How are you? Did you find your scissors?" Jules asked.

"No. I guess I'm as good as can be expected with some psycho killer running around. Someone is trying to set me up. Hey, I had a thought. You know what's going on around here. Can you see what you can find out from that sheriff? But be careful. I certainly don't want to draw any attention to my situation. Do you think you can help me?" He looked at her with his huge brown, puppy eyes.

"I can talk to him. Not sure what he'll share."

Jayden managed a half-smile. "Sorbonne wasn't the nicest person, but what a way to go." He pantomimed stabbing himself in the neck. He picked up a pack of cigarettes and a bejeweled lighter, stood, and stretched. "The police were all over the hair and makeup trailer looking through our stuff. The shears they found on Sorbonne were probably mine. I'm waiting for the next designer shoe to drop. It's a matter of time before the police come back." The thin twenty-something, with aqua and purple tinges in his bleached hair, waved his hand like a fan in front of his face. "I don't need this right now."

Jules stared at Jayden. She was surprised that he went from troubled and weepy to animated in a manner of seconds.

"Love the hair. What happened to the pink?" she asked.

"Perks of the job. I can try a new look anytime." Jayden waved his hand dismissively.

When he didn't say anything else, she asked, "Who else had access to this trailer?"

"Everybody. It's never locked. There are two other makeup artists here, Kat and Tess. And both turned white as a sheet when the police questioned us yesterday about our equipment."

Jayden, dressed in skinny jeans and a shiny purple oversized shirt, crushed his cigarette with his pointy-toed ostrich boot. "I've got to get back. We're going over the shooting schedule and what kind of setup we need for the rest of the week. Filming doesn't stop – even for death."

"Are you going to the memorial today?" Jules asked.

"Wouldn't miss it for the world. Can't you just see the drama," he said over his shoulder. "Everyone who hated her guts will be there singing her praises. She'll have a halo before the night's over. This murder will transform her from the Wicked Witch to Glinda in the pink dress. You watch." He left her with a half-smile. "Ciao, baby."

Before Jules could comment, Kat with her long chestnut hair in corkscrew curls and sunglasses, backed down the RV's steps with two oversized black bags. "Oh, hi. How are you?"

"I stopped by to see how everyone was doing," Jules said.

"Pretty good, considering. I think we're all in shock. Everybody I've talked to can't believe that Sorbonne is gone. I mean, who would do something like this? We've worked together for so long. We're like family." She gave a small shake of her head. "I can't believe it was one of the cast or crew. We're all hoping it's someone local."

Jules's brow furrowed. She couldn't imagine that it was someone from Fern Valley. "Does she have family?"

"Sorbonne didn't talk much about her personal life. She's married to a music producer. They had separate living arrangements. Sorbonne was pretty much a loner. She'd talk to Paul and Rod, but she was always too busy adjusting lines and doing revisions. She couldn't be bothered with us peasants." Kat pushed one of the bag's straps farther up on her shoulder.

"I thought you were close to her," Jules said, fishing for more information.

"Not really. We were friendly most days. I did her hair and makeup to stay in her good graces. And she liked to gossip, so she was always a good source of four-one-one on what was going to happen to the different actors. She liked to hint that she knew all the secrets before anyone else."

"Interesting. We only chatted a couple of times. I really didn't get to know her," Jules said.

"People either praised her or demonized her. Most folks were in the second camp, but she was a good writer. Her episodes always had a twist. She's been with the production company since the beginning." Kat paused and looked around. "I'm headed over to Kayleigh's trailer. She wants her hair and makeup done before the memorial."

"Do you need a lift?"

"Nah, thanks. It's only a few RVs over. Are you going to be at the thing tonight?"

Jules nodded.

"See you then." Kat fluttered her fingers in a quick wave.

Putting the cart in gear, Jules drove around the vintage trailers. All quiet. She headed down a slight incline to the amphitheater, a grassy knoll with wooden benches, the perfect spot for outdoor gatherings. In the past, it had been used for music concerts, outdoor movies, and a wedding or two. This was the first memorial service.

She looped around the seating area. Everything was set up, so she headed to the office to see what new tidbits Roxanne had gleaned.

Once inside the store, it took a minute for her eyes to adjust to the wooden building's interior. Her aunt stood at the counter, flipping through a magazine. "All well in the valley?"

"Pretty quiet. Lester's kept the grass manicured, so the amphitheater is good to go," Jules said.

"We're up to sixty-one today."

"Huh?" Jules looked at her aunt, who continued to page through her magazine.

"I've had sixty-one calls or texts asking if I can get them in to see a particular star. My favorites are the ones that want me to get them or their kid an audition. It's amazing how much talent folks in this town think they have."

"That reminds me. I need to talk to Rod or Paul to see if people can be on the property to watch the filming. If not, they'll have to take their chances in town for location filming. Bubba should have a good time controlling traffic. Speaking of law enforcement. Have you heard anything new about the investigation?"

"Not much. Matt has been working almost round the clock. I've only gotten a few texts from him, and they weren't about Sorbet. Hopefully, he'll have some time this weekend to get together." Her aunt closed the magazine and sighed. "He said he's called in Trooper Hughes to assist. It hasn't risen to the level of a task force like last summer's murder, though. Oh, he did say he was pretty sure Sorbonne wasn't killed in the house. But you already knew that."

Jules got a chill when her thoughts flashed to the guy in the green truck who skulked around her property last summer, looking for a small fortune that her dead guest had hidden in one of the vintage trailers. Jules apprehended the killer when he came back and threatened her staff. She'd proven that anything could be a weapon, including the cast iron skillet that she neutralized him with until law enforcement could take care of him.

She shook off the unpleasant memories. Normally, Fern Valley was a peaceful place, full of friendly people who enjoyed the beauty of the mountains. Now another murder tainted her resort.

"Jules?"

She realized she hadn't replied. "I'm sorry. I was thinking about something else. So, did the sheriff hint that they had any leads? Jayden, one of the stylists, is missing a pair of professional scissors."

"Interesting." Roxanne leaned forward. "Do you think she was placed under the house with her red-soled designer heels as an homage to the *Wizard of Oz* or whether it was the nearest place to dump the body? The sheriff did say that it looked like she had been dragged for a bit." Roxanne looked at her nails. "Might be someone's sick sense of humor."

"It makes sense she was dragged. There was no reason for her to be at that house. Jake hadn't finished it yet. The lights were all on at the house she was staying at – not the empty one."

Jake came through the front door before Roxanne could reply. "Hey. There's something odd out front."

"Define odd." Roxanne rummaged through the cabinet drawers. "We've had a lot of unusual lately."

"It's Jane Jenkins. She's out by the parking lot with a tripod, and she's talking a mile a minute and waving her arms around like a windmill," he said.

"Jane the Pain, our intrepid local reporter? She must be hot on the trail of some story lead or bit of gossip." Roxanne pulled out an emery board and filed her nails.

Jules followed Jake outside. On the other side of the split-rail fence surrounding the parking lot, Jane had set up a tripod with what looked like her phone. The reporter with the short, gray bowl cut paused to adjust her equipment and waddled back to her spot in front of the phone.

The pair walked closer as the reporter talked to the tripod. She stopped suddenly and looked at Jake and Jules. "I'm finishing up here. Would either of you like to answer a few questions about the most recent murder to rock Fern Valley?" The woman, who was as wide as she was tall, reached forward and turned the tripod toward them.

Jules cleared her throat. "Hi, Jane. Sheriff Hobbs's department is handling the investigation and all media queries. He has the most current information."

"I'm on assignment doing a video piece. And I've already talked to the sheriff. I thought I'd give you an opportunity to tell your side of the story." Jane's stare zeroed in on Jules.

"For the *Gazette?*" Jake asked.

"Maybe. Or maybe I'm freelancing." The forty-something woman with the haircut that looked like the Little Dutch Boy rolled her eyes at the couple. "And if you're not going to answer my questions, could you get out of my shot? I don't have all day. I need to get this posted before someone scoops me."

Jules waved, and Jake followed her back to the store.

The older woman said "Take two" and launched into a long description of Fern Valley, Jules's resort, and last summer's murders.

When they were out of earshot, Jules stopped. "Freelancing?"

Jake shrugged his shoulders. "There's a lot of buzz on social media about the filming. Emily said she heard some gossip sites are paying for storylines, spoilers, and pictures. Maybe Jane's trying to get her big headline or some cash."

Jules pursed her lips. "That's all I need are people sneaking around trying to get pictures of the stars or trying to figure out what's going to happen this season."

"I'm sure the true fans are looking for any details. The badder the better." Jake sported his signature grin. "Don't worry about it. You've got a crack security team. I'm headed to the barn. When the police remove the tape, I'm gonna finish the skirting on that tiny house. And I've got an idea for the fourth house's new look."

"Can't wait to hear. See ya for dinner?"

"Wouldn't miss it," he said over his shoulder.

"I'm headed to the amphitheater, but I could make something quick after that."

"Works for me."

Jules nodded and opened the screen door. "Come over about six-thirty?"

"Dinner with a friend?" her aunt asked before Jules could step inside.

"Something like that." Bijou greeted Jules and then followed her to the back office.

"Y'all look cute together," her aunt yelled from the front. "I'm headed out soon."

"If you see the sheriff, find out what news he has. I'm going to the memorial thing. Oh, if you go out front now, Jane is doing a video. She said she's freelancing."

Roxanne poked her head in the doorway. "Does she think she's a film crew now? I guess doing the calendar of events for the paper got boring. I might have to wander over there and photobomb her. Maybe I can get in her video."

Jules grinned at the thought of her stylish aunt popping up at random moments in Jane's video.

A few minutes before four, Jules checked her look. She fluffed her flattened curls and searched through her desk drawer for lip gloss.

"Come on, sweetie. Let's go see what's going on."

Bijou's ears perked up. They walked toward the amphitheater. As they got closer, they blended in with the steady stream of cast and crew. A couple of the guys stopped to pat Bijou.

The crowd, already three-deep, stood around the seated guests. No available seats in sight. Jules and Bijou made their way to the edge of the crowd and worked their way down the hill a few rows for a better view. Jules and her dog stayed on the fringe beside several people she hadn't seen before.

Rod Avery, Paul Bishop, and another man Jules didn't recognize edged their way to the front, stopping every few minutes to talk to someone in the crowd. When they finally made it to the front, a guy dressed head to toe in black handed Rod a microphone.

Rod cleared his throat. "Welcome, and thank you all for coming." The producer looked comfortable in a white dress shirt with rolled-up sleeves and a pair of khaki pants. He waved his arms to get the audience's attention.

The crowd noise subsided. Jules shifted her weight from one foot to the other. Bijou found a clump of grass to sniff. When she got tired, she plopped down and scanned the audience.

"Paul, Eric, and I thought we should get together and say a few words about the loss of one of our own. And a lot of you have had questions about the production. As most of you know, Sorbonne, our head writer, was found dead late Tuesday night. The police are investigating. I have no new details, but it saddens us all to lose one of our family. Sorbonne had been with the production since the beginning, and she was the only original writer still on the show."

When he paused, Paul Bishop took the microphone. "Sorbonne will be missed. But being as thorough as she was, all the scripts have been completed for this season, so her demise will not alter our production schedule. I don't anticipate any issues or delays."

Several loud whispers and some applause emanated from the crowd.

The other gentleman, with close-cropped salt and pepper gray hair, stepped forward. His tailored suit made the others look like they were dressed for Casual Friday. "Good afternoon. For those who don't know me, I'm Eric Renfield." A low murmur spread across the crowd. Jules looked around, trying to figure out who the speaker was. "It is good to see you all here. I know this is a sad occasion. I've spoken to our investors. They are willing to offer a ten-thousand-dollar reward for information leading to the arrest of Sorbonne's killer."

More murmurs drifted up from the audience.

"Thank you, Eric. And please thank all of our investors who make this project possible." Paul clapped Eric on the back. Turning toward the audience, he asked, "Would any of you like to come forward and say something in honor of Sorbonne?"

There were more whispers and a long, awkward pause.

"I will," Chavis Ratner yelled from several rows back. He jogged confidently to the front and stood by the trio at the bottom of the hill. It looked like he had been called to be a participant on a game show. He waved to the crowd, who applauded.

When the clapping subsided, he struck a pose and smiled. "It is a sad day for all of us, but we should all remember the good times with Sorbonne. Her words gave us a storyline that we actors bring to life. We are the embodiment of her words, and we give the show the success that it's known for." He stopped speaking and scanned the audience. Then he nodded and smiled a toothy grin.

"Thank you, Chavis," Paul Bishop said. "Anyone else."

No one came forward.

After what seemed like an eternity, Rod Avery said, "Thank you all for coming. Sorbonne's family is planning her funeral in California. If anyone needs contact information, see Sherri. She can give it to you." He pointed to a diminutive blond standing on the fringe in an oversized plaid, flannel shirt and messy bun.

"Okay," Rod continued. "We're going to keep to the filming schedule we posted yesterday. Rehearsals are tonight after dinner, and filming starts in and around the barn at six o'clock tomorrow morning. You have your call sheets. Please be prompt. We'll start the town scenes this weekend."

There were a few groans, and the crowd started to disperse. Most headed to the lodge for dinner. Jules made her way to where Sherri stood by herself. "Hi, I'm Jules Keene, owner of the resort. Could I get the contact information from you? We'd like to send a card or flowers."

"Sure." She jotted something on a sticky note and handed it to Jules. Two men in jeans approached, and Sherri, the production assistant, was sucked into their conversation about tomorrow's schedule.

Jules stuck the note to her phone and picked up Bijou. Sheriff Hobbs stood at the other end of the row. She almost didn't recognize him in his civilian clothes. He nodded and watched as the crowd filed out.

Jules waved to the sheriff and carried Bijou back to the cabin. She grabbed a pen from the counter and jotted down all the names she'd heard at the memorial.

After not finding anything interesting in the freezer for dinner with Jake, Jules pulled out hot dogs, chili, baked beans, and some leftover fruit salad.

As she assembled dinner, thoughts of the odd memorial service popped in her head. She couldn't decide what bothered her most: that the whole thing felt like a Chavis Ratner show or that it had all the markings of a business meeting where no one really cared about Sorbonne.

Chapter Five

Friday

Jules's alarm buzzed at the unearthly hour of five-thirty. She rolled over and tried to shake the haziness left over from a dream. Bijou lifted her head and rolled over on her back. Jules wanted to do the same, but she had to be ready for the first day of filming.

A quick, steamy shower and an espresso helped her feel more awake. She pulled on jeans and a sweater and tamed her unruly curls in a ponytail. She did several swipes of lipstick and mascara. It was subtle compared to Kat's handiwork with the airbrush and curling iron.

Bijou ran to the kitchen when she heard kibble hit the bowl. Jules settled in at the table with a bagel and a banana. Her cell phone vibrated, and a picture of Jake popped up on her screen.

"Hey, Boss. You might want to come over to the office."

"What's up?"

"We've got a slight situation, and I'd like you to see it before we decide to call the sheriff."

"Be right there." She let out a heavy sigh and slipped on a pair of tennis shoes. "Bijou, wait right here. I'll be back as soon as I can."

Jules halted in mid-jog as she approached the resort's office. Yelling and crowd noise emanated from the other side of the building. She poked her head around the corner and stopped in her tracks. Hundreds of people stood in the parking lot and along the fence line. Jake stood on the wooden porch with Rod Avery, another man dressed in all black with motorcycle boots and a petite blond in black leggings and a leather jacket.

Jules wormed her way through the crowd to the porch. She chided herself for not remembering to call Rod to ask what to do about onlookers. Now it was too late.

"This is Jules Keene, the owner," Jake said as she climbed the three steps. "You know Rod. This is Drake, head of the crew's security. And this is Poppy Carlson. She's…"

"The publicist." The woman looked like a Disney pixie if it wore leather and mirrored aviator glasses.

"And marketing guru," Rod added. "Poppy can spin anything to create a buzz for the show. And she's been hard at work on social media commenting about Sorbonne. By the looks of this crowd, she may have done too well." He grinned and looked at Poppy.

The blond looked up at the taller, older man and beamed.

"What's all this?" Jules asked, scanning the crowd. She recognized quite a few faces from Fern Valley, even the grouchy J. P. Gross, and his crony, Ralph Teagle, the owner of the local towing service, lurking on the fringes.

"That's what we're wondering. We didn't make the filming schedule public," Rod said. Jules thought she caught a hint of annoyance in his tone.

"We didn't either, but it's a small town." Jules turned and glanced at the growing crowd. "Looks like word got out and spread like wildfire."

The producer cleared his throat and shifted his weight. His focus shifted from Drake and Poppy to the two hundred or so people in the field.

"I say let them stay." Poppy surveyed the horizon. "If we're nice, we'll create organic excitement that we can keep going. If you're mean and send them away, you'll create a bigger buzz of disappointed fans. And people will try harder to sneak on the property and disrupt things."

"Do we have any caution tape?" Rod asked.

"I have some," Jake said. "I'll be right back." He headed toward the barn.

"Let's rope off the area and let them know they can stay behind the tape. They can't interrupt filming," Rod said.

"Do you want to tell them?" Poppy asked, pushing her sunglasses into her blond curls.

"You do it. And hype social media stuff while you're out there," the producer said. "That's what you're good at."

Jules caught his wink and grin before he returned to his somber self.

Poppy smiled and stood taller. "Anybody got a bullhorn?"

"Actually, I do. Be right back." Jules unlocked the store's door.

She rummaged through the closet and returned to the porch. "Here. Push this when you want to talk." Jules flicked the switch.

"Thanks." Poppy took the device and handed it to the huge man. "Get their attention, Drake."

He aimed the bullhorn at the crowd. "Ladies and gentlemen, may I have your attention please? Poppy has something you're really going to want to hear. Listen up. Heeeeere's Poppy." He sounded like an announcer at a professional wrestling match.

The dull roar from the crowd dissipated instantly.

"Thanks, Drake," she said, taking the bullhorn. "As you know, filming starts today for the fabulous *Fatal Impressions*. Who's a fan?"

She paused as the crowd went wild.

"We all are," Poppy continued. "People will be talking about this season for months. It's going to be something like you've never seen before, and you guys have front-row seats. In a few minutes, we're going to cordon off an area for viewing. You all were here first, so you get dibs on the prime spots. We'd like you to enjoy your day. Stay out of the way of the actors and equipment, and be as quiet as possible. The director gets testy if we do anything to get off schedule. If we get off schedule, the show will be late. And being late will make it much longer before you get to see the next season."

A rumble spread across the crowd that moved closer. The whooping and hollering started.

"Okay," Poppy said, waving her arm. "Just remember the rules. Have fun. Stay out of the way of production and be as quiet as possible. The guys will be here soon with the tape. And while you watch, make sure to post pictures and clips on social media. Hashtag *Fatal Impressions*."

The crowd cheered and settled down.

A few minutes later, the crowd whooped again. Jake came around the corner. He waved to the fandom as Drake joined him to plant stakes and mark off the viewing area facing the barn and the woods. As the borders appeared, people filled in the space and covered every inch of grass between the parking lot and the barn.

Jake and the security guy climbed the porch steps after they marked off an area about the size of a soccer field.

"We'll bring in safety fencing tomorrow and put it around the property. I'm sure the crowds will get bigger as word spreads," Drake said.

"Please let me know if you need anything else," Jules said.

Before he could answer, shrill squeaks and shouts emanated from the crowd. Then more screams. Chavis Ratner, dressed in all black leather and wearing Wayfarer sunglasses, walked around the building. He fist-pumped the air, and the crowd responded with more whistles and cheers.

"Chavis, Chavis, Chavis," echoed across the field.

He waved and did a quick run down one of the borders, slapping hands and taking selfies with adoring fans.

When he finished his meet and greet, he stormed up the porch steps and grabbed the bullhorn. "It's so great to see you all. Who's ready for another season of *Fatal Impressions?*"

The crowd went wild again. So much for Poppy's rules.

"I hope you all will hang out and watch the filming. This season is going to be so amazing. You'll love what Beau Staunton gets into this year." Chavis shook his fist in the air again and handed the bullhorn to Jake.

"Morning, Rod and other peoples," Chavis said. "Who's going to give me a ride back to the set?"

Jules opened her mouth, but Jake jumped in before she could volunteer. "I will," he said.

Minutes later, Jake pulled the golf cart around to the steps to more cheering. "Anyone else want a ride?" *If this continues, Jake will have a fan club before production ends.*

Rod and Drake shook their heads and descended the stairs. Poppy jumped in the back seat of the cart, and Jules slid in beside her.

"Onward," Poppy said as they left the cheering crowd in the background.

Jake sped around the field and the RVs to the barn. Scaffolding and booms blocked the view of the front of the building. Trolleys and carts with cameras and other gear covered the grass.

When Jake slowed to a stop, Poppy hopped out. "Thanks for the ride. Keep encouraging them to take pictures and talk about the production on social media."

Chavis stepped out and looked around, panning the horizon as if he were in slow motion. He paused and stared at the barn. Stretching to his full height, he strode with his head held high. It reminded Jules of the pomp and circumstance of British royalty or a bantam rooster.

"Jake Evans, chauffeur to the stars. Where would you like to go? I'm at your service."

Jules smiled. "How about RV land. I want to see who's over there and willing to chat. What are your plans for this lovely day?"

"I want to put the finishing touches on the Baum house. And then I'll do my rounds to check on production."

A few minutes later, Jake slowed the cart down by the first row of campers. Members of the crew milled around on the other side of the lodge.

"Thanks for the lift. Text me if you want to hang out tonight." Jules climbed out and surveyed the area.

"I'll bring a pizza," he said.

"Sounds like a date. Movie night?" Jules asked.

"You got it." Jake winked and sped off.

She rounded the corner and found Jayden smoking on the patio under the awning. Kat leaned against the step's railing, drinking sparkling water and looking at sheets on a clipboard.

"Hi, all," Jules said. "How's it going?"

"Normal first-day stuff," Jayden said. "Some of the actors," he coughed and said, "Kayleigh Bell and Ashe Lyons are habitually late, and that put us behind schedule. But we roll with it."

"With the morning rush over, we get a little break, and then we move over to the tents near the barn for touch-ups," Kat said. "How are things with you?"

"Good. We have about two hundred fans trying to get a glimpse of anything related to the series. Security had to cordon off an area."

"That always happens. They sneak in. They try to be delivery drivers. They bring drones." Kat took a swig of her water as Jayden crushed out his cigarette.

"Everybody doing okay after the memorial service?" Jules asked, looking to see if either reacted to her question.

"I didn't go," Jayden said. "I needed a break from peopling. You know, 'me time.' Heard I didn't miss much."

Kat scowled. "I went. Things are pretty much back to normal here now."

"It was a short ceremony," Jules added, hoping to fish for more information.

"Like I said before, she didn't have a lot of friends." Kat flipped through the pages again on her clipboard.

"I saw her with a guy by the tiny houses, and they looked pretty friendly," Jules added.

A frown crossed Kat's face. "More like a boy toy. She had a habit of picking up guys, usually young actors, and discarding them on a whim."

"Wasn't she married?"

"That doesn't mean anything around here," Jayden said. "After a long stint on location, most everyone plays musical beds. You know, being away from home for a long time and all that. Plus, she acted like queen cougar, attracting the actors who wanted to stay in her good graces. If she didn't like someone, she'd kill off the character with the stroke of a pen. She could and did end careers."

Jules raised her eyebrows.

"I'd love to stay and chat, but this boy has things to do. I've got to get my station straightened up and ready for the next wave. See you later." He climbed the steps and disappeared inside the RV.

Kat shrugged her shoulder. "I tried to stay on Sorbonne's good side. She could be brutal. She killed off characters in gruesome ways, and she complained to get members of the crew fired. People walked lightly around her. I think some of the actors hung out with her to get the scoop on what was going on. She didn't have scores of people singing her praises at the end. I'm sure a bunch are relieved that she's gone."

Jules pursed her lips and tilted her head. "Only Chavis spoke about her at the ceremony."

Kat rolled her eyes. "He likes the limelight and doesn't hesitate to find opportunities to promote himself. Every relationship he cultivates has to be one that will do something for him."

Jules paused. She had seen Kat in a liplock with the young actor. "I thought…"

Kat cut her off before she could finish her statement. "I have to go. It's going to be a busy day." She climbed the steps and let the door slam behind her.

Jules sensed a cooling in Kat's tone. "See you around," she said to the closed door.

The rows of RVs looked like a ghost town. She looped around and headed toward the barn. The scene switched from no one around to a buzzing beehive. People, mostly dressed in black, zipped around, shuffling equipment to different locations. Cameras on lifts and things that looked like black boxes surrounded the barn, where Lester stored his landscaping equipment and Jake assembled his tiny houses. They both would be displaced until shooting moved to another location.

"Jules, hey, Jules." Sherri, the production assistant, waved her clipboard and moved closer. "Hi," she said, catching her breath. "Do you have a few minutes to go over this week's schedule? I talked to Rod and Poppy, and they want to make sure that your team is aware of what's coming up."

"Sure. Do you want to talk here or in my office?"

"I'm sure it's quieter there." Sherri looked around at all the activity.

"And I have snacks," Jules said.

The assistant walked with Jules around the perimeter of the filming to the back of the office.

Once inside, Jules said, "Have a seat. What can I get you? I have coffee, tea, bottled water, and soft drinks."

"Do you have a Coke?" asked the production assistant.

Jules rummaged in the fridge and pulled out a soft drink and a bottle of water. She joined Sherri, who could pass for a college student except for the crow's feet around her eyes. "How are things going?"

"Pretty good for a first day after the head writer was killed, but we charge on." Sherri popped the top on her can and grabbed her clipboard. "Here's a copy of the schedule for the next two weeks. It's confidential and as always, subject to change. Poppy announces each day's filming on Instagram. So, wait for her post before you put anything out there. Today, we're filming in and around your barn and the woods. On Saturday and Sunday, we'll be at different locations in town, and you can read the rest. If you have any questions, all the key contact numbers are at the bottom. Just text me." She took a long swig of her drink.

Jules took the paper Sherri offered and added the contact number to her phone. "Thanks. If you need anything from me, let me know. I texted you my number."

"Cool. Oh, Drake and his crew brought in the plastic safety fencing. They'll cordon off areas on the property ahead of filming. The crowds will get bigger as news travels. I hope the sheriff's folks can control the crowds and the traffic in town this weekend. Drake hired more security guys." Sherri gulped more of her drink.

"I'm sure Sheriff Hobbs has it all under control. We've had a lot of calls and emails about the production, but we haven't been encouraging them to come on the property. Obviously, many of them did anyway."

"It always happens. We have superfans who follow the film crew. With social media, it allows the word to spread faster. We try to use the excitement to our advantage. Thanks for the drink. I've got to get back to the set."

Jules held the door for Sherri, who jogged down the steps and across the field toward the barn.

Jules picked up the sticky note on her desk and Googled Sorbonne's sister, Laura Daniels, who lived in Orange City, Iowa. She Googled Sorbonne next. Her page had a standard professional biography and a stern-looking photo. She found a link to Wikipedia with a wealth of information. She had married

John Carter, a music producer, in May of 1998. No children. No surprise there. Jules printed copies and created a Sorbonne folder. The writer's real name was Charlotte Daniels, from Orange City like her sister, and not Orange County like her biography touted. Interesting. The Hollywood glitz and glitter weren't always real.

Chapter Six

Saturday

A loud pop woke Jules from a deep sleep. She sat up in bed and listened for any other noises. She glanced at her phone on the nightstand. 6:08. Not hearing anything else, she chalked it up to a car backfire. Now wide awake, she decided to start her day. Bijou deferred, stretched, and yawned.

After a shower and her usual espresso, Jules felt ready to tackle the day. She grabbed a yogurt and said, "Come on, Bijou. Let's head to the office, and maybe we'll go to town later to check on the filming."

Bijou's ears perked up when she heard the magic "go" word. Jules opened the cabin door, and the morning chill made her wish she had brought a jacket. The pair walked briskly across the grass. The stillness in the mountain air seeped into her thoughts and calmed her like a cozy blanket.

She punched in the security code and zeroed in on the coffee maker. While her second cup of the day heated up, she started her computer and pulled out her notes on Sorbonne. Jules found the show's web page and quite a few fan pages. She added the printouts to her collection of random information.

Chavis Ratner's real name was Travis Miller, and he hailed from Orlando, Florida. Kayleigh Bell didn't have a stage name, and she was from Dallas, Texas. Ashe Lyons was born Ashley James Baker in Toledo, Ohio. She created a spreadsheet and recorded all the bits of information, mostly from the International Movie Database web page that listed everyone involved with the production. Ignoring the voice in her head that reminded her to stay out of the sheriff's investigation, she shut down her computer and tidied up her desk. "Come on, Bijou. Let's go for a ride and see what the filming is doing to our little town."

Bijou danced near Jules's feet, waiting for the signal to head out.

When Jules opened the door to her silver Jeep Wrangler, the terrier jumped in the front seat. The ride to town usually took about four minutes, but this morning, traffic came to a standstill at the outskirts, a first for Fern Valley. She could almost hear the complaints of some of the business council members who wanted to keep the area in a 1950s time warp.

Traffic beeped and creeped for what felt like miles. When she finally rolled into town, the deputy in the intersection directed her to the Baptist church parking lot, where she found one of the few remaining spots.

Jules locked the Jeep, and the pair hiked three blocks to the center of town. People stood shoulder to shoulder in the square. Crowds in Fern Valley. Another first for the one-stoplight town.

At the corner of Main Street, Deputy Dempsey stood in the middle of the road behind a sawhorse barrier.

"Hey, Charles. Busy morning?" Jules approached the barricade.

He nodded. "Yep. Word got out about today's filming. We've blocked off Main Street and most of the side streets. I think everyone in the tri-county area showed up here this morning. Sheriff had to call in backup from the state police." Charles leaned on the wooden barricade.

Jules looked up and down the street. A line circled the outside of Lula Belle's, the local gourmet sandwich shop. Good news for owners Mitch and Donna Hill. Even with all the chaos, sales were good.

"We're going to walk down to check out the filming." The terrier sniffed the air and watched all the hubbub around her.

"It's been pretty boring so far. They film something, and then they back up and do multiple takes of the same scene. It's hard to tell what's going on." Deputy Dempsey shifted his weight to his other foot. "It's gonna be a long day. I think they're here until about eight tonight."

"Do you need me to get you a drink or something?" she asked.

"Nah. I'm fine. I should get relieved here in about an hour or so. Have fun. Take pictures if you see any of the stars. So far, I haven't seen anybody famous." Jules was surprised he didn't ask to visit the resort. Everyone else in town had.

Bijou led Jules down the sidewalk toward the government center. All the streets in this area were blocked, too. Crowds lined the street and filled the grassy area near the library and the sheriff's office. Many came prepared with blankets, lawn chairs, and coolers.

Jules picked up Bijou, and they merged in with the bystanders. Jules had to stand on her tiptoes to see what was going on. She got a glimpse of rolling cameras and microphone booms. Lots of crew members zipped around. So far, no glitz or glamour.

The crowd closer to the filming started cheering and whistling, and the noise spread. Jules stepped off the curb and stretched for a better view.

Chavis Ratner, Derek Stone, and Kayleigh Bell walked across the street. Chavis waved to his fans. The director yelled something, and the actors found their marks on the street. They did the scene three times. Deputy Dempsey was right. Lots of repetition.

When Bijou started to get wiggly, Jules walked down the street, but the view was the same from the other side. People stood everywhere. She wondered where they came from. Fern Valley didn't have this many residents.

When boredom set in, Jules and Bijou headed back to her Jeep. She rolled down the windows and turned up the radio for the ride home. Since the police had blocked most of the side streets, traffic crawled inch by inch. While waiting for the cars in front of her to turn, Jules caught sight of Poppy in her rear-view mirror. The diminutive publicist in black jeans and a red leather jacket leaned against the brick wall of an office building and pulled out an e-cigarette. Jules watched her puff a cloud of vapor. Chavis, with his jacket collar pulled up to his ears, sauntered up to Poppy. He waved his arms around and stepped closer to the woman. Jules wished she could hear what they were saying.

Chavis leaned closer. Then he kissed Poppy, and Jules's mouth hung open.

Poppy stretched to drape her arms around the actor for a lengthy kiss that turned into a mini make-out session. As the car in front of Jules moved slightly, Kat Mason turned the corner. The stylist's body stiffened as she stared at the couple. Kat gestured as she yelled. Chavis turned and made a retort. Jules wished she had closed captioning. As Kat pointed at the two of them, traffic cleared, and it was Jules's turn to move. Part of her wanted to loop around and see what was going on with the love triangle, but another part of her wanted to return home to the normalcy of a non-Hollywood life. Jules decided to head back to the resort. She'd try to find out more about the Poppy/Chavis thing later.

On her way down the tree-lined entranceway to her resort, Jules's phone rang with an unknown California number. "Hello?"

"Jules, this is Drake Kelly. Rod asked me to reach out to you to see if we could get Sorbonne's things packed today."

"Sure. That's not a problem. I'm on my way to the office now. Why don't you meet me in front of her house in about ten minutes?"

"That works." The crew's security director ended the call.

When Jules opened the back door, Bijou ran through the darkened building to see if anyone else was there.

"Come on, puppy. I've got the key. Let's head out." Jules rummaged through the supply closet and found two empty boxes.

After dropping Bijou at home, Jules savored the solitude of the walk to the tiny house village. The weather was perfect. Thoughts of apple-picking and hikes to the waterfall bounced around her head. Jules snapped to the present when she spotted Drake, dressed all in black, staring at his phone in front of the tiny house. He stood and reached for the boxes as Jules climbed the steps.

She opened the door and took a step back. The head writer had only been in the house a few days, but it looked like a tornado had hit the place. Paper, empty food containers, clothes, and shoes covered almost every inch of the flat surfaces and some of the floor. In addition to the clutter, gray smudges dotted a lot of the surfaces where the forensic team had dusted for prints. Mel and Crystal would have to spend extra time to clean up this mess.

"I guess she wasn't known for her housekeeping skills," Drake muttered.

"Wow. We'll concentrate on her personal effects. I'll help you get those packed, and I'll take care of the trash later." Jules looked around the room, unsure where to begin.

"I'll start in the bedroom," he said. "Hopefully, most of this stuff will fit in her suitcases."

Jules spent the next hour picking up jewelry, scarves, and shoes. After checking the main room and kitchen, she turned the corner toward the bathroom and ran into the back of Drake.

"Oops, sorry," she said. "I didn't know you were there."

"I'm getting claustrophobic in here." Drake grinned. "I know this is a popular thing, but I couldn't stay in one of these. I feel like the walls are closing in on me. I can stand here and touch the walls on both sides with my outstretched arms." He demonstrated the narrowness of the hall. "I've finished in the bedroom and the bath."

"And I'm done in the other rooms. The rest of the stuff is trash. Take a look and make sure I didn't miss anything."

Drake poked around the other rooms. Satisfied that they had all of Sorbonne's things, he carried two suitcases and an overnight bag to the front door. Jules added her two boxes to the pile, and the director of security gave the front room a once-over.

"It looks like we got everything. I'll take this stuff to Sherri, and we'll get it shipped out on Monday to her family."

"I'm going to head over to the office to get trash bags and the golf cart."

"Thanks for your help." He picked up the two suitcases and lumbered down the stairs. "I'll be back for the rest of this in a minute."

Jules made a quick round trip to the office for basic cleaning supplies and the golf cart. Crystal and Mel would take care of the heavy-duty cleaning on Monday.

About an hour later, Jules had filled three garbage bags of trash. Her stomach rumbled, reminding her that it was past lunchtime. She reached down to pick up one last magazine and got distracted by the pile of paper underneath it. The crumpled pages looked like a script. Jules piled all the pages together to give to Rod.

Running out of steam for this project, she tied all of the trash bags and loaded them in the back of the golf cart. After a quick run to the dumpster, she headed home to see what she could throw together for lunch.

Jules settled in at her kitchen table and savored the simplicity of a peanut butter and honey sandwich. She flipped through the discarded script pages. None were in any order, so there was no storyline to follow. Jules tried to arrange them by page numbers, but she quickly discovered they were not from the same document.

On one page, Kayleigh's character was kidnapped and would only appear in non-action scenes with her captors. A handwritten note in the margin read, "Pregnant." Jules's eyes widened. Sorbonne did have access to a lot of secrets that the paparazzi would kill for.

She flipped through about forty more pages. One with green and purple edits in the margin caught her attention. In block letters, someone had penned in the margin "Die, Chavis! You deserve it" next to his character Beau Staunton's lines. And from the remaining paragraphs on that page, it looked like Chavis got lost in the woods and was being chased by hungry wolves. In red ink, someone had made notes about adding a vicious wolf attack. In the other margin, there was a note for Ashe Lyons's character to follow the vultures to find Chavis's character's body. The revelation of that scene would create a firestorm on social media.

Sorbonne didn't mince words. Jules wondered if these were the actual scripts or revisions that had been discarded. None of the pages had a date on them. She would add the tidbits she gleaned from the scripts to her notes on Sorbonne and make copies before she gave them to the producer. At the very least, she'd found some juicy gossip for all the time it had taken to clean the mess Sorbonne left. Would the secrets in the scripts be enough to motivate someone to kill the head writer? And did Chavis know about his character's fate?

Chapter Seven

Monday

Bijou hopped down Jules's porch steps and danced around between her legs. The Jack Russell was way more enthusiastic on a Monday morning than Jules was. She and her staff had a little break since most of the weekend's filming happened in town. She wondered if the Sheriff's Department survived the crowds and traffic jams and if Fern Valley would be the same after *Fatal Impressions* and the murder. Today, the crew set up camp at the edge of the woods behind the barn. Before Jules could snap Bijou's leash in place, the dog tore off on a barking jag toward the RVs, and Jules had to give chase.

When Bijou darted between two RVs, Jules heard shouting and wailing over the barking. Two state troopers dragged Jayden down the metal stairs of the makeup trailer. The stylist bucked like a bronco when the taller trooper hoisted him to the patio. Jayden crumpled like a wet noodle. The troopers each grabbed a leg in addition to an arm. They half-carried, half-dragged him across the patio toward the parking lot. Jules scooped up Bijou to calm her down and get her out of the fracas.

Jayden yelled, "Stop! Stop it. You're hurting me. You have no reason to come up here and drag me out like I'm some sort of criminal."

"Mister Diamond, you are under arrest for the murder of Charlotte Daniels. We told you that inside."

"Who the heck is that? I don't know anyone named Charlotte." Jayden freed one arm from the taller trooper's grip and flailed it around. "This is so uncalled for. And so unfair. I didn't kill anybody."

The shorter trooper ducked to avoid Jayden's swing. The other trooper scowled and grabbed Jayden's arm and pulled it behind his back, and cuffed him. "Charlotte Daniels went by Sorbonne. We are arresting you for her murder."

Jayden went limp like a petulant three-year-old. The officers lowered him to the ground.

"You can make this easy or hard. Your choice," the shorter trooper grunted.

Jayden looked around and rose to his feet. When he noticed people watching, he yelled, "This is reprehensible. You're targeting me because I have a past. You have no proof. This is all a huge mistake. I'm being framed."

The two officers guided Jayden to the blue and gray cruiser. The crowd that had gathered to watch the drama slowly drifted to whatever they had been doing previously as the cruiser kicked up a small dust cloud as it bounced down the maintenance road.

Jules turned to leave as Kat descended the stairs with two black nylon bags.

"Are you okay?" Jules asked.

"Why wouldn't I be?" Kat's mouth formed a straight line. "You think you know someone. I'm always surprised what people will do." She threw one bag over her shoulder and disappeared between the row of RVs.

Jules caught a glimpse of the stylist knocking on the door of a large trailer that looked more like a tour bus. She disappeared inside when a young brunette with long, straight hair opened the door.

Jules shrugged off Kat's attitude and headed to the office to see if the news of Jayden's arrest had spread across the resort.

Bijou and Jules jogged up the steps to the store's porch. She opened the screen door, and Bijou barged in.

Roxanne, in her tailored denim shirt, khakis, and chunky orange necklace, put her phone down and picked up the dog. "Where have you all been?"

"We went for a walk and bumped into some commotion over at the RVs."

A puzzled look crossed Roxanne's face.

"Two state troopers arrested one of the stylists for Sorbonne's murder."

Her aunt's mouth formed a small "o."

Before Jules could comment further, Lester, the groundskeeper, raced through the front door. After stopping to catch his breath, he said, "I have news. The police scanner has been hot today."

"Are you okay?" Roxanne asked.

"Fine. Just a little winded," the older man said. "I heard on the scanner that the police have made an arrest, and they're going to have a press conference later today."

"Two troopers took the male stylist away," Jules said.

"Wheeeee doggie," Lester declared. "I guess the sheriff got his man."

"That would be nice. I haven't seen much of him lately. He's been working almost around the clock," Roxanne mused.

"Well, I'm headed back home in case anything else comes across the airwaves. I'm sure the film crew will be relieved that the hunt for the murderer is over." The screen door slammed behind him.

Something nagged at the back of Jules's thoughts. Could Jayden really be responsible for Sorbonne's death? She shrugged off the gloomy feeling. "I've got to head to town to do some errands. You okay if I leave Bijou here?"

Roxanne nodded. "We'll be fine. What else could happen?"

Jules needed to clear her head of thoughts of murder and Jayden's arrest. After stopping by the bank and the drug store, she made a quick stop at Honey's Fruit Stand on the edge of Fern Valley for ten pots of fall mums and a bag of apples. The fall flowers were what the tiny houses needed to brighten up the area and make it more festive. After stuffing them in the cargo space, Jules slammed the door of the Jeep and headed to the resort.

She followed the long line of cars down the resort's driveway and dodged pedestrians in the graveled lot. Fans wandered around the parking lot and gathered near the cordoned area. She hoped it was because of the show and not the murder.

Parking in front of her cabin, she jogged over to the office to get the golf cart.

After loading all the mums, she drove slowly across the resort and gave the film crew a wide berth. She didn't want to interrupt filming or have to dodge equipment or cameras. The tiny house village looked eerily empty. Starting at the Beatrix Potter house, Jules placed burnt orange sunburst mums on each side of the porch.

Yellow was the color choice for the Baum house. It looked like a normal fall day, no trace of the police tape and no indication that they had found a body here. Jules eyed the porch with the bright flowers.

The deep purple mums were perfect for the Rowling house. Jules climbed the three steps and deposited one flowerpot on each side. The burst of color looked great next to the white railing and the purple door. Of all the houses, this was her favorite. Jake had built a tiny reading nook under the stairs to the loft, and he'd put 9 ¾ on the front door as the house number. Harry Potter fans would love all the little touches from the wizarding series.

Jules leaned on the banister and looked out at the woods. Everything seemed to be under control. The crew, looking like ants in constant motion, milled around the tree line. Drake and his guys had corralled the onlookers into a viewing area that seemed to expand each day.

As she turned away, Jules noticed something on the wooden post on the other side of the steps. About a foot over her head, there was a brownish smudge. She spotted another one down near her ankle. When she stepped back, there were several more on the porch's decking. She pulled out her phone and snapped several shots. She texted Sheriff Hobbs and added the photos for good measure. The smudges looked like dirt, but on closer inspection, Jules let out a gasp when she realized they were drips. Blood?

Jules plopped down in the golf cart. Her phone rang. "Hi, Sheriff."

"What did you find?" It sounded like Sheriff Hobbs was chewing something.

"I was putting out fall flowers, and I noticed some marks on the porch of one of the tiny houses. It looks like something dripped down the post. I think your guys might want to take a look at it."

"I'll send someone out. Can you cordon off the area?"

"Sure, but I have a guest staying there. Should I move him?" she asked.

"Which house is it?" Jules could hear tapping in the background.

"The one Rod Avery is using."

The sheriff paused. "I'll get someone over there as soon as I can. I don't think you'll need to move him. They'll collect evidence, and then you can do what you need to do."

"Thanks. I'll be waiting in front of the house." She hoped it was dirt, but she had a sneaking suspicion that it wasn't. Why was the blood on the Rowling house and not where Sorbonne had stayed or was found?

Jules knocked on the door. "Housekeeping." No one answered. She sat on the porch to wait.

Twenty minutes later, Jules spotted a police cruiser heading her way down the maintenance road. The sheriff parked in the front lot, and he and a guy in a navy windbreaker hiked over, each toting several black bags. None of the fans seemed to notice the police presence.

"Hey, Jules," Sheriff Hobbs said when they were close enough to the golf cart. "What did you find?"

"I noticed this on the post, and when I checked it out, I found a few others. I was hoping it was dirt."

The sheriff stepped closer for a look and nodded. "This is Ben Thomas. He's one of the forensic guys."

"Nice to meet you," said the man with the salt and pepper buzz cut who leaned over and pulled out gloves and a digital camera from one of the bags.

"Anybody in the house?" Sheriff Hobbs asked.

Jules shook her head. "They're filming right now."

Sheriff Hobbs and Jules stood nearby and watched Ben meticulously photograph, catalog, and measure every square inch of the post and porch decking. Then he used a variety of tools to take samples of each of the stains.

When Jules started to fidget, she slid into the front seat of the golf cart to wait, and the sheriff joined her.

Almost an hour and a half later, Ben called out and startled Jules. "I'm wrapping it up here. I've collected and tagged the evidence. Sheriff, could you come over and help me? I'm going to tent off an area to do a quick test with Luminol on the porch to see if there's anything else we can't see. I need you to hold this black cloth around it to block out as much light as we possibly can."

Sheriff Hobbs rose and climbed the three steps. Ben sprayed the area and pulled out a black light. The brown spots and some drips not noticeable before glowed a bright blue under the light. Ben photographed these and began packing his gear.

"So, it's definitely blood?" Jules asked.

"Most likely, but we can't say for sure until the results come back from the lab. There are a few other substances that react to the chemicals, but my hunch is that it's blood traces. I'll get everything shipped tonight. Oh, and I may have a partial print from the spot on the post," Ben said.

"Good work. Maybe some of the missing pieces are starting to fall into place," Sheriff Hobbs said.

Ben finished repacking his camera and picked up his gear.

Sheriff Hobbs said, "I'm gonna stop by Jules's office for a minute. I'll meet you back at the car."

"Hop in. I'll give you a ride over." Jules dropped Ben and his gear at the sheriff's car, and then she and Sheriff Hobbs tooled over to the office.

Bijou greeted Sheriff Hobbs with enthusiastic yips. After a few pats, he leaned over the counter to talk to Roxanne. Feeling like a third wheel, Jules scooted into her office.

A few minutes later, Sheriff Hobbs popped his head in the doorway. "The film crew over at the barn?"

She nodded.

"I'm going to talk to the producer. Hopefully, he'll cooperate. If he doesn't, I'll be back with a warrant for the key."

Jules let out a deep breath that she didn't realize she was holding. Was the show's producer somehow connected to Sorbonne's death?

Chapter Eight

Tuesday

Jules cranked up a jazz station and cruised into town. She circled the block where Lula Belle's sat next to the offices owned by J. P. Gross. Her goal this morning was to try to get in to see Jayden at the county lockup. Thoughts of his arrest bumped around her head all evening and jumped on her train of thought every chance they got. Jules wanted the chance to ask him some questions.

She turned on a cross street near the government center to find parking. After a quick mirror check, Jules slammed the Jeep's door.

A wave of warm air, combined with a heavy antiseptic smell, hit her as she opened the glass doors. The beige and grey decor looked like it was last updated when pet rocks and disco balls were the rage.

Ashley Sharpe greeted her from behind a thick glass window. "Hey, Jules. It's kinda crazy here today. If you're here to see the sheriff, he's going to be tied up for a while. Is there something I can help you with?"

"I was hoping to stop in and see Jayden Diamond for a few minutes."

"Uh, let me check. I know he's back there. Not sure if he can have visitors, though. Sheriff said no press."

"I'm not with the press." Jules smiled.

"True. Then I guess it's okay. Let me buzz someone to take you back." The perky receptionist pushed several strands of hair that escaped from her ponytail off her face. She picked up the phone and talked in low tones. When she was done, she looked at Jules. "Have a seat over there. Mike Cooley will be out in a minute or two to get you."

Jules tried to get comfortable in the plastic chair to no avail. Mike Cooley, a former all-county wrestler from Jules's high school days, interrupted her squirming when he opened the thick oak door and said, "Hey, Jules. Follow me. You can visit for about fifteen minutes. But I need you to leave your personal belongings in a locker. No phones." He pointed inside a workroom with a wall of small metal lockers.

"Not a problem." She set her belongings in one of the square lockers, and he gave her the key.

"Any weapons on you? Even though I've known you for ages, I'm still going to have to pat you down before you go in. You can't touch him, and you can't give him anything."

"I don't have anything on me."

The deputy, who still sported a stocky wrestler frame, stepped forward and patted her down. "Okay, follow me."

Her shoes squeaked on the institutional tile floor as she followed Mike through a warren of halls to an interrogation room.

The battleship-gray door creaked when Mike opened it. Jayden, sitting on the other side of a scarred oak table, looked up. His thin wrists were cuffed to rings in the tabletop, and he wore ankle restraints over his jeans. He looked like he had aged ten years since yesterday.

"Jayden, are you okay?" Jules sunk into the plastic chair across from him.

Awkwardly, he tried to bury his head in his cuffed hands. "I knew this was going to happen. I had a record, so they zeroed in on me. Jules, I didn't kill her. She annoyed me on good days, and I despised her on bad days. But I didn't kill her." The young man sobbed into his folded arm.

"Jayden, I want to help you. Do you have an attorney?"

He sniffed. "My mom found some lawyer. He's supposed to show up this afternoon. I'm stuck here until who knows when. And it could be longer if that lawyer doesn't do his job."

"I need you to tell me what you know about Sorbonne."

"Why do you want to help me?" he sniffed.

"She died on my property, and I need to make sure the murder doesn't damage the resort. It's all I have, and I've worked too hard for it to be ruined." One of the chair legs scraped the well-worn tile floor as she shifted in her seat.

"You believe me?" Jayden looked up at her with his bloodshot eyes. A puzzled look crossed his face. "I don't know how much good my new lawyer will do."

"I do. I think you were set up. Someone was doing a bad parody of the *Wizard of Oz* with Sorbonne's murder scene, and I think your rainbow scissors were the perfect prop. Who knew you had them?"

"The makeup trailer was hardly ever locked. People come and go all day. The scissors were in a case in my drawer. Anybody who's ever been in the trailer knows the stuff's never locked up."

That didn't help. "Who knew you had a record?"

"Everybody. I didn't try to hide it. Or the addiction problem. I've kicked that, and I'm working on the anger management crap."

"Did they know the details of your arrest?" Jules asked, staring at the stylist.

"Probably a few people. I shared it with Kat, Tess, and Rod. Somehow Sorbonne and Chavis found out. Loose lips, you know. They joked sometimes about me stabbing someone. It didn't really bother me. That awful night had nothing to do with my clients. It was a fight that got out of hand. We were all high. The other guy said something that made my blood boil, and I stabbed him in the hand with my shears. He didn't die. He got a little of what was coming to him and about ten stitches." Jayden slumped down in his chair. His shoulders sagged.

Jules felt sorry for Jayden. He looked more like a lost kid than the over-the-top stylist. "I'll see what I can find out. Anybody you suspect in Sorbonne's murder? Any information could be helpful."

"Nobody liked Sorbonne. I'm sure the suspect list would be long if they looked past me. She was always tattling on the crew to Rod. And she threatened to write the actors out of the script if they didn't do what she wanted. They were all scared of her. I don't know who died and made her queen."

"There are other writers," Jules said. "How did she get all that power?"

"Who knows. She probably had dirt on someone. She would cozy up to anyone she thought could help her. She remembered everything, and she'd throw it back at you if she could. I think Eric, our executive producer, brought her in on the project. Sorbonne always acted like the favorite child. She's been around since the beginning."

"Anyone else?"

"Tell the cops to look at her paramours. Being married and old didn't stop her from catting around like she was some hot commodity. She fancied herself a cougar, but she was really more like a saber-toothed tiger. That's where I'd start looking." For a moment, a glimmer of hope flashed across his face.

Jules nodded. "I've got to be going. If you need anything, please have the sheriff call me. He knows how to get in touch with me." Jules rose and knocked on the metal door.

"Thanks for coming. I hope my lawyer can work his magic, and I'll be out of here soon." Jayden let out a long breath.

"Take care," Jules said.

A deputy unlocked the door, and Jules waved over her shoulder to Jayden, who slouched again in his seat. The heavy door clanked behind her.

On her way to the Jeep, she tried to shake off the feeling of melancholy that weighed heavily on her. Her gut told her that Jayden didn't kill Sorbonne, but she needed proof. Maybe the blood evidence would exonerate him, but the killer was still running around loose. The sheriff wouldn't be too happy with her nosing around in his investigation, especially when he had someone in custody. But it did happen on her property, and she was pretty good at uncovering information.

Chapter Nine

Wednesday

A buzzing burrowed into Jules's brain. She sat up and shook off the remnants of a dream. When she realized it was her phone, she fumbled in the dark and eventually found it on her nightstand. 12:48. She didn't recognize the number. "Hello."

"Jules, Jules Keene?"

"Yes." Jules didn't recognize the soft female voice.

"Jules, it's me, Poppy Carlson. I need your help."

"What can I do for you?"

"I went into town with some of the crew. They took the car back, and now I'm stuck. I can't find an Uber driver anywhere near here. And you're the only one who's answered your phone. Can you come and get me?" the publicist slurred.

"Where are you?"

"We were at some place called Red's. Some guy at the bar gave me directions to your place, and I started walking, but I ended up in town. Everything around me is closed. I'm near some place called Lula Belle's, and next door, there's a glass door with "Gross Landscaping" on it. That's funny," she snickered.

"Stay there. I'll be there in about ten minutes."

"Okay. You're a peach. See you soon." Poppy giggled.

Jules grumbled and found some jeans and a sweatshirt. "Why can't she call Drake or Rod?"

Bijou looked at her, but she didn't have the answer either.

About fifteen minutes later, Jules drove slowly down Main Street toward Lula Belle's. Everything was dark except for a couple of streetlights. She looped around the block in case Poppy started walking again. No publicist in sight.

She pulled into a parking lot down the street and dialed Poppy's cell. It rang and rang. When the perky voicemail finished, she said, "It's me, Jules. Where are you? I'm in front of Lula Belle's."

Jules disconnected and retraced her path through town. She tried Poppy's phone again, but it went directly to voice mail this time. Dropping the phone in the passenger seat, she cruised around the block a third time and looked down side streets and in parking lots for the young woman.

Her frustration rising, Jules drove back to the resort. She hoped she would find Poppy along the route, but she had already gotten lost once this evening. Jules pulled into the lot by the office. Still no Poppy.

She jogged over to the back door and let herself in. She flipped on a light and waited for her laptop to wake up. Deciding against a cup of coffee, she looked up Poppy's vintage trailer number. A5, the 1954 Airstream that Jules had decorated in honor of Elvis's first recording with Sun Records.

Jules shut her laptop and turned off the lights. She powerwalked to the vintage trailers. No lights. No signs of life. She knocked on the aluminum door and waited.

As she stepped off the stairs and decided to return to her Jeep, the door opened. A sleepy Rod Avery in a black T-shirt and lounging pants opened the door. "Jules?" Light from inside the trailer pooled out and around Rod. He rubbed his eyes and ran a hand through his gray buzz cut.

Jules hoped he couldn't see the surprise on her face when he opened Poppy's door. "I'm sorry to disturb you at this hour, but is Poppy here?"

"No. She went out with friends. What time is it?" He looked at his watch. "Almost one-thirty. She doesn't usually come in until after two or three."

"I got a call from her that she needed a ride, and when I went into town, I couldn't find her. I was checking to see if she was here." Jules tried not to fidget.

A look of concern flashed across his face. "No, she's not back yet. When did she call?"

"About one o'clock."

He pulled out his phone and dialed. He disconnected when the call went to voice mail. "I have some missed calls, too. I think we should go back into town. Gimme a minute to get some shoes."

A few minutes later, Rod followed Jules across the grass to the parking lot. She unlocked the Jeep, and he climbed inside.

"I'm sorry to disturb you, but when I couldn't find her, I was worried. She said she was at Red's Honky-tonk and planned to walk back to the resort but ended up in town. I told her to stay at Lula Belle's, but when I got there, she was nowhere to be found. I looped around the block I don't know how many times." Jules tried to keep the panic out of her voice.

The producer frowned. "She thinks she's invincible. I love her spirit, but sometimes, she takes chances that aren't always the best choices."

"I'll show you where I looked before. See if you can get her on the phone." Jules clipped her seatbelt in place.

Jules sped toward town as Rod texted and called to no avail. She drove down Main Street and slowly down the side streets near Lula Belle's.

After about a half hour, Jules pulled into an empty parking lot and fumbled for her phone. She got Poppy's voicemail again. She checked the Facebook and Instagram sites for *Fatal Impressions*. The last post was at nine last night.

Rod broke the silence. "Let's head back to the resort. I'm sure she's caught a ride with someone, or she's crashing somewhere."

"You sure?"

He nodded. "She's a night owl. But she's always a professional. She'll be at work on time."

Jules put the Jeep in gear and drove at a snail's pace, still scanning the roadside for Poppy.

When she pulled in next to her cabin, he said, "Night. Thanks for trying to find her. I'm sure she'll turn up with a reasonable explanation." Rod slammed the passenger door and jogged toward Poppy's trailer.

Jules hoped Rod was right, but she had a sinking feeling in her stomach.

After tossing and turning for the rest of the early morning hours, Jules decided to get up and shower at seven. Maybe a couple of aspirin would help get rid of the dull headache pounding behind her eyes.

The hot shower and the caffeine and sugar combination helped. She checked her phone to see if Poppy had ever responded. No missed calls or texts from the publicist and no new posts to any of the show's social media sites. Jules, with Bijou in tow, strolled to the office to do some work and get her mind off the early morning phone call.

When they climbed up the back steps, Roxanne, who sat at the other desk flipping through folders, greeted them with a wave.

Jules set down her keys and phone on the desk. "You're here early."

"I decided to tackle the accounts this morning to make sure everything's up to date."

"I got a strange call from the show's publicist in the wee hours of the morning. She said she was with people at Red's, and she needed a ride back. She couldn't get an Uber."

Her aunt snickered. "In Fern Valley?"

"That's when it got weird. I told her to stay put, and I'd pick her up in town where she walked from Red's, but I couldn't find her anywhere. I drove back and checked her trailer."

A look of concern flashed across her aunt's face.

"I knocked on her door, and Rod Avery answered" Her aunt's eyebrows shot up several inches. "He said that it wasn't unusual for her to stay out late. But he must have been a little bothered because he went back to town with me to search for her. We never found her. He was pretty confident that she got another ride or crashed with someone. I hope he's right."

Roxanne frowned. "I guess he knows her best. I wonder how long their thing's been going on? There's a big age gap."

Jules shrugged. "I'm going to see if Poppy showed up for work." She picked up her phone and exited through the back door.

Bypassing the fan viewing area, Jules made a straight line for the barn.

Sherri stood behind the hurricane fencing with her clipboard at the ready.

"How's everything this morning?" Jules asked.

"Good. Filming's underway already. I emailed you an update on the locations for the next two weeks."

"I appreciate it. Have you seen Poppy this morning?"

"No, but Rod's over there. He'll know where she is." The woman's ponytail bounced as she pointed with her clipboard.

Jules waved and walked toward the producer, who stood near a group of younger guys dressed in black.

Rod looked up from his vinyl binder. "Morning." The guys from the crew walked off in different directions and blended in with the activity on the set.

"Did Poppy make it home?" Jules whispered.

A frown crossed the producer's face. "No. I haven't heard from her. She's usually not this irresponsible. I'll deal with it later. I need to get back to work." Rod slammed his binder shut and jogged toward the cameras.

Jules dialed Poppy's number again, hoping the publicist would answer. The call went straight to voice mail.

Not having any leads, Jules walked to the lodge to find the front doors locked. She circled the building. The catering crew had the kitchen door propped open, and Jules wandered in. Two cooks chopped onions and peppers on the large aluminum table. They paused and watched her approach.

"I'm Jules Keene from the resort. Have you seen Poppy Carlson today?"

Both men shook their heads and returned to chopping.

Jules strolled through the kitchen to the dining room. A man in jeans supervised two women cleaning the tables in front of the oversized fireplace.

"Good morning. I'm Jules. Have any of you seen Poppy Carlson this morning?" The two women hesitated and looked at the man.

"No. But it was busy in here. She might have slid through the chow line without me noticing. If I see her, I'll let her know you're looking for her."

After thanking them, Jules retraced her steps and headed out the kitchen's back door. She made one last stop at Poppy's trailer. Jules's constant knocking was acknowledged only by silence and a few chirping birds.

Jules hoped the publicist would show up after lunch. She returned to her office and pulled up the *Fatal Impressions* Instagram and Facebook accounts. No new posts since yesterday.

"What are you up to?" her aunt asked from the other side of the office.

Before Jules could comment, Lester blew through the front door. The screen door slammed in his wake. The groundskeeper stood in the doorway waving his arms. "You're not going to believe this. You are not going to believe this. It happened again."

Roxanne stared at him. "What happened again?"

Lester paused. "The police found a body in town this morning. It's a good thing they're filming here today. I heard they had a bunch of the streets blocked off, and they're calling it a crime scene." Lester paused. Jules had not seen him this hyped up since some teens hijacked his riding mower and took it for a joyride across the field into the meadow.

"Another body. Oh, my stars," Roxanne said. She pulled out her phone and tapped a text.

Jules's stomach dropped to her feet.

"They didn't say officially who it was, but I heard the police and EMTs talking on the scanner. It's one of the gals from the film crew."

Jules's knees felt weak. She slid into her chair and grabbed the armrest to steady herself. "Which one?" she blurted.

"That little, tiny blond gal. Pixie? I can't remember her name."

"Poppy?" Roxanne asked with a pained look on her face.

"Yes, that's it. They found her behind one of J. P. Gross's buildings about an hour ago."

First Jayden's arrest for Sorbonne's murder, and now this. Why hadn't Poppy waited for her in town? Jules rose and headed to the refrigerator for a Coke, hoping it would settle the bats in her stomach. "Anybody else need a drink?"

"No, thanks. I wanna get back. I don't want to miss anything on the scanner." Lester turned and slipped out the door.

"Let me know what you hear," Jules said to the back of the groundskeeper.

"Holy cow," Roxanne said. "I was supposed to have lunch with Matt today, but that's probably unlikely now. Last night didn't work out either. He and his crew were here searching your other tiny house late into the evening."

"Did he say whether he found anything?"

Roxanne shook her head.

"I can't believe it. I tried to find Poppy this morning. I should have kept looking," Jules whispered.

"Why'd she call you?" her aunt asked.

"She said no one else answered the phone. I feel terrible now."

"You can't blame yourself. You got up at oh-dark-thirty and tried to find her when none of her friends or coworkers did." Roxanne walked over and patted Jules's shoulder. "This is not your fault. You can't take the guilt for this. You were trying to help."

"Thanks. But she ended up dead," Jules said, wiping the tears that leaked out of the corner of her eyes.

After composing herself, she dialed the sheriff's number. After the beep, she said, "Sheriff Hobbs, this is Jules. I heard about Poppy Carlson. I thought you might want to know that I got a call from her early this morning. Call me when you can."

Jules opened her spreadsheet. Maybe looking through her collection of random notes would help her find something. She had seen Sorbonne, Kat, and Poppy locking lips at different times with Chavis Ratner. Could either of the two survivors on this list know anything about the murders? Jules shuddered. Neither woman deserved to die. Jayden had a criminal past, and the police thought he was Sorbonne's killer. But if both women were killed by the same person, that could help Jayden because he couldn't be the guy. Her curiosity got the best of her. She felt compelled to keep digging to see what she could find.

She searched for all she could about Poppy Carlson. There were thousands of posts by her, but not a lot of information on her biography. She left college in her sophomore year to be a social media influencer. Jules wondered when she met Rod Avery and how serious their relationship was. He had seemed concerned but not overly crazy that Poppy hadn't returned after a night out.

Jules's phone buzzed and vibrated on the desk. "Hello, Sheriff."

"Hey, Jules. So, when did Poppy Carlson call you?"

"It was almost one. She said she had been at Red's Honky-tonk, and she was going to walk back to the resort. She said she got mixed up, and she was near Lula Belle's."

"Not even close," he replied.

"I know. I told her to stay put, and I drove to town to get her. When I couldn't find her, I went back to the resort and knocked on her trailer to see if she was there."

"And?"

Jules walked him through the events of the early morning hours.

The sheriff cleared his throat. "I'll send someone by to talk to you and Rod. We're going to be tied up in town for a while. Tell Roxanne I'll text her when I can and not to wait on me for lunch or dinner."

"Will do." Jules disconnected. She stood and stretched. Exhaustion, with the help of caffeine and sugar, had turned into nervous energy. "Sheriff said that he'd text you later and that he'd most likely miss dinner. Are you going to be here for a while?"

"Yup. It sounds like any plans I had are going to be canceled. I'll hang out here."

"I'm going to run into town. I'll be back soon."

"Be safe. Bijou and I will let you know if anything happens while you're gone," Roxanne said.

Filming was in the woods again today, so no traffic in Fern Valley. She cruised by Lula Belle's and let out a gasp when she saw the heavy police presence. As she signaled to turn to circle around the block, she spotted the barricades and a deputy she didn't recognize. Jules did a quick turn and parked across the street.

She jogged around the block and stood behind the crime scene tape. A forensic team worked painstakingly in the alley. Police tape cordoned off the entrance near a large blue dumpster that was the last place anyone saw Poppy alive. Jules shuddered.

After forty-five minutes of watching techs take pictures and measurements, Jules decided to head back and come up with a plan to ferret out more information from the film crew.

Chapter Ten

Thursday

The sheriff's heavy boots thudded on the wooden floor of the store. "Hey, Jules. Hey, Rox. I like the sweater." He pointed to Roxanne's pink cashmere that she had paired with her signature pearls.

"Good to see you, too, Matt. Gettin' any sleep?"

"Not much. A lot going on lately."

"Let me get you a cup of coffee while you chat with Jules. You've got a look of all business in your eyes, so I'm guessing you're here to see her." Roxanne winked at her beau.

"I'll make it up to you. I promise," he drawled.

"I know you're good for it." Roxanne winked again as she retreated to the office.

"Jules. You got a few? I need to get your statement."

"Come on back." Jules waved her hand toward the Dutch door.

Sheriff Hobbs settled in one of the vinyl chairs at the table and pulled a notebook and pen from his front pocket. "When did you last hear from Poppy Carlson?"

"About one o'clock. She said she needed a ride back from Red's. She complained that she couldn't get an Uber."

"In Fern Valley?" He shook his head and continued to jot notes.

"I guess the bouncer told her that we don't have a local taxi service. She ended up on Main Street near Lula Belle's and J. P. Gross's place."

Roxanne set a steaming mug on the table in front of the sheriff. She patted his shoulder and returned to the store.

"Then what?" he asked.

"I drove into town to get her. But I couldn't find her. She didn't answer my texts or calls. I went back to the resort and knocked on her trailer, hoping she was there." She paused, and when the sheriff looked up, she continued, "Rod Avery answered her door."

"Describe his demeanor."

"He seemed pretty calm. It was obvious that I woke him up. He said Poppy tended to stay out late. He went back to town with me, but we couldn't find her."

"And?"

"We came back here. He was pretty sure she got a ride with somebody. He seemed okay with it."

"Anything else?" The sheriff took a sip of his coffee.

"She didn't show up for work. And then we heard about what happened…." Jules's voice trailed off.

"Can you think of anything else that's related?"

Jules shook her head.

"My guys have interviewed Rod Avery, and he let us search the trailer and the tiny house where you found blood."

"Any leads?" Jules asked, hoping he was in a sharing mood.

"What you found on the porch rail was definitely blood. The lab is running more tests. We also got a partial print, but so far, no hits in the database. We'll keep at it."

"So where was Sorbonne killed?"

"We found an earring in the grass near the house where she stayed. And then there were the bloodstains you found on the house with the purple door. There was an area in the grass that was trampled and worn. The best guess is that she was killed outside and dragged to where we found her." The sheriff closed his notebook.

"What about Poppy?"

"She wasn't stabbed," he said, rising. "Thanks for the coffee."

Jules hoped he would continue, but he leaned over to pet Bijou. Then he pulled the bottom half of the door shut behind him.

The sheriff stopped at the front counter, where he spoke to Roxanne in low tones. Not wanting to eavesdrop, Jules flipped open her laptop and added what the sheriff said to her collection of random data.

Later that evening, Bijou was in no hurry to return home after her walk. Neither was Jules. The chilly night air and the brisk jaunt helped clear Jules's head. They wandered around the RVs toward the tiny houses.

A bouncing light inside the Potter house caught her attention. She moved closer, standing in the shadows in case someone was watching. She paused. A small light bobbed in and out of view from the front window. Jules edged closer. Curiosity got the best of her. She moved nearer to the porch.

The light bounced around and disappeared. She pulled out her phone, not sure whether to call Jake or the sheriff.

The light was back and moving around again. She inched closer to the railing. The bright dot looked like a fairy dancing in the dark window.

She shook off the distraction and focused on the house. The light wiggled and disappeared.

Jules waited and listened. The front door creaked, and Bijou growled. Jules leaned down and patted the dog to quiet her.

The door opened and closed. A shadowy figure stepped off the porch.

The person checked his cell phone, and the device created enough light for Jules to see Chavis Ratner's face. Bijou growled and barked.

"Bijou," Jules commanded.

Chavis sauntered closer, and Jules turned on her flashlight app. "Oh, hi, Chavis. How are you this evening?"

"Uh, good," he replied, stopping near her. He ran his hand through his hair as Bijou let out another growl. "I'm out for an evening stroll. Lovely place you have here."

"I hope you enjoy it."

"I've got to get back. Toodles." He strutted toward the RVs.

That was odd. What was Chavis doing in Sorbonne's place, and how did he get inside? I could kick myself for not confronting him.

Jules rushed home to put Bijou in the cabin. She searched through her hall closet for her Mag-lite flashlight.

She jogged first to the office for the key and then back to the tiny house. Jules found the front door unlocked. She let herself in and flipped on the downstairs lights. The drawers were slightly ajar, and the knickknacks on the bookshelves were askew. What was he looking for?

The items on both nightstands looked moved, and someone had sat on the bed. Mel and Crystal would never have left a rumpled bed.

The kitchen cabinets had been searched, too. Some of the doors and drawers hung open slightly.

As Jules turned to leave, she heard the front door open. Panic welled up inside. Is *Chavis back? I should have locked the door.*

Not seeing any weapons handy, she flipped her flashlight upside down to use the long, black handle as a bat. She stepped toward the doorway with her Mag-lite held high. Jules held her breath, listening for any noise.

Someone's heavy step echoed through the house.

Jules willed her heart rate to calm down. She took a deep breath and lunged forward with the loudest, primal yell she could muster.

"Jules!" Jake yelled as he grabbed the flashlight she wielded. "What are you doing here?" Jules released the handle, and Jake took it from her.

"When Bijou and I went for a walk, I spotted a light inside this house. It turned out to be Chavis Ratner. I wanted to see what he was up to and how he got in." She took a deep breath. "He was searching for something, and the door was unlocked."

"So, either someone left it open, or he jimmied the lock." Jake locked the door and stepped out on the porch.

Something rattled around the doorknob. The lock clicked, and Jake stepped inside. He returned a credit card to his wallet.

Good skill to have. That explains how Travis probably got the door open.

"I'm going to look around outside," he said.

While Jake was gone, she did another walk through the house. Nothing looked like it was missing, just rifled through. Jules retraced her steps and turned off the interior lights.

When she heard footsteps on the porch, Jules opened the door.

"Nothing weird out there. Everything looks okay," Jake said, stomping on the porch to knock loose the grass and dirt from his boots.

"Nothing's missing inside either." Jules flipped off the foyer and porch lights and pulled the door shut behind her. Then she shook the knob to ensure it locked.

"I'll walk you home if that's where you're going."

"Yep." Jules grabbed his hand. No one else was out. A few lights glowed in the windows of the vintage trailers.

They stopped on her porch. As she unlocked the door, Bijou ran from window to window to get a good look at who was there.

Jake hugged Jules, and she let the warmth envelop her as she got lost in the embrace. Thoughts of murder and Chavis vanished. Jake leaned over and kissed her, and his kiss turned into a mini make-out session. A jolt of excitement surged through Jules and almost curled her toes.

Before she could speak, he interrupted her thoughts of a rendezvous when he said, "See you tomorrow." He turned and headed toward his cabin.

Bijou danced around until Jules picked her up for a kiss. "I wonder what Chavis was searching for," she said.

Bijou cocked her head to one side.

"He tried to be cool about it, didn't he, but he was definitely hiding something."

Chapter Eleven

Jules had been at her desk since the orange and pink streaks showed over the mountains. She had caught up on all the resort emails and the ones from the business council. She'd even put the finishing touches on her newsletter and created the next business council agenda. Staying busy helped her shake off the feelings of guilt about not being able to help Poppy.

Now, she stretched and brewed another mug of coffee. Filming was back at the barn and around the woods today. As soon as Roxanne got in and settled, she would nose around the resort to see if she could find out more about Chavis, Kat, and Rod.

Bijou stirred in her puffy pink bed. The store door opened, and Bijou jumped into security mode. Her yips turned into a happy dance when she saw Roxanne open the dividing door.

"Hey, y'all are here awful early." Her aunt dropped her insulated lunch bag and bright pink Versace purse on her desk. "I need caffeine."

"Late night?"

"I stayed up waiting for Matt to call. He and his team were working on the murders. He couldn't talk until about one-thirty. I hope he gets some sleep soon. He's dead on his feet." Her aunt sighed and settled in at her desk.

"Any news?"

"Not really. You know how he is. Matt doesn't talk about work much.

He's got a state trooper helping out on the Sorbonne murder. He said the investigators were going to regroup today and put together a war room for both murders. Right now, they think there are two different killers, but I guess they'll know more after the crime scene stuff comes back."

"Interesting. I went to see Jayden earlier this week."

"The hairdresser they arrested?" Roxanne chose a strong coffee pod and put her mug under the machine's spout.

"Yep. He said he didn't do it, and no one liked Sorbonne. And that a lot of people were scared of her."

"That doesn't surprise me. Learn anything that would help the sheriff?" her aunt asked.

"No, not really." Jules logged off her laptop and stood. "I'm going to check out today's filming. Bijou, hang out here with Aunt Roxanne."

The dog raised an eyebrow but didn't stir. Their conversation interrupted her mid-morning nap, and no one had any treats. Jules stepped out the back door. Crowds had already formed in the parking lot and the fenced-off area in the field. She walked in the opposite direction to avoid the people on the grass. No complaints yet from her fellow business council members about the swarm of people. Hopefully, everyone was spending money in town.

Jules cut through the amphitheater toward the cabins. As she edged closer to the barn, she noticed Lester on the front porch of his cabin. She sped up to catch him before he headed to work. Stopping in front of the rustic cabin, she waved.

"Good morning, Jules. What brings you out this way?" The groundskeeper tied his work boot and stood.

"Just checking on things. How are you?"

"Good. Sleep deprived. I howled too late the last few nights, listening to the police scanner. They were burning up the airwaves with those murders. Lately, it's been all about that little blond girl. Such a shame."

"Anything interesting?"

"A lot of it was chatter," Lester said. "Police checking in and out of places. The forensic team was on site in town for a long time. The sheriff's folks have been putting in some late hours. I doubt Miss Roxanne will see much of her boyfriend in the next few weeks. Oh, J. P. Gross had a meltdown when he found out the body was behind his property. It took the sheriff and a trooper a bit to calm him down. He did a lot of ranting about the evils of Hollywood. I heard that from Milton, who heard that from Pete."

Jules hoped Lester didn't see her roll her eyes. That would mean the next business council would be raucous with J. P.'s gripes. He never missed an opportunity to take a jab at her since he had gladly taken on the role of her nemesis. "Anything about the other murder?" she asked.

"Right now, they're treating them as two different cases, but I heard them talk about sharing notes and working together since they're both linked to the Hollywood people. Do you think this will affect the filming?"

"It hasn't so far. I'm headed over to get the scoop. Let me know if you hear anything else. I hope they find the killer or killers before it scares off customers."

"Will do, Boss." Lester waved as Jules continued her walk.

The film crew faced the woods on the far side of the barn. A few people milled around near the tree line. She hiked over to the orange fencing and scooted closer for a better view of the lighting crew arranging booms and equipment. Black boxes, carts, and wires covered the entire area.

Tired of waiting for the filming to start, Jules cut through the space next to Jake's cabin. She ducked behind the barn and peeked around the corner. A row of white canopied tents lined her field. It looked like booths in a craft show. Under one, Kat arranged her gear.

Jules strolled by the line of tents. The first was empty. She slid under the canopy of Kat's tent and said, "Hey, there. How are you?"

The stylist jumped.

"I'm sorry. I didn't mean to startle you."

"It's okay. We're all a little on edge lately," Kat said.

"I'm sorry to hear about Poppy."

Kat shrugged her shoulder and continued to unpack brushes and makeup containers. "It is what it is. Nobody can explain it, and we're all wondering if it's a pattern or two separate incidents. Everybody'd probably be relieved if it were the latter, but we still have two dead bodies."

"Any indication that the two murders are related?" Jules asked as she pretended to look at the styling items Kat had arranged on a plastic table.

"Who knows. We never had any problems before." Kat paused. "They both worked for the production company. I'm sure Rod and Sherri are running around trying to figure out what to do next. They're trying to put on a strong face for us. He said this morning that filming will continue as scheduled."

"Wasn't he close to Poppy?"

Kat raised an eyebrow. "If you're asking if they were a thing, then yes. And yes, there was quite the age difference. They were together, but they didn't flaunt it. I don't know how serious it was. I think there was some kind of understanding." Kat continued to rearrange her things on the table. She pulled a metal and black stylist chair in front of a freestanding mirror. "He was close to Sorbonne, too, but not in a romantic way. He was probably the only one on the set that Sorbonne admired. She liked take-charge kinds of guys with lots of power. And for some reason, he seemed to like her. Most people couldn't stand to be around her for long periods of time."

Before Jules could respond, Kayleigh Bell and a young brunette burst under the canopy. They were laughing and chatting.

Kat's glum demeanor changed instantly. Her face lit up with a bright smile. "Hi, Kayleigh. Hi, Reagan. I've got this spot all ready for you." She patted the chair's seat. "Jules, have you met Kayleigh and her assistant, Reagan? Jules owns the resort."

Kayleigh Bell, who wore harem pants and a blousy tunic, dropped in the chair and kicked off her shoes. The other woman pulled out her phone and stood behind her. Her rapid tapping was the only sound in the tent for a few seconds.

"It's so nice to meet you," Kayleigh purred. "Kat, I need you to do something about these dark circles. I haven't slept well in a couple of nights. And my feet hurt already, and we haven't even started the day."

Kat pulled out her foundation airbrush and tested the spray on her wrist.

Jules was going to say something to Reagan, but she didn't look up from her phone. "It's nice to meet you both."

Jules continued her walk and found a spot near the barn to watch the crew's activity. Teams of people in black shirts moved constantly. She lost count of how many light and mic checks they did. The cameras pointed toward the woods, but so far, there was no action.

From her vantage point, Jules spotted Drake Kelly in all black with shiny aviator sunglasses, talking to two men she didn't recognize. She slid around the orange fencing and sidled up to the men to see what was on the docket for the day. "Hi, Drake." Waving as she approached, the men stopped talking and looked at her.

"Hey. Everything okay?" Drake scrutinized the horizon, always watching.

"Fine. I was going to ask you the same thing. I wanted to check in to see if you all needed anything," Jules said.

"All's well. We're here today and tomorrow, and then we're back in town for a while. This is C.J. and Titus, my crack security team. Guys, this is Jules, the owner." The two men resembled linebackers, and Jules wasn't sure which man was which.

Both men nodded as Drake continued to scan the tree line. "We're planning out our coverage for filming and trying to keep the lookie-loos corralled. Every once in a while, one of them sneaks in through the woods. We had to stop work this morning for a punk with a drone."

The men nodded again. Jules shifted her weight from foot to foot.

"Seems everybody's got one lately and wants to use it as a spycam," one of the men said.

When no one said anything, Jules broke the silence. "I'm sorry to hear about Poppy."

Drake shook his head. "It's sad and shocking. She'll be missed. She always did a good job of promoting the show and knew how to get people hyped up on social media."

"Did she have any problems with anyone?" Jules looked for a reaction from any of the men.

"Nah. Everybody liked her," said the first guy.

"Except Sorbonne," the second man added, shaking his head.

"Well, we know she's not the killer." Drake smirked and scanned the nearby field. The crowd grew by the minute.

"I'm going to check in with Rod and Sherri." Jules looked around to see if she spotted either the producer or his assistant.

"He's over there under that big tent." Drake pointed to the tent that looked ready for a wedding.

"You've got the crowd control down pat," Jules peered at the crowds behind the fence line.

"Yup," Drake said. "Two buses came in about an hour ago."

"Part of the production?"

The director of security shook his head. "Nope. Full of fans here to watch the filming."

Jules's eyes widened. She hadn't realized how popular *Fatal Impressions* really was. She made a note to check on the porta-potties. They would probably need a few more at this rate. She waved over her shoulder and headed toward the barn, where Rod and several men in black stood off to the side. The one with the clipboard waved his arms, and the camera crew moved closer.

Rod and his staff looked busy, so she stayed out of their way. Although she was in no hurry to go back to work, no other opportunities to chat up the film crew about Sorbonne or Poppy's deaths materialized. When she started to get fidgety, she moseyed back to her office. She was a little disappointed at not uncovering any new information.

After a raucous greeting from her terrier, Jules straightened her desk and found the stack of script notes from Sorbonne's house. She copied them and put the originals in a folder. Then she texted Sherri to see if Rod had a few minutes to chat.

Before Jules could dive into any new tasks, her phone dinged with a text. **He's free now at the barn.**

Jules tapped as a return message. **Be right there.**

She grabbed the folder and her phone and zipped out the back door. Jogging across the field, she dodged cables, boxes, and equipment, littering the grass. Spotting Rod by a large camera, she gingerly stepped over wires and headed his way.

"Sherri said that you had a few minutes. I hope I'm not interrupting. I am so sorry about Poppy."

"I keep expecting her to walk through the front door at any time." He took a deep breath. "We're on a tight schedule, so there's not much wiggle room to postpone filming. I gave them a short break for the crew to set up the next scene, so I have a couple of minutes. What can I help you with?"

"When we cleaned Sorbonne's residence, we found these. I'm not sure if they're important or not. Some looked crumpled." She handed him the folder of script pages.

He flipped through the loose pages. Rod paused and stared at one. A frown crossed his face. He flipped through a few more. "Thanks. I think these are discards. There weren't any others, were there?" His eyes looked tired, and his face had more gray stubble than she remembered.

"No. This is it."

"Thanks. We have spies everywhere who are always trying to get a line on the upcoming storyline. Some want to leak spoilers, and others want a ransom to keep quiet. That's why we always film two or three different endings for each season. Even the actors and crew don't always have an idea of which cliffhanger scene will air."

Jules nodded. "Drake and I packed Sorbonne's belongings, and he took her personal stuff. I found these during the cleaning later."

"I'll check them out. Thanks." The producer looked distracted. His eyes darted around the field as he talked.

"I'm guessing that the sheriff will be by to look through Poppy's trailer if he hasn't already. Do you want us to pack her items?"

"A state trooper came by this morning. I'm back in the tiny house I'll have Drake or Sherri call you when the cops are done with Poppy's trailer."

Jules stifled the urge to ask more questions. He was all business and didn't seem too broken up over the murder of his girlfriend. "I'm sorry for your losses."

"Uh, yep. It's tougher on some of us than others, but we've got a job to do," he said with a half-smile.

Jules said, "I'll wait to hear from your folks."

He nodded and strode over to several gaffers and a light rig. Yesterday, he had been helpful in her search for Poppy. She hadn't spent much time with Rod before, but he seemed odd today. She had expected to see more grief. He looked like he hadn't slept much lately. But he seemed ready to get back to the predictability of work.

She strolled toward the tents on her way to the tiny houses. In the second tent, she heard voices and laughing. She paused. Chavis Ratner spun around in the stylist chair as Kat stood nearby with a makeup brush held high.

"Come on. Sit still," she said. "Quit fooling around. I need to finish here. Derek and the others will be in shortly."

"You don't want to have any fun lately." He pulled her closer and kissed her neck. Kat pulled away. "What's wrong with you? I'm working here. Plus, I'm not in the mood right now. I've got a lot of things to do."

"Work never stopped you before." Chavis stepped closer. His smile looked like a leer to Jules.

"Keep your voice down. You don't want anyone to hear you. And aren't you even the least bit concerned that you were involved with both of them?" Kat frowned at the actor, who kept trying to take the brush from her hand. "You need to be careful."

"*We* need to be careful." He ran his hand through her hair. "Nope. You're involved, too."

"Purely professional. You're probably on a suspect list," she said, readying a thick barrel brush.

"It doesn't really affect me. Life goes on. Everything's good, and if you think about it, it probably turned out well for you, too."

"Really?" Kat paused and stared at him. "The police will look closer at you when they find out you were concerned about the script changes."

"Why should I worry? They've got their man. And Sorbonne promised me she'd completed her rewrites. I'm safe. And I'm connected to you, too, and you're not dead." His smile formed a thin line across his face.

Jules's eyes widened. She took a couple of steps back, so they wouldn't notice she was eavesdropping. On a whim, she clapped her hands and said, "Hey, Kat. Are you around?" as she stepped under the tent.

Both Kat and Chavis stared at her.

"Oh, hi, y'all. I was doing my rounds, and I was hoping to catch Kat before she got slammed with work."

"I'm kinda busy." Kat stepped away from Chavis and arranged the brushes and makeup containers on her table. "What do you need?"

"I had a few questions for you, but I can come back later. Hi, Chavis. You made my staff's day when you took selfies with them at the store."

He stood and straightened to his full height and hit her with his most dazzling smile. "Anything for fans. What kind of questions?" Chavis took a step closer to Jules, and his stare felt like it bore into her. "Maybe I can help."

Although she knew that she should probably be quiet, Jules wanted to see if she could shake things up. "I was curious. When my crew cleaned Sorbonne's house, they found some script drafts. I thought I heard Rod or somebody say that the scripts for the season were already written."

Chavis stiffened. "They are. Sorbonne was a pack rat. She never threw anything out."

"But sometimes there are changes." Kat looked up from her equipment. A half-smile crept across her face.

Chavis glared at Kat.

"So, do you all know what's happening this season?" Jules asked, watching Chavis. "That would be a great secret."

"Of course. The actors do." Chavis waved his arm and turned his head toward Kat.

"I thought they said that y'all film two or three endings. You know, to throw off suspicions about the cliffhangers." Jules glanced at Kat and then stared at Chavis, who fidgeted in place.

"That's a given," he smirked. "But some of us know things. Some of us have connections." He turned on his heels and ducked under the canopy. "See you around, Kitty Kat." He went from nervous to cocky in a few seconds flat.

"They don't want spoilers out there ahead of the season. And they give everyone talking points about what to hype. Bloggers and fans go to great lengths to find out secrets. I never quite understood it," Kat said. "Well, I guess I'm free for a while. What did you need?"

"I had a couple of questions. The night that Sorbonne died, there was a lot of noise around the tiny houses when the police were there. I was curious. Rod, or anyone else for that matter, never came out to see what was going on. Any ideas why?"

Kat raised one eyebrow. "He probably wasn't in that evening. He spent most of his time at Poppy's." After a pause, Kat said, "When you're on set, you're thrown together, and things happen. Rod likes blonds, and I got the sense that Poppy would do anything to further her career. A win-win for both. A hit show can do a lot for a publicist."

Jules nodded. "I went to see Jayden. He said his mother hired a lawyer."

"I hope he's doing okay. He swears he's innocent, but the police must have their reasons if they arrested him. He has a temper and a past. You never know about some people." Kat's voice trailed off. She shrugged her shoulder. "Maybe Sorbonne pushed him too far. It wouldn't surprise me." She looked past Jules and focused on something in the distance. "Anyway, I've got to get ready for the touchups. The actors will be here shortly. Do you need anything else?"

"No, that's it. See you around." Jules backtracked out of the tent and did a quick walk by the tiny houses. Jake had finished the latticework under the Baum house. The little cottages made up a tiny, vacant neighborhood.

Jules pulled out her phone and dialed Sheriff Hobbs as she strolled to the office. After his long voicemail message, she said, "I forgot to tell you. I found something in Sorbonne's house when I was packing her things. I think you might be interested."

By the time she got back to her desk, her phone dinged with a text from the sheriff. **What did you find?**

Pages from some scripts with notes.

I'll stop by tomorrow on my way in, he replied.

Chapter Twelve

Monday

Jules finished her yogurt. Instead of begging for a lick, Bijou barked and zoomed to the Dutch door. Sheriff Hobbs made his way inside and petted her after closing the door behind him.

"Hey, Jules. I heard you stopped by to see Jayden Diamond." A slight scowl darkened his face.

"I did. I wanted to see how he was doing."

He raised an eyebrow. "That's it?"

She nodded and hoped he wasn't fussing at her for snooping around his investigation. Jules changed the subject before he could comment further. "I want to thank you for stopping by this morning. I know you're terribly busy." She rummaged through the pile of notes on her desk and pulled out a folder with copies of the script that she had made for him. "I found this when I was cleaning up after Sorbonne."

He took the folder and thumbed through it.

When he didn't respond, she said, "There are some handwritten notes on this that may be of interest to you. It's not a full script."

"Discards?"

"Probably, but the notes about the cast were interesting. Didn't know if it would help you or not. These are copies. I gave the originals back to Rod Avery. He seemed to be concerned that the storyline would leak out. Then he acted like they were outdated pages with no value. I don't know the whole story, but I had heard that Chavis was worried about Sorbonne writing him off the show. When I chatted with him yesterday, he seemed much more confident that his role was secure."

An emotion crossed the sheriff's face, but Jules wasn't sure whether it was anger or concern. "Thanks. How are you all doing?"

"Everything seems to be humming along here. The Hollywood people are interesting."

The sheriff raised his eyebrows.

"They're a little more cavalier than we are…." Her voice trailed off.

"How so?" He pursed his lips.

"Forget love triangles. I think some of them are up to rectangles or pentagons."

Sheriff Hobbs stifled a laugh. "I know. We've encountered some of the gossip in our interviews. They seem to be a curious bunch."

Jules had hoped to get an idea of where his investigation was going, but so far, he hadn't shared much. She took a deep breath and decided to ask. "Do you think it's someone local or someone from *Fatal Impressions*?"

"The murders were different, but there are some commonalities."

"Like what?"

The sheriff frowned and didn't continue.

"But Jayden was in custody, so he can't be the lone killer of both women," Jules added.

"Yep. My guys are working on it, and we've got some help from the state police. Anything else you want to tell me about the night Poppy called you?" He pulled a small black notebook out of his shirt pocket.

"No, only that she wasn't where she was supposed to be in town. I went there twice and couldn't find her, and she never answered my calls or texts."

"Well, she definitely encountered someone else. You may have heard we found her in an alley behind J. P.'s buildings on Main Street. She was sitting up with her back leaning against the dumpster. An insurance agent came into the office early, and he noticed her when he took out the trash. He thought she was sleeping at first. But she had marks around her neck. We found her long scarf and purse in the dumpster. We'll know more when we get the full autopsy results back. If you come across her phone, let me know. We couldn't find it at the scene." He pocketed his notebook and paused. "Keep an eye out and call me if you see anything suspicious. I don't think there's reason to panic. Be alert and aware of your surroundings." The sheriff stood and adjusted his gun belt. "Tell Jake hello for me." He put on his hat and strode to the front door.

Surprised that the sheriff shared any details, Jules turned on her laptop. There could be two killers, but two murders in the same week seemed coincidental to Jules. She grabbed her cell phone and called her friend from college, Gwen Pierce. Gwen, who went by the moniker Pixel for her forays into the gaming world and the dark web, was a whiz at finding information that normal people didn't have access to.

After several rings, she heard, "Hey, Jules. What's up?"

"Hi. I hope I'm not bothering you. I have another favor if you're not swamped with work."

"That's no problem. I've been meaning to call you, but it felt a little silly."

"What's up?" Jules asked.

"I wanted to ask you about *Fatal Impressions*. I heard that you're right in the middle of ground zero."

"That's an understatement. I've got a resort full of actors and crew. And the place has been packed with spectators. Some of them even come by the busload."

"Sounds awesome. I love that show."

"Then you need to come over. I'll give you a tour. My staff went nuts when they met Chavis Ratner."

Pixel giggled. "I would too. So, what can I do for you?"

"Well, the show is what I'm calling about. One of the writers was killed and left under one of my tiny houses. The police arrested one of the stylists for the murder."

"Hmm," Pixel said.

"But that's not all. Then the publicist was killed in town. That's two murders in one week." Jules sighed and rubbed her temples.

"That's nothing for a big city, but it's noticeable around here. How about you give me some names, and I'll see what I can find."

"You're the best. Then we can meet for lunch. My treat," Jules said.

"And a backstage tour of the film set?"

"Of course. What works with your schedule?" Jules asked.

"Today's good."

"Perfect. I'll text you the list of names. Where do you want to meet for lunch?"

"How about Pop's Diner about one, and then we can swing by your place. I'll see what I can find about the names on your list," Pixel said.

"See you then." Jules disconnected and texted her the names of the key players.

"Okay, sitting around here isn't going to shake up anything. Let's go for a walk, Bijou." The terrier danced around Jules's feet.

The pair trekked across the grass to where a line of people crossing the grass looked like an endless stream of marching ants with lawn chairs and coolers. She had no idea where all these people were coming from.

Not that interested in the crowd of fans, Bijou led the way to the tiny houses. They walked around the Baum house. Hopefully, she'd have time this weekend to start working on ideas for Jake's new project. She couldn't wait to see what ideas he had for the next build. Each one had a different surprise for the guests. To save space in the Baum one, Jake had built a revolving bookcase for the library. Jules added her design touch by putting grey, black, and white books on one side. She used books with bright colors on the reverse side of the bookcase. It doubled the storage area, and guests could switch from black and white to color, like in the movie. It would be fun if Jake could incorporate some kind of tower design into the new house.

A door slammed, and Bijou turned and yipped. Rod Avery slung a black backpack over his shoulder and descended the stairs of the Rowling house.

"Good morning," Jules said.

"Hey, there." The man in jeans and a maroon pullover leaned down to pet the terrier. "I see you brought your assistant."

"She's in charge most days." Jules laughed. "How are things going?"

He straightened up. "Filming's our focus for now. We're bouncing between your place and town over the next few days. The location and accommodation have been great. Thanks."

Jules smiled. "Glad to hear it."

The producer disappeared into RV land. Bijou tugged on her leash, wanting to follow her new friend. Jules guided the terrier toward the barn, and they stood on the edge, watching the setup. So far, the crew appeared to be the only ones moving around the set.

When Jules and Bijou became restless, they meandered toward the fan area and the office. A loud whoop rose up and echoed across the field. Chavis Ratner and Derek Stone stood in front of the barn waving, and the crowd roared.

Back in the office, Jules had enough time to check her email and make several calls about the upcoming business council meeting. The council had divided up into teams to plan three weekends to attract guests to the town in December. The ideas so far included a parade of lights, concerts, a Taste of Christmas, and a walking tour with carolers and holiday treats. Jules was excited about all the interest in the holiday festival. Elaine, Kim, and Darlene volunteered to collect all the ideas to make sure each weekend was packed with things to do. Jules made a note to get with Elizabeth Rhoney at the bookstore to share holiday social media feeds to create a buzz like Poppy did for *Fatal Impressions*.

When it was close to lunchtime, she set the phone's auto-attendant and shut Bijou in the back office. Jules cruised down the resort's main entrance, dodging fans who were still walking in from the main road. When she turned toward town, she found cars parked on both sides of the two-lane Baker Road as far as she could see. It occurred to her that she'd have to hire security to direct traffic if this kept up.

She dodged pedestrians and drove slowly to Pop's on the edge of downtown. The 1950s-themed diner had been a fixture in Fern Valley for years. The current Pop, the grandson of the original owner, kept the tradition alive. The diner, known for its pizza, cheeseburgers, and extra-thick milkshakes, was the town hangout after high school football and basketball games.

Jules had to tour the lot twice before she found parking near the kitchen door. After a hike around front, she found a line that looped out the door and around the corner. A young guy in a black leather jacket and slicked-back Elvis hair and sideburns collected names on a clipboard.

Not seeing Pixel, she added her name to the list and found a spot to lean against the wall. After scrolling through her Facebook feed, she noticed her petite friend walking up the sidewalk.

"Hey, there. I haven't seen you since last summer. We need to hang out more often." Pixel hugged her.

"It's been crazy lately." Jules sighed.

"Tell me about it. I'm still teaching an adjunct class at UVA, and my day situation is busier than ever. It's great to see you." Pixel pushed her jet-black hair behind her ears. The ends of her hair looked like they had been dipped in purple dye.

"Keene. Party of two," the Elvis-lookalike yelled.

The two women followed him inside through the art deco doors to a room in the back decorated in Buddy Holly, Big Bopper, and Ritchie Valens memorabilia.

Marsha and her pink bouffant hairdo dropped off two menus. "How are you gals doing? Can I start you all off with drinks?"

"Uh, I'll have an unsweetened iced tea." Jules closed her menu.

"How about you?" Marsha said, looking at Pixel.

"I'll have a glass of water with lemon. I know what I want if you want to do lunch orders now, too. I'll have the jalapeño veggie burger with onion rings."

"I'll have a side salad," Jules said.

"Be back in a flash." Marsha disappeared into the kitchen.

"So, what's it like to hang out with *Fatal Impressions* people every day?" Pixel's eyes sparkled. "You know my gamer friends would kill for that opportunity. Everybody is crazy about that show."

Jules smiled a half-smile. "It's interesting. It's not what I thought it would be. They film the same scene over and over. And none of it's in order, so it's hard for me to follow a story. I have no idea what's going on."

"I want all the dirt on Chavis Ratner." Pixel leaned forward like she was getting ready to listen to a secret.

"He made my part-timer's day when he took a selfie with her. He's friendly when fans are watching, and he has lots of female friends." Jules wrinkled her nose.

"What's he like when nobody's watching?" Pixel pulled out her phone.

"Cute, but arrogant. He acts like he's blessing us with his presence," Jules whispered.

Pixel giggled. "I still want to meet him. He looks like the guy next door. You know, the Captain America type. Okay, here's what I found about the names you sent me. I didn't find a lot on Sorbonne. She seems to have created a new persona and a new life and left the old Charlotte behind. Maybe it's because she put a baby up for adoption the summer after she graduated high school. She also had some kind of car accident later, and she declared bankruptcy when she couldn't pay off her medical bills. Not sure if any of those facts matter. I had to dig to find the baby news." Pixel paused.

"Wow, that doesn't sound like the carefree teen years. Maybe that explains a bit of why she was the way she was."

"Let's see what else I found. Poppy Carlson was twenty-five. She has been a social media influencer for the last four years. She actually quit college to do that full-time. And she's been seen on the arm of a string of rock stars and Hollywood bad boys over the years. Gossip sites have her linked to Chavis Ratner and producer Rod Avery, who, by the way, is fifty-six." Pixel raised her eyebrows and took a breath.

Jules jotted notes on the back of an envelope she found in her purse. "Speaking of Rod, did you find anything on him?"

"He's been married three times. Only wife number one was his age. Her name was Cara Jones-Avery, and they had three kids, Zach, Michael, and Brittany. Married in 1983 and divorced in 1996. He met his second wife, Delia Tate, on the set of *Careless Whispers*, a rom-com he produced and she starred in. She was twenty-four when they married in 1997."

Pixel paused and glanced at her phone. "Oh, sorry. Work junk. Rod left wife number two after five years for Tricia Scott, a makeup artist, on the set of *Red Dawn Rising*, a short-lived military-themed TV show. His marriage to Tricia, a twenty-two-year-old, lasted two years. He's been single ever since, but there are photos of him around Hollywood with other actresses younger than his kids. I dug up some tax problems from the nineties, but it looks like that was paid off and settled before it went to court."

"You've been poking around all kinds of sites. That's a lot of information. I ran out of paper to take notes on." Jules took a deep breath. "Rod and Poppy definitely had a thing going. And he was staying in her trailer," Jules added.

Marsha interrupted with their lunch. "Here you go. I'll be back in a few with refills. Enjoy."

"Thanks." Pixel bit into her veggie burger.

Jules put her napkin in her lap. "A lot of the cast and crew definitely have active social lives."

Pixel's eyebrows shot up under bangs. She continued to munch on her veggie burger.

Marsha breezed in and dropped off refills. "It's crazy busy in here today. I'm going to leave the check now. But don't hesitate to holler if you need anything else." The waitress zipped over to another table.

Pixel set down her burger and flipped through the notes on her phone. "Let's see, Jayden Diamond was born Jayden Holmes in Baltimore. He ran away a couple of times and eventually ended up in Los Angeles. He started out as a makeup assistant and bounced around between production crews, drag shows, and upscale hair salons. He was homeless for a while, but things improved. He's been with *Fatal Impressions* for the last three years."

"He said he did time."

"Yep. Got that right here." Pixel scrolled through her phone. "He got busted a couple of times for solicitation and selling weed. And the big one was when he got in a fight and stabbed a guy with scissors. He seems to be clean since that arrest. My sources hinted that it was a fight stemming from a love triangle. He served some time for it. I couldn't find any more arrests after that."

Jules polished off her salad. "I went to see him in jail. He swears he's being framed."

"Because of his past?"

Jules nodded. "His scissors were used in Sorbonne's murder. They found her under one of my tiny houses. The one themed for L. Frank Baum's books."

Pixel stifled a giggle. "Somebody had a thing for the *Wizard of Oz*."

"It gets worse. She was wearing Christian Louboutin stilettos, and the shears had a metallic rainbow shine to them."

This time, Pixel didn't try to stifle the giggle. "Either clever or kinda trite."

"She wasn't killed where she was found. A couple of days later, I found blood on the porch of the Rowling house where Rod was staying."

"Be careful. You've got a kook running around." Pixel popped part of an onion ring in her mouth.

"But that's not the end of all the weirdness. Poppy had been at Red's Honky-tonk the night she died. She started to walk home, but she got lost. They found her in town. It's not like we have a wild nightlife down there. The sidewalks still roll up after dark."

"Any theories of how these could be related?" Pixel asked, pushing her plate away.

"I found some script pages in Sorbonne's place. They weren't all from the same episode, but there were notes in the margins." Jules leaned forward and whispered, "One note said that Kayleigh was pregnant."

"Awww," Pixel said. "She's married to ex-boy band singer Emory Aames. They're cute together. I like her character."

"She's always wearing baggy clothes, so it might be true." Jules took a sip of her drink.

Pixel raised her eyebrows. "Anything else?"

"There was a note about killing off Chavis Ratner's character," Jules whispered.

"No!" her friend said a little too loudly. People at the table across the aisle stared.

"Chavis and Rod acted like they were early drafts, and the script for the season was already done. Chavis was pretty adamant that his role continued into next season."

"Whew. You had me worried for a bit. He's a nice guy in the show. Everybody likes him as Beau Staunton." Pixel cleared her throat and leaned forward. "Okay, how was he supposed to die?"

"A wolf attack."

"No way." her friend said. "His character lived in the mountains and befriended wolves. They turned on him? Not cool."

"And then buzzards were supposed to lead Ashe Lyons's character to the mauled body."

"Nooooo!" Pixel repeated. "That can't be how it ends for him. I hope he's right about a new storyline. It would be terrible if they killed him off. Thousands of female fans will be outraged. Not a smart move. Let's talk about something else. I don't even want to think about it." Pixel winked at her. "So, anything else exciting going on in your life?"

Jules smiled and hesitated.

"Do tell," her friend said.

"Well, I sort of started seeing Jake."

"No way. That's great. But what's sort of?" Pixel stared at her.

"We've been pals for years, and he works for me. I don't want to draw too much attention to a relationship. It's awkward. He's so different from the Idiot. And I haven't dated much since the divorce. I like slow and steady."

"Good for you. You need some fun." Pixel wiggled her eyebrows.

Jules nodded. "He's great."

"And good looking. Here's my two cents. Don't worry about what others think. Life's too short to care. Be happy."

"Thanks," Jules said. "I'm getting used to the idea of having someone else around now. It's nice not to spend all my nights at home with my DVR. What about you?"

"I met this guy online. He's a gamer. He lives in Richmond, so we don't see each other that much. But it's fun so far. Nothing serious. Right now, work and the class I'm teaching keep me pretty busy."

Marsha returned to pick up their plates. Jules grabbed the check and put down her credit card.

"Thanks for lunch," Pixel said. "Next time, it's my treat."

"It's the least I can do for all the info you uncover for me. You're my best resource." Jules winked at her friend.

They vacated the table when Marsha returned with the receipt, but their conversation spilled into the parking lot for another twenty minutes.

"Do you want to come back to the resort now, or is another day better?" Jules asked.

"I thought you'd never ask. I am dying to see the behind-the-scenes stuff. I'll follow you if that's okay."

Jules bobbed her head. "See you back at the ranch." Before they pulled out of the lot, she had an idea and texted the resort cleaner, Mel Carson. **Let me know when you go to do the Rowling house.**

Her phone binged seconds later with a response from Mel. **It's first on the list tomorrow A.M.**

Pixel parked her black Prius behind the Jeep at Jules's cabin.

"Let's head over to the office, and I'll get you a VIP badge," Jules said.

After a quick stop for a nametag and lanyard and introductions to her staff, Pixel and Jules hiked to the edge of the woods where gaffers and other crew moved equipment. Pixel snapped photos of everything.

After an hour, they still hadn't seen any filming. Jules said, "Hey, I have an idea. Let's walk over there to the tents. Maybe we can see some of the actors there."

Pixel and Jules wandered over to the little tent city. Jules peeked under the tent canopy. Ashe Lyons sat in the chair while Kat touched up his makeup. The thirty-something actor with reddish-brown hair chatted with Kat. She ran a hot comb through his hair and sprayed the results. The top resembled a pompadour, but the sides were shaved close to his head.

"Hi, Kat," Jules said, ducking under the tent canopy. "This is my friend Pixel. I was showing her around the grounds."

"Ashe Lyons," Pixel blurted out. "Kix Burton is such a great character on the show."

"Ashe, I'm about done here." Kat removed the plastic drape and dusted the actor's shoulders with a small brush.

"It's always great to meet a fan." Ashe stood and extended his hand. Pixel hugged him.

"Jules, can you get a picture?"

"Here, Kat will take it, so you both can be in it. Kat, take several," Ashe said, pointing to the stylist. After a couple of serious and goofy poses, Ashe continued, "Thanks, y'all. See ya around."

"Pixel, this is Kat Mason. She does hair and makeup for the cast. And she's been with the production company since the beginning of the show," Jules said.

"Nice to meet you," Pixel said. "So, I bet you know all the secrets."

"And I know how to keep them," Kat said with a sly wink.

Then after a long pause that made Jules fidget, she added, "Thanks for being our photographer. We're going to continue our walking tour."

"The craft line opens soon. Everybody's there if you're looking for stars," Kat said as she straightened her station.

"Thanks for the tip. See you around." Jules followed Pixel outside.

"Well, we have time to kill until five. What do you want to do?" Jules asked.

"How about if I keep poking around the list of names to see what else I can find, and I come back another night to meet the cast? I've got class at six-thirty."

"Deal. I'll check the schedule and give you some dates."

The friends walked back to Pixel's car and chatted for a few minutes in the driveway. Jules's phone buzzed as Pixel drove down the road to the resort's entrance.

Dinner tonight? Jake texted.

b

Her phone binged with his reply. **Nacho Mama's? 5:30?**

It's a date. She added a heart emoji and a smiley face.

Chapter Thirteen

Tuesday

Jules awoke from a deep sleep at four-thirty in the morning. Unsure what caused her to stir, she listened for any strange noises. All was quiet except for Bijou's steady snores. Jules's mind raced. Not being able to shut out the thoughts of the two murders, she got up and pulled on her robe and fuzzy slippers. She padded down the hall to the kitchen, poured a glass of milk, and settled in at the table with her notebook.

Her doodles turned into a list of names. She drew lines connecting Chavis, Kat, Sorbonne, and Poppy. She added Jayden and his history. Then she added more lines that connected Jayden to the others. She listed other *Fatal Impression* names and jotted what she knew of them in the margins. Then she sketched tiny houses and noted where Sorbonne and Rod stayed and where the blood was found.

She stared at her diagram, but nothing pointed to a killer. Her gut feeling was that Jayden didn't kill Sorbonne. But how could she prove it? And who else had a reason to kill the two women?

After a quick shower, Jules downed her breakfast and a jolt of caffeine. She laced her work boots and wiped her hands on her jeans. "Bijou, you're on guard duty here. I'm going to meet Mel and Crystal over at the tiny houses. Be back soon."

The Jack Russell scurried into the den and jumped on the couch for a morning nap.

Jules pocketed her keys and walked to the tiny houses. The tranquil morning provided the perfect backdrop. As she walked farther, the peaceful setting morphed into a beehive of activity near the woods. The crew, carrying boxes and equipment, wandered in and out of the trees.

A few minutes later, she plopped down on the porch of the Rowling house to wait for the mother-daughter cleaning pair. She pulled out her phone and texted the sheriff. **Cleaning trailers and tiny houses. Do you have everything you need where Rod stayed?**

A few seconds later, her phone dinged with his response. **We're good. Didn't find anything inside the house.**

Jules didn't let that discourage her. She wanted to take a peek, and with a guest staying there, she needed a cleaning or maintenance reason to go inside.

Mel and Crystal pulled up a few minutes later in the golf cart with a vacuum, mops, and cleaning supplies. The pair hauled everything onto the porch.

Mel knocked on the door, "Housekeeping."

When there was no answer, she unlocked the door and held it for her daughter. Jules picked up the vacuum and carried it inside. While the mother-daughter pair split up and divided cleaning tasks, Jules poked around in the living room. Nothing was out of place. Rod was much neater than Sorbonne. No personal effects. She lifted the lid on the storage bench. Empty. The bookcases contained only her decorative items and books. And even the secret reading room under the stairs was filled only with books and overstuffed pillows. Disappointed, she popped into the kitchen and bathroom for quick searches. Not finding anything, she searched the pantry, downstairs closet, and the bedroom in the loft.

On the nightstand, Jules spotted a black, three-ring binder. She flipped through the tabs. The binder held four scripts. She skimmed the cast list on the coversheet of each. Chavis was slated to be in each of them. On the floor next to the bed, she found a pile of psychological suspense novels and two more black script binders. Chavis appeared in all episodes of these. She flipped to the end of the last one and let out a breath. Chavis's character was still alive, and he had quite a few lines. The last binder was missing the final two scripts. She snapped pictures of all the binders and the empty slots. Where were those last two scripts? And what did Rod say about cliffhangers? She hunted around the room but didn't find anything that looked like the last two episodes.

When Crystal climbed the steps to clean the bedroom, Jules returned the binders to their original location and descended to the main room.

"Mel, Crystal. Thanks for letting me tag along today. I'm going to head back to the office."

"See you, Jules," floated in from the kitchen, where Mel stacked the tiny dishwasher.

Chavis was adamant that he wasn't cut from the show. Not having any other leads to pursue, she decided to take a walk over to the set.

Behind the barn, the gaffers, key grip, and prop master moved around in organized chaos. They dragged equipment in and out of the woods. Jules inched closer to get a better look under the several large oaks. When her eyes adjusted to the darkness of the tree canopy, she spotted Rod, Sherri, and Paul, the director, huddled off to the side of a small clearing. Chavis Ratner lay on the ground near a rotting log.

When someone off-camera yelled "Action," Kayleigh Bell stumbled through the underbrush and rushed to Chavis's side.

Jules was too far away to hear the lines. She stepped forward, determined to figure out what was going on. Two other male actors appeared, and one had a gun. As Jules moved closer, someone put a hand on her shoulder, and she yelped.

"Cut," someone yelled on the set. "Let's pick it up at Kayleigh's last line."

"Sorry. I thought you heard me," Jake whispered, pulling her in close for a hug.

"I think we're going to get in trouble for interrupting their scene." She grabbed his hand and led him toward the grassy area on the other side of the tree line. "I think I squealed too loudly."

"Didn't mean to scare you. What's up?"

"Just hanging around." Jules pushed a curl out of her face. "What are you up to this fine morning?"

"One of the gaffers said that they would be wrapping up at the barn tomorrow, so I was going to see if I can get back in there and start on a new house. I got an order from Kurt Marino. He's moving back to his parents' place after his divorce to keep an eye on them, and he wants to be on their farm, but not in the same house. He liked the design of the Baum house. This will delay the construction of the fourth house for a while."

"Congrats. It's great news about the custom order."

"He picked out the design. I'll show it to you tonight. Wanna grab dinner in town?"

"Two nights in a row?" she asked, and he nodded.

A little after six, the hostess at the Good Thyme Bistro seated Jake and Jules in a cozy corner near the front window.

They flipped through the menus until a waiter appeared. "Hi, I'm Dan. What could I get you all to drink tonight?"

"I'll have an unsweetened iced tea," Jules said.

"Same," Jake replied.

When the waiter left, Jules asked, "So tell me about the order for the tiny house."

"Kurt Marino wants me to make a more modern version of the Baum house. It's going to be his bachelor pad on his parents' farm. He wants less cottage and more modern."

"Got pictures?"

The waiter returned as Jake was flipping through his phone. "What can I get for you tonight?"

"I'll have the grilled chicken Caesar salad," Jules said.

"Uh, I'll have the spaghetti with meatballs," Jake replied.

"Any appetizers?" When Jake and Jules shook their heads, the waiter picked up the menus and disappeared in the back.

"Here," Jake said. "These are some new designs." He scrolled through a slideshow as Jules peered over at the screen.

"They're cool looking. They remind me of beach homes. They could be popular as vacation homes. Maybe we ought to try that as a marketing angle."

"I'm up for it. So, what's going on in the *Fatal Impressions* world?" Jake set his phone down and looked at Jules. "You didn't mention anything last night about the filming."

"You know about Jayden's arrest. I stopped in to see him in jail. He still insists on his innocence. There's always a whole lot of hanky panky involving Chavis, Sorbonne, Poppy, Kat, and Rod. I need a scorecard to keep up with the goings-on. Oh, and I found some discarded script pages in Sorbonne's house. She'd made some juicy notes in the margins about the actors. When I gave them to the producer, he acted like they were old versions. Not sure what to make of that."

"I've been hanging around the sets while they were filming by the barn, and I hear chatter while I'm helping Lester keep the fan area trash free. The security guards are annoyed that the actors keep mixing in with the spectators. Kat is always mad at Jayden because he's careless. And Ashe and Derek talk bad about Chavis behind his back," Jake said.

"Keep your ears open. You never know what'll be important. And thank you for taking care of the trash. It never occurred to me that we'd have that many visitors show up to watch. I need to find a way to pass out pamphlets. Roxanne thinks we should have a themed tour next summer for folks to see all the locations used in the show."

Jake nodded. "You've got to plan something to coincide with the airing of the show. Fern Valley's own Hollywood premiere."

Before Jules could answer, the waiter returned with their dinners. "Be careful of the plate. It's a little hot." Dan pointed to the spaghetti. "Can I get you anything else?"

Jules shook her head.

"Well, then. I'll check back with you in a little while."

Jules took several bites. When the lack of conversation bordered on boring, Jules asked, "So, anything new in your world?"

"When I was at the lumber yard, I got a couple of leads on folks who want to see the tiny houses. One is a writer, and he thinks it would be a great workspace in his backyard. Another guy wants one for his grown kid who's still living at home."

"You're turning this into quite a business."

"With your help." He winked as he took an oversized bite of his dinner. When he finished chewing, he said, "Wanna take a vacation when the season winds down? There's a tiny house operation in South Carolina. I thought we might be able to stop there on the way to Myrtle Beach or Charleston."

Jules raised an eyebrow. "I love Charleston and Savannah. Lots of cool bed and breakfasts and restaurants. Sounds like fun. We have a little break around Thanksgiving. The film crew would have cleared out by then, and the weather's not too terribly cold. Let's find some dates. I can make reservations."

"Or we can drive south and stop when we feel like it. There will always be a hotel." Jake took another bite of his sandwich.

"I'm a planner, but I'm up for an adventure. Pick the dates." Butterflies bounced around Jules's stomach. She hadn't been on a real vacation in a while. *Wow. An adult relationship and a road trip.*

Jules looked around the restaurant that was once the town's pharmacy. Hints of its past appeared in the current décor. The old soda fountain had been repurposed as the bar.

The waiter interrupted Jules's daydream when he stopped by with refills. "Can I get you all anything else or a dessert menu?"

"I'm good," Jules said.

"The check, please," Jake said, wiping his stubbled chin with the cloth napkin.

When the waiter returned, Jake paid the check. "So, what else should we do tonight?"

"How about a walk around town? Are you in any hurry to get home?" Jules dropped her napkin on her plate and pushed it to the middle of the table. After Jake paid the check, the pair stood, and Jules slid her hand in Jake's and led him outside toward Lula Belle's. Dusk had settled, and the streetlights had started to pop on.

"Where are you taking me?" he asked.

"I want to see something," Jules said as they walked farther down the block. All the businesses in this part of the street had already closed for the evening. At the corner, they turned at the cross street. Jules slowed her pace at the alley behind the row of brick buildings. There was no trace that this was a crime scene earlier in the week. She pulled out her phone and turned on the flashlight. The blueish-gray dumpster stood alone in the alley with a stack of wooden pallets next to it.

Jules circled the dumpster. The dirt and gravel had been disturbed on the far side. "This is where they found the publicist." Jules scooted some pebbles with her boot. She peered at the ground around the dumpster. "Hey, what time does Red's open?" Jules looked up at Jake, who leaned against the brick wall.

"I didn't picture you as a honky-tonk kind of gal. In fact, I don't think I've ever heard you talk about the club scene," he said.

Jules shrugged her shoulders. "It's a new day." Then she crinkled her brow. "Fern Valley has a club scene? There's only one bar."

Jake shrugged, and the couple walked down the alley and around the block.

"I'm curious about who Poppy was with that night, and I thought maybe we could do some snooping."

"The doors open around nine. Karaoke usually starts around ten," Jake said.

"Wanna stop by?" she asked as they approached his red Mustang.

"Sure, Nancy Drew." Jake grinned and held the door for her. "What about the sheriff?"

"Why would he care if you and I go to the honky-tonk?" Jules slid into the leather seat and clicked the seat belt in place.

Jake jumped in, and a minute later, the Mustang roared to life. They sped through town and pulled into a gravel lot. Several cars and trucks dotted the lot on the side of the building with a large red door. Barnwood planks covered the building's front façade, and a neon sign flashed on the overhang by the double doors.

"Let's go around back. I'm sure the front's locked at this hour. They don't open for a while." Jake grabbed her hand and led her around the side next to a green dumpster and an open cargo van full of amps and musical equipment.

Jules followed Jake down the narrow hallway where dishes and cleaning supplies sat on aluminum shelves lining the outside of the long walkway. He slowed as he approached a closed door. He looked around. Not seeing anyone, he knocked on the thick door.

Jules heard a faint "come in" from the other side. Jake held the door, and she stepped into a paneled office outfitted with black lacquered furniture. The "I Love Me" wall of framed photos with celebrities spread around all four walls.

"Jake," the redheaded woman behind the desk drawled. His name sounded like it had four syllables. "How have you been, baby?" The pink fringe on the woman's western outfit fluttered as she came around the desk and hugged him. "It has been so long since you've darkened our doors. How are you? We miss you." Her hair, the color of a red velvet cake, was piled high on her head, reminiscent of some country singers from the seventies.

"Carleen, it's good to see you. Jules, this is Carleen Taylor or Red. This is my…uh…boss, Jules Keene."

Before Jules could comment on his introduction, Red interrupted with, "I know who she is, Sweetie. She's Bob's girl. Roxanne's niece. I've lived in these parts for more years than I'd like to count. Welcome, it's nice to meet you. Have a seat." She shook Jules's hand with a lot of enthusiasm. "What brings y'all here?" Red slipped behind the desk and settled back in her chair.

"The publicist for the film crew staying at the resort was killed in town, and she was last seen here. She left and walked back to the resort, but somehow, she got turned around. And well, you know how it turned out," Jake said.

Red leaned forward in her chair and folded both hands on top of the papers on her desk. "Sheriff's already been here and collected the security feeds. The little gal was here with a rowdy table at the back. It caused quite a stir with the locals."

"Do you still have copies of the feed that we could see?" Jules asked.

Red paused and looked at Jake. "I guess it wouldn't hurt. She turned and tapped on her keyboard. When she located the file, she pointed her screen toward them."

Jules spotted Poppy, Chavis, Kat, and several of the crew at a long wooden table that overlooked the stage. Red fast-forwarded. People came and went from the table. It was almost comical to watch them zip around the screen. By eleven, Poppy, Chavis, and two men were the only ones at the table. Poppy leaned over and said something to Chavis. He patted her arm, and she left. Red sped through the feed. Several women in tight outfits joined the table, and Chavis left with two of them about one that morning.

"Thanks," Jules said. "Did this include your parking lot cameras?"

"Yup. We caught her talking to my bouncer Gabe. Then she walked outside to vape with a guy in black and a tall gal. About ten minutes later, she walked through the lot and turned toward town. She was by herself then."

"Do you still have the vaping footage?" Jake asked.

Red tapped on her keyboard and then pointed to the screen.

Jules and Jake watched Poppy, Kat, and one of the guys from the crew in front of the bar. The man lit a cigarette, and the others chatted. Jules wished the feed had sound. Red turned off the video as Poppy disappeared into the parking lot.

"Any problems while the film crew was here?" Jules asked.

"Not really. They were loud and definitely outsiders. Chavis Ratner caused a stir when he walked in. I don't know how much some of the good ol' boys liked having their dates drool all over the actor. But he's a cutie patootie. It looks like he left with a couple of the local gals. Probably the highlight of their year."

"Thanks for all of your help. We appreciate it." Jake stood.

"Y'all don't be strangers. I miss seeing you 'round here, Jake. Come on back anytime. It was nice to finally meet you, Jules."

"Thanks for all the help." Jules followed Jake out, and he shut the door behind her.

"This way." He pointed to the narrow hall to the right.

Jules trailed him down another long, darker hallway. They passed a swinging door to the kitchen and the bathrooms, which took up most of the hallway that opened to a brightly lit bar area. Jules blinked several times for her eyes to adjust to the glare. The bar sported every type of cowboy memorabilia imaginable. Tables surrounded the large dance floor and an elevated stage. The long bar, with seating for over twenty, was made of thick dark wood, and some kind of gold medals or coins were embedded in the poly finish.

Gabe Henderson, the head bouncer, stood watch at the end of the bar where a blond bartender sliced fruit into aluminum pans.

"Hey, Gabe," Jake said as they approached.

Gabe, who played linebacker in high school, stood and wiped his hand on his black jeans. "Hey, Jake. I haven't seen you in ages. I heard from Ashley over at the sheriff's office that you've become domesticated." He winked at Jules and clapped Jake on the shoulder.

"It's nice to see you. It's been a while," Jules said.

Gabe extended his hand. "Good to see you, too. I heard you were back in town after your divorce. Sorry to hear about your dad."

Before Jules could continue, Jake interjected, "Hey, we stopped by Red's office, and she said that the gal who was killed in town talked to you before she left."

"Uh-huh. Sad. She'd been drinking, but she didn't seem impaired. She asked for an Uber or a taxi. I told her she wasn't in New York or Los Angeles. She was going to call someone. Then she went outside with some woman. Later, that publicist came back and asked for directions to your resort."

Jules nodded. "Somehow, she ended up in town. Did you see her get in a car with anyone?"

"Nope. I was inside working the door that night. We had a scuffle at the pool tables, and I had to break that up. By the time I got that all straight, most of her party had left."

"Any odd behavior?" Jules probed.

"Nope. She was on her phone a lot."

"How did she act when you talked to her?" Jake asked.

"I told the sheriff all this when his folks were in here questioning us. She seemed nice. She didn't want to be bothered by the locals when they asked her to dance. She was in a grouchy mood that got worse when Fern Valley didn't meet her big city standards for car service." He shrugged his shoulders. "That's about it."

"Have any of the film people been back since?" Jake asked.

"The tall girl came in here one night this week with some guys. I don't think any of the actors have been back. I'm sure I would have heard about it. They suck all the oxygen out of the room when they show up."

"Thanks, man. I appreciate it," Jake said.

"Don't be a stranger. The gang's still here every week for karaoke. I'm sure they'll be in later tonight. You should come back."

Jules raised her eyebrows but didn't say anything. *Jake and karaoke. Interesting.*

"We'll stop by sometime. If you think of anything else, give me a call," Jake said.

"Will do. I heard your new business is going well. I want to stop by one day and get a tour of your houses. My brother's looking for something to put on his property by the river for a fishing cabin. I'll tell him about you," Gabe said.

"Thanks. Come on by. We have models set up at the resort." Jake handed him a business card. He reached for Jules's hand, and she followed him out the front door.

They hiked around the building to his car. The temperatures had dropped dramatically since dinner.

"It was kinda fun nosing around," Jake said, shutting his door. "I think I'm now officially your sidekick."

Chapter Fourteen

Wednesday

After another restless night, Jules showered, pulled on jeans and a sweatshirt, and put on the kettle for hot tea. She couldn't find the page where she doodled the film crew connections, so she opened a blank document on her laptop and mapped out what she knew about both murders. The players overlapped. One victim was beloved, while the other was prickly with many enemies. Lots of people with motives for Sorbonne's murder. Jules had trouble finding anyone with a grudge against Poppy. Was there another connection between the two besides Chavis and that they worked on the same show?

When the kettle whistled, she made a mug of Earl Grey tea and added honey. Sorbonne wielded power that could end careers, and she had the boss's ear. But Poppy had a happy role that lifted everyone up in celebration. Opposite sides of the coin.

Jules tapped her temple with her index finger. She had forgotten about Poppy's trailer. No one from the crew had called about Poppy's things like Rod said they would. She reached for her phone and sent a flurry of texts to the sheriff to confirm that his folks were done with Poppy's trailer and to Pixel to see if she wanted to come by and watch the filming.

A few seconds later, her phone dinged with a response from Sheriff Hobbs. **You're up early. We're done.**

She clipped her keys to her belt loop. "I'll be back soon," she said to the dozing terrier.

After a quick stop at the office for the main key, boxes, and the golf cart, Jules dragged the boxes inside Poppy's Elvis-themed trailer. Her phone vibrated, and she dropped one of the boxes.

Dinner tonight would be great, Pixel texted.

They're filming all day. Come by anytime.

2 works for me.

Jules sent a check and a smiley emoji and started her search in the bedroom. Small piles of clothes covered every flat surface, and everything had been rifled through by the investigators.

The only task in the kitchen was dumping the trash that overflowed with takeout containers. Jules would have to get Crystal and Mel over here to scrub down the flat surfaces that were dotted with dust from the fingerprint search.

She spent the next few hours packing clothes and personal items in Poppy's suitcases. She filled one gym bag with shoes and boots. The social media guru must have had a different pair of shoes for every outfit. She also had six leather jackets. Jules resisted the urge to try on the pink one with metal spikes.

On her last pass of the bedroom, she did a quick check under the mattress. Nothing there. When she dropped the mattress back in place, she bumped the nightstand and knocked off a romance novel that clattered to the floor. A piece of paper fluttered out of the book. She picked up the torn, white envelope with a Captain America notecard inside with a message scrawled in blue ink. "Forget about him. You're wasting your life. It's a job. Let's see where this goes." *No signature.*

She took a picture of it and the novel. Jules flipped through the book one more time to see if there was anything else. Then she checked the room and found thirty-five cents under the bed.

When she was satisfied that she had packed everything that belonged to Poppy, she stacked the suitcases and boxes by the front door. Dusting her hands on her jeans, she surveyed the vintage trailer once more.

Sheriff Hobbs crossed her mind, and she pulled out a phone and tapped in a text to him about the note. It may not be more than a love note, but she didn't want to take a chance. She slid the note in her back pocket with her phone and dumped the book in the nearest box.

Pulling the door behind her, Jules jiggled the knob to make sure it was locked. She drove around the trailers and circled the lodge.

Her phone dinged with a text from Sheriff Hobbs. **Put it in an envelope for me. Be by later.**

She spotted Sherri and Drake near the barn. Jules parked as close as she could without interfering with the film setup and jogged over to the pair. "Good morning. How are you?" Jules asked.

"Great," Sherri replied. "But it got a little chilly here last night. I'm a California girl. Anything below seventy-five to me is arctic. Brrr."

Drake took another slug from his to-go cup and wiped his mouth with the back of his hand.

"I packed all of Poppy's things in her trailer, and I'm going to have my cleaning crew work their magic tomorrow. Who should I give the suitcases and boxes to?"

Sherri paused and looked at Drake. It looked like she was about to say something.

"I can come and get them. You have time now?" Drake asked.

"Sure," Jules replied.

Sherri looked at Drake again. Jules wasn't sure what she was trying to telegraph to him.

"Okay. It was only Poppy's stuff, right?" he asked.

"Yes. Clothes and personal stuff."

"Okay, good," Sherri said to Drake. "Put it in the work trailer, and I'll get it shipped to her parents."

Drake nodded and followed Jules to the cart. That was an odd exchange, but Jules shrugged it off. She retraced her path and parked in front of the restored Airstream. After she unlocked the door, Drake loaded Poppy's things in two trips.

"That's all of it," he said, rubbing his hands together. "The work trailer is over in the field." He pointed past the trailers and tiny houses.

Jules put the cart in gear as Drake climbed in. They bounced across the grass, and she slowed when she approached the oversized RVs and trucks. "Which way?"

He pointed to a large navy and gray one. As Drake moved Poppy's stuff inside, Rod exited a nearby RV and put on his sunglasses.

"Everything okay?" Rod asked.

"Just fine. Jules packed up Poppy's things. Sherri said to put them inside, and she'd take care of them."

Rod nodded and walked toward the barn.

"Thanks for cleaning all that up." Drake filled the entire space of the RV's doorway.

"Not a problem. I'm sorry that we had to do it again," Jules said.

As Jules put the cart in gear, Drake said, "Any news from the police?"

She shook her head. "The sheriff said the two investigating teams are sharing information, but as of a few days ago, they're treating it as two separate murders."

"What are the odds of two random killings within the same week? Let me know if you hear anything."

"Will do," Jules said as she headed home to pick up Bijou. She would spend a few hours in the office catching up on resort and business council work until Pixel arrived.

A little after two o'clock, Jules's phone dinged with a text from Pixel, **I'm in the parking lot. Where are you?**

The office. Meet you on the porch. She forgot to ask Jake about dinner, so she sent a text to him, too. **Dinner tonight? Pixel's here.**

What time? He responded.

Fiveish. See you then.

Jules remembered the Captain America note in her pocket and dropped it in a white envelope. She scrawled the sheriff's name on the front and left it on Roxanne's chair.

"Come on, girl. Let's go meet Pixel." The terrier bounced around, ready for an adventure.

"Hey, y'all," Pixel said from the front porch swing. "I love what you've done with the place. Those tiny houses are adorable."

"They're Jake's creations. He's finished three, and now he has orders for some more. He'll be glad to get the barn back after the *Fatal Impressions* people leave. They're over there by the woods today."

"I saw that your lot was full. I had to park in the grass near the main road. Crazy fans?"

"They've been here faithfully every day. Come on."

Bijou's ears perked up, and she danced at Pixel's feet.

"Aren't you adorable." Pixel leaned over to pet the terrier and got a nose lick in the process.

"I'm going to drop Bijou off at home before we tour the set. It'll take a minute."

Pixel followed them to her cabin. Jules added food to Bijou's bowl and refreshed her water. "There you go. You guard the house until we get back."

"I like your place. You've redecorated it since it belonged to your parents."

Jules nodded, and Bijou jumped on the couch and found the perfect spot.

"So, what's the storyline this season?" Pixel and Jules picked their way across the grass to the edge of the woods.

"It's hard to tell. Nothing is linear. Rod, the producer, told me that they film multiple endings, so not even the actors and crew know which cliffhanger will air," Jules said.

"I've followed a fan group online since season one. I love the plot twists. The show's known for its surprises," Pixel said.

"I hope the head writer's death won't affect the scripts going forward. I know she had a lot of control over it. Hopefully, the remaining writers will continue to put out quality stuff."

"It will be interesting to see if it changes. I'm hoping it won't. The writing was excellent. That's part of what made the show so good." Pixel's eyes darted around, taking in all the activity.

"This is the area where the crew works. Let's see if anyone is around." Jules led the way to the smaller canopied tents.

Kat, the only one nearby, pulled brushes and bottles out of a travel bag.

"Hey, Kat. How're things? I'm showing Pixel more of the set."

"I'm a huge fan of the show. It's all anybody at work talks about when there's a new season."

Kat smiled. "It's good to see you again. What do you do?"

"I'm a computer programmer and data specialist." Pixel looked around the tent.

"And she's a college professor in her spare time." Jules didn't mention her extracurricular hacking activities.

"My friends are crazy about the show. We have watch parties for the season openers and finales. I'm so excited that you all are here in Fern Valley," Pixel said.

"It's a cool show to work on. We're like family, dysfunctional at times, but a family." Kat moved small black containers to the drawers. Then she wrapped the cord around a professional-sized hair dryer.

Before anyone could respond, Reagan and Kayleigh breezed in. "Kat, we're here. And it's my fault that we're late again. I felt out of sorts this morning, and it took a while for me to get moving. But I'm here now for you to work your magic."

"No problem. Have a seat." Kat patted the black vinyl chair.

"Kayleigh, this is my friend Pixel. And this is Reagan." The assistant had her nose buried in her phone. She looked up when she heard her name.

"It's so nice to meet you. I am such a fan," Pixel said to the blond actress.

"It's great to meet you, too. I'm loving autumn in the mountains. I've lived in Los Angeles for so long, I've forgotten what it's like to truly have four seasons."

"We'll let you all get to work. We're going to check out some of the filming, so I hope we'll see you around later," Jules said. She and Pixel ducked under the canopy as Kat went to work on the actress.

"This is fun," whispered Pixel.

Shouts emanated from the large, white tent. The pair quickened their pace and moved toward the loud voices.

"You'll do the scene the way it was written," Rod Avery boomed.

"I talked to the writers, and they thought it would be better my way. I'm surprised they didn't give you line edits and new pages." Chavis spat out the words. "The new lines are much better." He turned his head away from the producer.

"We're not changing the script. Paul's orders. So forget about it. I don't know why you're vying for more camera time. Nothing's changed around here," Rod picked up a metal travel mug. "End of discussion. And I suggest that you make every effort not to be late again today." The producer stormed out of the tent and brushed past Jules and Pixel without saying a word.

Chavis noticed the two women standing near the tent poles. He straightened his back and stood taller. Running one hand through his hair, he turned on his dazzling smile.

"This is my friend Pixel. I'm showing her around this afternoon," Jules said.

His demeanor and countenance changed in an instant. "It's lovely to meet you," he said, stepping toward them with an easy gait.

"I hope we didn't interrupt anything," Pixel said.

"Not at all. Just a little discussion with some creative differences. It'll all work out. What can I do for you all?"

"Would you mind if I got a picture?" Pixel asked. "I'm such a fan."

"Not a problem," he said, flashing an overly white smile.

"I'll take it," Jules said, reaching for the phone Pixel offered.

Chavis pulled Pixel in close and wrapped one arm around her waist. After a couple of shots, he said, "Gimme that. Let's do some selfies. They're always fun. You get in the picture, too."

Chavis mugged for the camera with his signature suave grin.

After a few minutes, he handed Pixel her phone and pulled her closer to him. He kissed her on the lips. Then he waved on his way out. "See ya around."

Pixel looked stunned.

"And that was Chavis Ratner," Jules said with a grin.

Pixel smiled the same goofy smile that Emily had when she'd met the actor. When Pixel finished posting her photos, the pair walked around the barn to the woods.

A loud cheer emanated from the fan area. Kayleigh Bell and Derek Stone stepped into the open doorway of the barn. The crew moved more equipment, and filming eventually started. Pixel took photos of everything.

Jules checked her watch. It was almost five. "You hungry yet?"

"Getting there," her friend replied.

"Let's head over to my cabin, and I'll get dinner started. Is ravioli okay with you? Jake is going to stop by."

"Oh, good. I finally get to swap stories with the boyfriend." Pixel rubbed both of her hands together. "Bhwahhhhh."

Jules wrinkled her nose and winked. "You and Jake know most of my secrets."

When Jules opened the door, Bijou pounced on the women. After dog greetings, Pixel and Jules settled in at the kitchen table.

"Do you eat cheese?" Jules asked.

"Yup. I'm not vegan. I try to eat mainly veggies. I do eat eggs, cheese, and a cheeseburger every once in a blue moon."

"I was struggling to figure out what to fix that you would like. I'm going to bake the ravioli, and I'll throw together a salad while we chat," Jules said.

"Let me help." Pixel stood as Jules pulled ingredients from the refrigerator.

By the time the entrée was in the oven, Pixel had all of the veggies sliced and the giant salad ready to go. Jules pulled out breadsticks and spread them on a cookie tray.

"All done," Jules said, wiping her hands on a paper towel. "I'll set the table, and then we wait."

"I've got a lot of chatter on my Chavis pix on Instagram. We look pretty good." Pixel handed her phone to Jules.

Jules scrolled through the series of photos of the actor with them. "You do look good." She paused when she stopped on one that Pixel must have taken when they first arrived. Chavis, with his hand on something on the table behind him, stood facing Rod. Jules didn't remember this. She must have been engrossed in the men's conversation. She increased the view on the photo and zoomed in on his hand. Chavis had his hand on a black and stainless knife. Jules gasped. She looked again to make sure she saw what she thought she saw. "Hey, Pixel. Do you mind if I send these to myself?"

"No. Help yourself. Are you a closet Chavis fan?"

"I'm going to put together an album after the filming. Roxanne thinks we should do a 'they filmed it here' event next year when the show airs."

"That could be lucrative for you. I'll help you spread the word to the fan groups."

A knock on the door animated Bijou and interrupted their conversation.

Jake stepped inside and kissed Jules. Butterflies banged around in her stomach. He handed her a Boston cream pie.

"Dinner's almost ready. Y'all have a seat, and we'll catch up," Jules said when she recovered from the giddy feeling.

"Oh, we plan to exchange the most embarrassing Jules stories that we can think of to make you squirm." Pixel laughed.

Jake took the chair against the wall. "You're on. I knew her when she had braces and pigtails. I'm sure I could think of a few, like when she'd practice her best Spice Girls moves out behind the barn when she thought no one was watching."

A flush crossed Jules's face.

"You didn't know I knew about that?" Jake grinned, and Jules caught a gleam in his green eyes.

"Oh, I knew her in college at JMU. Go Dukes! That's when she was trying to be Miss Sophisticated and Sexy and walk in heels across campus. She almost broke her ankle in those four-inch heels," Pixel said.

"If I remember correctly, I ditched those the first week of freshman year and moved on to jeans and Vans like a normal college kid."

"I have pictures before and after." Pixel pulled out a chair and sat down.

The three dug into the giant salad and laughed through dinner, the Boston cream pie, and the sunset.

"It's getting late, and I have to get online tonight and finish grading projects. Thanks so much for the tour of the filming and dinner. I had a great time. And Jake, it was great to share stories with you. Next time, I'll bring pictures. Knowing Jules, she probably burned the ones she had."

"I don't remember having any." Jules hugged Pixel at the door. "Do you want me to walk you to your car?"

"No, I'll be fine. It's across the way. Thanks again. Call me when you can meet for lunch."

"Will do." Jules shut the door behind her friend.

"Let me help you do the dishes."

"My hero. Most everything can go in the dishwasher. I really only have to wash the metal pan and wipe down the counters."

After restoring order to the kitchen, Jules asked, "What do you want to do tonight?"

"Did you ever finish all the seasons of *Fatal Impressions*?" Jake plopped on the couch next to Bijou.

"Yep. But I want to watch the last episode again." Jules sat down next to them. "You know, for research. I want to see if there are any hints about the characters or where the next season is going."

Jules snuggled next to Jake on the couch, and Bijou wormed her way in between them. A quiet night at home felt comfortable and just right.

Chapter Fifteen

Thursday

Jules dropped her purse on the desk and headed for the coffee machine as Bijou ran to greet Roxanne.

"You're in late this morning. Rough night?" Roxanne picked up Bijou and gave her a treat from her stash in her desk.

"No. Pixel and Jake came over for dinner. And then Jake and I binge-watched a bunch of *Fatal Impressions*. Now, I'm dying to see what happens with this season."

Before Roxanne could comment, they heard the front screen door open and heavy footsteps on the wooden floor. Bijou yipped and tore through the open door to the store.

"Hey, Bijou," Sheriff Hobbs said. "Where's everybody?"

"Back here, Matt," Roxanne called.

The sheriff stepped through the open doorway. "Morning, y'all. How're things?" He leaned over and kissed Roxanne. "Good to see you."

"You, too. It's been a while. Anything new going on?"

"Jules texted me that she found a note in Poppy's house."

"Oh, I put it on your desk." Jules walked over and picked up the white envelope. "I was packing Poppy's things, and it fell out of a book on her nightstand. It looked like a love note. I didn't know if it meant anything to you."

"We'll see. We don't want to discount anything yet."

"Oh, and something odd happened yesterday. Again, I don't know if this is anything, either. I was showing my friend Pixel around the set, and we stopped by the tents near the barn. When I was flipping through the pictures, I noticed something looked odd in one of them. We were under one of the tents, and Chavis and Rod were arguing over some script changes."

"Send it to me." Seconds later, the sheriff's phone dinged, and he looked at the picture.

"You may have to enlarge it. Look at Chavis's hand," Jules directed.

"Hmmm. Might be just a prop, but probably worth looking into," he said.

"I don't remember seeing a knife when we were under the tent. And I don't know if he took it with him or left it on the table." Jules tugged on the hem of her sweater.

"How would you characterize his interaction with Rod?" Sheriff Hobbs asked, pulling out a small black notebook and pen from his shirt pocket.

"It was heated, but not threatening. Rod put his foot down about the changes Chavis wanted. He was clear there would be no alterations."

"Okay. I'll let the team know. They're working round the clock on both murders."

Roxanne looked up at the sheriff. Before she could speak, Jules asked, "Do you think Jayden really killed Sorbonne?"

The sheriff hesitated. "Don't breathe a word of this to anyone. No. I think we may cut him loose soon. A witness said she saw him near Sorbonne's house. So far, we have no other concrete evidence or witness accounts. According to his phone records, he was on a call to a friend in California until about two-thirty the next morning. His friend and the phone records verified his alibi."

Jules plopped down on her desk. Her knees felt weak. This confirms her gut feeling that someone set up Jayden. "Uh, Sheriff, did you all figure out whose blood we found on the porch?"

He paused and furrowed his brow. "It wasn't Sorbonne's or Rod Avery's. We're not sure who it belongs to right now or how it got there."

Thoughts banged around in Jules's head like bingo balls in a tumbler. Who could have set up Jayden, and who had an injury that would have left blood on Rod Avery's porch? There had to be a connection. She racked her brain, trying to remember anyone with a bandage recently.

Jules was startled when the sheriff said, "Thanks, y'all. I'll see you around. Roxanne, dinner tonight?"

"Sounds perfect. Why don't you come by my place when you're done with work, and I'll have dinner ready," her aunt said, hugging the sheriff.

When the sheriff exited through the store, Jules looked at her aunt. "You're cooking?"

"Of course not. That's what takeout is for." Roxanne winked at her niece.

Jules straightened her desk. "We're headed out soon. Have fun tonight."

While Bijou dawdled, Jules pulled out her phone. After about six rings, she heard a "Hey there. What's up?" It sounded like Pixel was out of breath.

"I need a favor. It's about one of those photos you took of Chavis. It's bothering me."

"What did you see?"

"In one of the candid shots you snapped of Chavis and Rod, look at the actor's hand. He's resting it on a knife on the table behind him."

"Hang on." A few seconds later, Jules heard a faint, "Well, shoot. That's exactly what it is. I never noticed it while we were standing there."

"Me either. If you have some time, could you poke around the secret parts of the internet and see what you can find on Chavis Ratner? All I could find was the fan stuff about him and the show," Jules said.

"I hope it's a prop," Pixel said with a sigh. "Sure, I'll see what I can find. Thanks again for dinner and the tour. It was the highlight of my week."

"Come back anytime," Jules said.

"I may take you up on that, especially while the film crew is still in town. See ya." Pixel clicked off.

The workers had started breaking down for the day, and the fans began to trickle out toward the parking lot. Near the cabin, Bijou yipped and pulled on her leash.

Jake sat in the golf cart in the driveway. Jules let go of the leash, and the terrier tore off to greet her buddy.

"Hey, whatcha doing here?" Jules asked as she neared the cart.

"I had an idea I wanted to run past you. How about heading over to Red's tonight. It's usually quieter on Monday nights, but the regulars are always there. We can divide and conquer and see what other information we can find."

Jules raised an eyebrow. "Sounds good. Not sure if I have anything to wear."

"Casual is fine unless you're thinking about making your karaoke debut. Then you'll need a hat and cowgirl boots."

"I don't think we'll have to worry about that. What time do you want to head out?"

"How about if I pick you up about six-thirty? We can grab a quick dinner and be at Red's by eight," he said.

"Sounds like a date. See you in a bit." Jules picked up Bijou as Jake did a quick turn and headed toward the woods.

She spent the next hour trying to find the right outfit and finally landed on a pair of skinny jeans, a cream camisole, and a leopard print cardigan. She curled her hair into corkscrews and tried to recreate Kat's makeover sans the airbrush. "Well, Bijou, that's about as good as it gets. I hope this look is more CMT than *Hee Haw*." Bijou raised one eyebrow and rolled over on the fuzzy red bathmat.

Jules picked up the loose items on the counter and returned them to the cabinet drawers. "You're in charge of security while I'm gone." The terrier zoomed toward the couch and her plush blanket while Jules flipped through her notes on Sorbonne and Poppy.

A little after six-thirty, a knock on the door jolted Bijou into a greeter mode.

"'Bout ready for a raucous evening?" Jake asked as Jules opened the door.

"Hopefully, it's not too rowdy. This is Fern Valley, and we're snooping, er working tonight. What're you thinking of for dinner?"

"How about sandwiches? Lula Belle's is always good."

"They close now at six in the off-season. How about Good Thyme Bistro or Pop's?"

"Pop's," he said.

She grabbed her black leather jacket. "Onion rings, yum."

"Sounds like a plan." Jake waited for her to lock the front door.

On their way down the maintenance road, they had to pause for the few remaining fans to cross the parking lot with their coolers.

Jake parked in front of the silver diner that had expanded over the years with multiple additions. He held the art deco door with the little porthole window, and Jules ducked under his arm and entered. The scent of french fries wafted through the air and made her stomach growl.

"Two, please," he said to the teenager with the greased-back hair and white T-shirt at the host stand.

"This way." The teen picked up two menus and led them to the back room decorated in wall-to-wall Mickey Mouse Club.

Jules scooted into the red vinyl booth, and Jake slid in beside her.

A few minutes later, a teen waitress in a pink poodle skirt and saddle oxfords approached. "Hi, I'm Lily. What can I get for you all tonight?"

"A grilled cheese sandwich with onion rings and an unsweetened tea," Jules said.

"I'll have the double-decker cheeseburger with fries and a vanilla Coke." Jake closed his menu.

"It should be right out in a few minutes." Lily twirled in her skirt and pranced back to the kitchen.

"So, what's the plan tonight?" Jules turned so she could see Jake better.

"I thought we could get there early to get a good seat and mingle with the regulars. Someone must have seen or overheard something. If I know them, they'll live to talk about their encounters with the stars," Jake said.

"I still think the murders are related somehow. And my hunch is that it's someone connected to *Fatal Impressions*."

"I don't think it's someone from town either. A random stranger doesn't seem to fit with the two crimes. Too coincidental," he said.

The waitress approached with their drinks. "Your food will be out in a few minutes." Jake nodded, and she moved on to another table after she carefully placed the glasses on cardboard coasters.

"There are so many overlapping relationships. Some good and some bad, and the production folks, the crew, and the actors are all mixed up together. And there are so many romantic involvements."

"Love and hate are powerful motivators for a lot of things, including murder." Jake raised one eyebrow.

A few minutes later, the waitress returned with a tray loaded with oversized dishes and condiments. "Here you go. Enjoy. Watch the plates. They're hot."

Jake and Jules ate in silence until he pilfered one of her onion rings.

"Help yourself. I'm not going to finish all of this." She nibbled on the crust of one of the sandwich triangles. "Okay, Sorbonne and Chavis had a thing. Chavis and Kat had a thing going, too. And Chavis and Poppy were an item, even though Poppy was also involved with Rod."

"Sounds like a soap opera, *As the Stomach Turns*."

She stifled a laugh as her somber mood took over. "Sorbonne was stabbed with Jayden's fancy styling shears. And Poppy was strangled." Thoughts of the two murders continued to flick across her memory.

"Both are up close and personal kinds of killings. The kind where passion is involved." Jake drug a fry through the ketchup and made it disappear in one bite.

Jules looked at him out of the corner of her eye.

"What? I watch *CSI*."

"You're right. I think that makes our argument that they weren't random crimes committed by strangers. Both of the women probably knew their killer." Jules took one last bite of her sandwich and pushed her plate away.

"We need to stay alert," he said.

"And find the connection," Jules said as Lily appeared again.

"I know you're not done yet, but can I get you all any dessert? We have key lime pie on the menu tonight."

"Sounds great, but I think I'll pass. What about you?" Jules asked. Jake shook his head, and Jules continued, "Just the check then."

Lily pulled out a black folder, and Jules grabbed it before Jake could. "My treat." Jules slid her credit card inside and handed it to the waitress.

"Thanks for dinner. Let's go see who's hangin' at Red's," Jake said.

Jules hoped she knew what she was getting into. Jake seemed like he had been a fixture at the honky-tonk for quite a while.

After a quick ride through town, they pulled onto the gravel lot that contained a few cars and trucks. The neon sign over the front door cast a red hue on the planked porch and barn wood of the building's facade when it pulsated every few seconds.

Jake held the door for her and paid the cover at the hostess stand. Jules grabbed his hand and followed him past the bar around to a small group of tables that faced the dance floor.

When the waitress in Daisy Dukes and a red and white checkered shirt tied in a knot right above her belly button ring approached, Jake ordered a beer. "What do you want?"

"Can I get a Coke for now?" Jules asked.

The waitress glared at her and returned to the bar.

"Interesting place," Jules said, rolling her eyes.

"It gets livelier as the night goes on. It used to be known for line dancing, but it's mostly karaoke now."

"I didn't know you sang."

"I'm a man with many talents. The karaoke was alcohol-induced one night when I was here with a bunch of friends. It became the thing to do after that. You should try it sometime." Jake winked at her.

Jules pursed her lips and nodded. Then she shook her head. "I can't carry a tune even with a bucket. I'll stick with being the audience."

The waitress sashayed back to the table and plunked their drinks down." She handed Jake a small tray with the tab.

After he paid for the drinks, Jake said, "Let's move to the bar. That way, we can hit up the locals. You okay?"

"Sure." Jules picked up her Coke and followed Jake to the end of the bar, where two women sat, sipping white wine and chatting.

"Hi, Ellen and Doreen. How are you?" he asked, putting an arm around each of the women.

"Why, Jake. I haven't seen you around in a month of Sundays. Come here and let me hug you around the neck." Doreen, the shorter of the two women, stood and grabbed Jake in a bear hug around his waist.

"This is my girlfriend, Jules," he replied when the woman ended her extended version of a hug. "Jules, this is Doreen and her sister Ellen."

"So, you're the one who finally tied a rope around Jake," said Ellen, the larger woman with a graying pin curl perm. "We haven't seen him in ages. Hope you didn't forget about us."

Jules smiled. Before she could reply, Jake interrupted. "Hey, were y'all here the night the crew from that TV show was here?"

"They've been here almost every night," Doreen added. "But sadly, I've only seen the actors in here once. And that was the night that little girl disappeared. Tragic. Some weirdo, if you ask me."

"Anything unusual that night?" Jules scooted closer to the two women's barstools.

"A big group of 'em came in that night. They were laughing and talking loud and buying rounds of drinks for anyone at their table. Two women, the petite blond who got herself killed and a taller woman with long curls, were with the group. The women kept leaving the table and returning."

"Where'd they go?" Jake asked.

"Bathroom or outside. One of them had one of those fancy e-cigarette thingies," Doreen said.

"Did they mix with the locals?" Jules asked.

"Are you kidding me? The whole group made it clear that they wanted to be left alone. They had some big bodyguard discouraging people from even breathing their air. That sweet Chavis Ratner was the only one who talked to us peons. He was nice enough to sign autographs and take pictures. The rest of them acted all stuck up." Ellen took a long swig from her wineglass.

"Anything else memorable about the evening?" Jake asked.

"Other than that hunky Chavis?" Doreen asked. "I'd take him home any night. He looks like he could use a home-cooked meal."

"One of the roadies or whatever he was…maybe their security guy…he almost got in a fight. Some drunk was hitting on the tall woman in the group. I don't know who she was. Anyway, the big dude grabbed the guy and drug him out to the parking lot. Not sure if there was a fight outside or not. Only the big dude in black returned to the party," Ellen added.

"Did anyone talk to the women? Or see them leave the final time?" Jules asked.

"Nah. They were up and down so many times. I wasn't really paying that much attention. They mostly kept to themselves." Ellen drained the last bit of her drink.

Jake motioned for the bartender. "Their next round's on me," he said, dropping a twenty on the bar.

"Jake, you're a doll." Ellen reached up and squeezed his bicep.

"Oh, wait. I do remember something," Doreen said as the bartender set two more white wines in front of the women. "I was in the little girls' room when that tall woman and her short friend came in. They were loud and fussing. Someone had spilled a drink on the tall woman's jeans, and she was trying to use the cheap ol' paper towels to soak it up. She was madder than a wet hen, especially when the shoddy towels disintegrated into bits of wet schmutz. Anyway, the little girl kept apologizing, but the other one acted all mad. She said something like she'd remember this too as she stormed out of the restroom."

"If you think of anything else, call me. It's been good to see you," Jake said.

"Now, you don't be a stranger, you hear me. We miss having you around. Karaoke isn't the same without you. And I'm sure Red misses you, too." Doreen winked at Jake.

"See ya soon," Jake said over his shoulder as he guided Jules to the edge of the dance floor before she could comment.

They headed to the pair of pool tables in the back, where Mike O'Rourke aimed at one of the solids across the table. The owner of the private security firm pulled back, and the cue ball hit the red ball and stopped by the back pocket. Mark straightened up and said, "Hey, Jules. Hey, Jake. It's good to see you."

The guy next to him, Anthony Rizzo, leaned forward and knocked several striped balls in. When he missed the third, he came over to the trio. "Hey, there."

"It's good to see you, Anthony. I hope you've fully recovered." The mountain of a man shook her hand. Jules had not seen him since last summer when he chased a killer into the woods while on patrol at her resort. His abduction put everyone on edge until the sheriff's office found him injured, but alive, at Honey's Fruit Stand.

"It was nothing. I'm back to normal. It's all part of the job."

"The concussion didn't hurt his pool game any," Mark said. "It looks like he's going to take more of my beer money tonight. What brings you two here? This isn't one of your regular haunts."

"The publicist for the film crew staying at Jules's resort was last seen here before she turned up dead in town. We're asking around to see if anyone noticed anything when they were here."

"They've been in here a few times. Set up court over there with all those tables. Seems they have their own security staff," Mark said, pointing to the alcove full of tables on the other side of the dance floor.

"You know you're my security team. I appreciate all the help you provide at the resort. The crew hired their own security and cooks. I was hoping they'd use locals, but they brought guys with them. They have their own support staff, too." Jules sighed.

"Their security guys need to learn some manners," Anthony added. "A couple of times, they roughed up some of the guys who were trying to chat up the actors. They acted like they owned the place. Not too endearing with the locals."

Mark nodded and took a swig of his beer.

"Were either of you here the night the publicist was murdered?" Jake asked.

"Nah. We were working a job in Charlottesville," Anthony said. "You might try some of the barflies. They seem to sit on their perches every night."

"Will do. Y'all take care. I'll call you in February to start making plans for the spring and summer seasons," Jules said.

"'Preciate it. See you around," Mark said. Anthony nodded, and the men returned to their game. Jake and Jules looped around the bar. Classic country music blared through the speakers, and a few couples claimed the dance floor.

"You wanna dance?" he asked.

"I'd love to."

Jake took her hand and led her to the dance floor. It was nice to be out on a date, even if was a cover to dig up information on the film crew.

After several laps around the dance floor to Garth Brooks and Brooks and Dunn, they found spots at the bar. Jules sipped ginger ale, and people watched.

A little before nine, Jules asked, "Anybody else you want to talk to?"

"We've probably found out all we're going to tonight. Everybody seems to tell the same story."

"I need to let Bijou out." Jules rose and flipped her purse strap over her shoulder.

"You just don't want to be here when karaoke starts." Jake winked as he followed her to the front door.

Chapter Sixteen

Friday

Jules woke when Bijou stirred in her bed. The sun streamed in through the sheer curtains. Jules stretched and wondered if she had anything in her kitchen for breakfast. She missed not being able to run over to the lodge before work.

After a quick shower and an espresso, she found enough bread for toast with honey butter. She packed up her laptop and poured coffee into her to-go cup. "Come on, Bijou. Let's go see who's in the office."

Jules's phone binged with a text from Sherri. A quick peek let her know that starting tomorrow, filming would be at the resort for most of the next week and then in and around Fern Valley after that.

Jules popped in the back office where Roxanne sat at the other desk. "Good morning. You're in early," she said to her aunt.

"I wanted to get all the bills paid, sales tax filed, and payroll done, so I can sneak out a little early. Sheriff Hobbs promised to take me to dinner tonight. He got called into a meeting yesterday and didn't leave work until after nine. Dinner at my house was quick before he headed out to check on his night crew. I'll be so glad when they get these murders solved." Roxanne sighed.

"Me too," Jules said, plugging in her laptop. "Before I dive into resort work, I'm going to walk around the set since they're going to be in town for the rest of the week."

Jules's first stop was hair and makeup. Three people sat in patio chairs under the camper's awning.

Jayden jumped up, whooped, and ran toward her. He picked Jules up and spun her around.

When her feet landed back on the ground, Jules said, "Welcome back. What happened?"

"They didn't have enough to charge me. My phone records are my alibi. Who knew that flapping my gums all evening would get me out of hot water? I'm a free bird. Tweet. Tweet. It feels so good to be out. I made my lawyer take me to Charlottesville and do the drive-thru at Mickey Dee's. The food and the vibe in that jail were awful. It's going to take me weeks to get back to being myself. My locks need some attention, and I need a spa day after all that bad energy. And thankfully, I had a job to come back to. I love it here with Kat and Tess." He leaned over and threw one arm around each woman for a group hug.

Kat looked up from her phone. "Hi, Jules. Welcome to Jayden's celebration. Have you met Tess yet?"

"No, I don't think so." Jules stepped forward and shook the brunette's hand.

"It's nice to meet you. And it's great to have our full crew back. Kat and I have been hoping to keep up with schedules without our bud Jayden. We're going to have to go out soon to celebrate." Tess pushed her long brown bangs off her forehead.

"There's only one place in town, and it's a redneck bar. It'll do if you need a drink." Kat's voice trailed off as she flipped through images on her phone. "It's very, uh, rural here."

"I don't care," Jayden said. "I'm so happy to be back. There's nothing anyone could say or do right now that would burst my bubble. My lawyer said that the police are looking more and more at the possibility that there was one killer. And that means it's not me. Oh, happy day!"

A frown crossed Kat's face, but she didn't comment.

Tess looked around. "I guess the actors will be rolling out of bed soon and heading over. It's almost time to work our magic."

Jayden jumped up and clapped his hands. "I can't tell you how thrilled I am to be back." He grabbed Kat's hands and pulled her up. "Come on. Let's get going. Today is going to be fabulous."

"Oww," Kat whined. "Calm down and let go. I hurt my hand last week, and it's still sore. I'll be inside in a minute." She waggled her hand and looked down at her palm.

"Oh, sorry," he said, stepping back. "Didn't mean to open an old wound. I'm going in. I am back in my element." Jayden opened the RV's door and disappeared into the camper.

"I guess I better head in, too. Ashe is my first customer of the day." Tess beamed. "You, Miss Kat, have the perfect Chavis lined up." Tess winked and climbed the camper's steps.

"I don't know how perfect," Kat muttered and followed Tess inside.

That was curious. As she turned to leave, Ashe Lyons and Chavis Ratner rounded the corner. The two actors continued their conversation as they passed Jules and headed up the RV steps. Before he shut the door, Ashe said, "Oh, hi. I didn't see you there. Are you waiting for someone?"

"No, not really. Just answering a text before heading off to make my rounds. Y'all have a good day."

"See ya. Love that southern accent. I'm going to have to use that sometime." Ashe winked and disappeared inside.

Jules wanted to join them, but she couldn't think of a plausible reason. She turned to leave but changed her mind. She might not get the chance again to snoop with the actors present.

Pulling the door open, she climbed up the steps. Kat and Chavis stared at her from Kat's station. Jayden arranged brushes and containers of gel and mousse.

"Sorry. I don't mean to barge in. I know you're working, but I haven't had much time to watch the goings-on while you're still here at the resort. I want to get some pictures for my newsletter and website. I hope y'all don't mind."

Tess applied gel and a curling iron to the long part of Ashe's hair.

"No problem," Ashe said. "Come on in. We were listening to Kat and

Chavis have a spat."

Kat pursed her lips and returned to work on Chavis. She rubbed gel on the tips of her fingers and jabbed them into his spikey hair.

"Owww. Not so rough," Chavis whined.

Kat continued to spike Chavis's hair while Jules moved around the room, taking candids with her phone. Jayden and the actors mugged for the shots.

"Here," Chavis said, standing. "You come and get in the shot. I'm sure Kat or Jayden would be willing to take our picture."

When nobody said anything, Tess reached for Jules's phone. "I will." Come on over here between Ashe and Chavis. "Say, cheese."

"Cheeeeeeeese," the group said as Jayden jumped in with his beautiful smile.

"That one is to celebrate my being sprung from the pokey," Jayden said, returning to his station.

"Thanks so much, everyone. I'll let you get back to your work. See you around." Jules scooted out of the RV.

The cool, crisp fall morning called to her. She decided to wander over to the set to see if she could ferret out any other information under the guise of taking photos.

Next to the woods, Kayleigh Bell sat on a log, and Derek Stone stood next to her. A crowd of extras stood behind him. Jules was too far away to hear the lines, but she heard the director yell, "Cut."

Someone in black ran into the shot and gave Kayleigh a bottle of water. After she handed it back and he stepped out of the scene, filming began again. Jules moved closer and snapped shots of the cast and crew.

Jules stood on the outskirts and watched them film parts of the same scene twelve times. When her legs started to ache, she skirted around behind the cameras and headed for the office.

She didn't get very far before her phone dinged with a text from Pixel. **Found some stuff. Want to meet for lunch?**

Where? Jules replied.

Pie in the Sky at 12.

See you then. Jules pocketed her phone and picked up her pace. She had enough time to freshen up and drive to town.

"Hey, Roxanne," Jules yelled as she opened the door to the office.

"I'm up front" drifted in from the other room.

"I'm going to meet Pixel for lunch. I should be back in plenty of time to get Bijou, but if I'm not, could you call Jake to pick her up before you leave."

"Will do. She'll supervise while I restock the brochures this afternoon."

"See ya in a few." Jules picked up her purse and slipped out the door.

Deciding to take the back roads to the restaurant, she cranked up some smooth jazz for the ride. The leaves had started to turn, and the sun magnified the autumn colors. Soaking in the beauty of the Blue Ridge Mountains, she forgot about the murders for a little while.

She pulled into a spot in front of a row of brick buildings where Pie in the Sky sat between a new art supply store and a gallery. Not seeing Pixel, she found a table near the window facing the door.

Jules, lost in her Instagram feed, saw a shadow descend over her table.

"Sorry I'm late. I had every intention of heading out on time, but I got distracted by a text. Have you ordered?" Pixel asked, sliding into the empty seat.

Jules shook her head, and right on cue, the waitress approached the table, "Can I get you something to drink?"

"Water with a lime slice, please," Pixel said.

"I'll have an unsweetened tea," Jules added.

The waitress nodded and set down two red menus.

When she returned with the drinks, the pair ordered personalized mini pizzas.

"It's been crazy, but I had some time to poke around the dark web, and you'll never believe what I found. Not the stuff you see on fan web pages." Pixel sported her best impish grin.

"Do tell," Jules said, leaning forward.

"Well, it seems that old Chavis got married to his high school sweetheart the summer after graduation. They hightailed it to Los Angeles, and she worked as a waitress to pay the bills while he auditioned and did odd jobs."

"All the fan pages list him as Hollywood's most eligible bachelor."

"How can that be, you ask?" Pixel raised her perfectly manicured eyebrows. "It seems that when he signed with the studio for his first production, a soap opera, they wanted him to be their newest heartthrob. Rumor has it that the studio funded the divorce and paid for the wife to return quietly to Florida. She must have signed an NDA because I couldn't find anything else about it."

"Hmmm. That might break a few teens' hearts, but it probably wouldn't matter that much since he's single now."

"I thought it was interesting how the Hollywood machine controlled people's lives. That led me to some reading about what the studios and music companies did to their stars to manipulate them. Not pretty. Anyway, that wasn't the worst of it. It seems Mr. Chavis likes to gamble, and he's gotten in trouble several times by making large bets that he couldn't cover. The show has tried to quash stories and rumors about his bad habits. When he got into hot water last time, the executive producer, Eric Renfield, bailed him out. Rumor has it that that was the last straw. If he didn't get it together, they would kill off his character and be done with him."

"That jives with the balled-up scripts I found in the writer's place. When I took it to the producer, he glossed over it by claiming the pages were from an old script draft."

"The wolf story, huh?" Jules nodded, and Pixel continued in above a whisper, "He may not be the best human, but I like his character. I hope they keep him around."

"Did any of your deep sources say how Chavis reacted to the studio's ultimatum?" Jules asked.

"Not really. There was some mention that he was on his best behavior, especially on set. He didn't want to lose his meal ticket." Pixel lowered her voice.

The waitress dropped off their food, and the pair paused their conversation.

When the waitress was out of earshot, Jules continued, "I wonder if that was a motivator for his relationship with Sorbonne. Somebody told me that she had a thing for younger actors."

Pixel flipped through her phone. "I found something to that effect. Let me see." She swiped her phone several times. "Here it is. It's an interview with 'tude that Sorbonne did for *Xcel*, an online tabloid. The writer asked if there was someone in her life, and Sorbonne snapped back with, 'Yes, there are some gentlemen in my life.' Later the reporter asked if Sorbonne considered her relationships with the actors to be one-night stands, and her chippy answer was, 'Why no. I consider them to be auditions, and it's up to me whether or not they get a call back.'"

Jules's eyes widened. "She never minced words."

"Her dance card alone should provide a list of suspects that will keep investigators busy for a while." Pixel bit into her veggie pizza.

Jules blew on her mushroom and sausage pizza and then poked holes in the cheese with her fork. "Sheriff has his hands full."

"Let's see what else I found about the cast and crew," Pixel said. "Oh, here. Tess Anillo had a thing with Rod Avery, but it ended when he took up with Poppy. It's rumored that she's been seen with Ashe Lyons recently."

"I need a spreadsheet to keep up with this group and who's dating whom. So, there's another connection to Rod and Poppy." Jules cut up her pizza.

"I think that's all I found. Oh, wait, I know where Eric Renfield's money came from. He got a pretty good nest egg when his father died and left him a security company. He parlayed that in the early 2000s to an international company that provided security to famous people and to companies with staff based in former war zones or other dangerous places like the Mid-east. He's loaded. He's the executive producer on this show, as well as several other movies in the last ten years. He's pretty much retired from his day job, but he likes hanging out on the sets with the Hollywood folks."

"You always find the good stuff lurking around the corners of the dark web. I hope the sheriff's team can wrap this up soon. I have a business council meeting next week, and I'm sure there will be complaints about the ills of Hollywood permeating our idyllic valley."

"You didn't cause any of this." Pixel paused and took a sip of her water.

"I know, but I'm the one who gets blamed for always trying to bring new visitors to the area." Jules put down her fork and let out a sigh.

"You're doing what's best for everyone. Stop beating yourself up. You had nothing to do with the murders."

The corners of Jules's mouth turned up into an almost smile. "Thanks."

"All done with these?" the waitress asked. When the pair nodded, she continued, "Did you all save room for dessert? Do you want refills in to-go cups?"

"No, thank you," Jules said.

"I'll take a refill to go," Pixel said.

"All righty then. Be back in a snap." The young waitress with aqua hair and multiple piercings in both ears turned on her heels and ducked into the kitchen.

When the waitress returned with the check, Pixel grabbed it, and Jules frowned. The waitress set the to-go cup down.

Pixel shrugged and picked up her drink. "What? I'd pay ten times more than this to hang out with the *Fatal Impressions* cast," Pixel said.

"I appreciate all the research you've done for me. And thanks for lunch."

The women continued their chat long after the waitress cleared the table.

"It's been great to see you. I need to head out soon." Pixel reached for her bag and rose.

"The filming will be back at the resort next week."

"I'll be back, too. My pictures were a hit on Instagram." Pixel's eyes sparkled.

The women hugged and parted ways in the parking lot.

Jules enjoyed the warmth of the afternoon sun on the drive back. Her desire for fun outside and the urge to check on the film crew battled in her head. She compromised and decided to take Bijou on a walk.

They trekked over to the meadow and around the barn. Craft services had the back door of the lodge's kitchen propped open and grilled scents wafted out. Bijou sniffed the air. Steak night. Jules's stomach rumbled even though she had had a late lunch.

Bijoy and Jules made a wide circle around the cabins and the empty tent city. On the last part of their excursion, the pair walked around the RV lot. Jules heard loud voices, and Bijou froze. Her ears pointed up, and she let out a low growl. Jules tugged on her leash and led the small dog toward the noise. Curiosity got the best of both of them.

"I said no!" a male voice bellowed.

Jules stuck her head around the back corner of a large brown RV. Rod Avery stood with his back toward her. He waved a hand around and stepped toward Chavis Ratner. "The end. No more discussions. Do not bring it up again. We are going with the existing scripts. Nothing changes. Drop it. And I don't want you bothering the writers again. They don't have the patience for you like Sorbonne did. I'm tired of hearing that you're stalking them. Do not ask again, or I personally will have the script changed to put you in a coma for the next three seasons."

Chavis blanched as Rod stepped closer toward him.

"I'm done with you." The producer spat out the words, threw both of his hands in the air, and stalked off between two nearby RVs.

"If I'm in a coma, do I still get paid?" Chavis yelled at Rod's back.

The actor rested his head in his hands. Bijou barked, and Chavis looked up. Concern flashed across his countenance. Nonchalantly, he ran his hands through his hair.

"Oh, hi. I didn't see you there," he said.

"We were on a walk. Everything okay?" Jules asked.

"Of course. Why wouldn't it be? Everything's peachy here. And you didn't see or hear what you thought you did. And if I see any kind of leak to the media about a script change or my character, I'll sue you and your resort." Chavis turned and ambled toward the lodge.

Jules's eyes widened. Chavis went from fear to anger in less than fifteen seconds. "What brought that on?" Jules asked Bijou.

The dog turned her head.

"Never mind. It's a beautiful day. Too nice to let the likes of him ruin it. Come on, puppy. I'm thinking about pulling one of the hammocks out for some afternoon relaxation."

Chapter Seventeen

Saturday

After finishing the resort's newsletter and the agenda for next week's Fern Valley Business Council meeting, Jules grabbed her camera and headed to the barn. She decided the cover of taking pictures would give her the best excuse to continue to nose around the cast and crew. Jules poked her head in the open door of the lodge and snapped a few pictures of the workers cleaning up the remains from breakfast and prepping for the lunch rush.

Tired of watching the food prep, she made her way to the tent city. Several guys set a gun, bowls, a radio, and other props on a cart.

Jules inched closer. "Do you mind if I take some photos for the resort's newsletter?"

The older guy with the salt and pepper beard replied, "Help yourself."

"Thanks." She snapped photos of the cart, the crates full of things, and the two men. "Hi, I'm Jules. You've got quite a collection here."

"Yup," the older guy replied. "If it's in a scene, we have it. And we often have to keep stuff from earlier scenes in case we have to do a flashback or it needs to be part of the storyline. I'm Bradley Taylor, the prop master, and this is Topher Smythe, who's training to take over when I retire. He's also the armorer."

The younger man with long black hair and a nickel-sized gauge in each ear nodded. Jules must have had a puzzled look because he added, "I'm the one on the set designated to monitor and care for all the weapons and ensure set safety."

"How do you keep all of the stuff straight?" Jules asked, poking through the open crate.

Topher replied, "It's all barcoded. We have an inventory system to keep up with three seasons' worth of stuff."

Jules snapped more photos. "Who keeps track of what should be in each scene?"

"There's a script coordinator who checks the script, scene, and the shot for continuity. Years ago, they called them script girls, but we've evolved over time," Bradley replied. "They have to make sure it's right, or the scene may have to be reshot."

"What do you do with all this stuff after filming?" Jules poked around the three open crates.

"This isn't even a tenth of what we have for this show. There's a warehouse at the studio," Topher interjected. "We keep everything. Sometimes, we reuse it or repurpose it. Bradley and his crew are whizzes at fixing or crafting anything. They have a workshop back in L. A. that would put Santa's to shame."

"And Topher's teaching us how to use computers and the new 3D printer. He's been able to make stuff that we can't buy anymore," Bradley added.

Topher looked at the list on his clipboard and made some notes. "And if the show gets canceled, it either gets auctioned off or swallowed up by another production that the studio has. Some of the famous stuff ends up in museums or private collections." Topher added a black backpack and a canteen to the collection on the cart.

"Your inventory includes the weapons for the show?" Jules asked, thinking of the knife in Pixel's picture.

The older man looked up and paused. "We have what the characters would have or use. And that includes weapons, food, drinks…everything. The production company sells product placements for the name brands you see. You'll often see sponsored stuff on the cabinets and tables. And yes, we have weapons for this show. There's a whole collection of knives, guns, and swords that Ashe, Chavis, and Derek use mainly. Though Kayleigh has been building up quite an arsenal this season herself."

"I was looking through my pictures recently, and I saw a knife on the table behind the actors. I was curious."

"They're all fake," Topher added. "We only have blanks on the set, and the knives aren't sharp. I guess you could bludgeon someone with one, but they're really for show."

"Smile," Jules said as the two men paused for a photo. "Thanks for all the good information. I never realized what it took to make a TV show or a film. I am in awe of the work that goes on behind the scenes."

The men returned to the props, and Jules wandered through the rest of the empty tents toward the RV city. She took some pictures of the campers and a squirrel that was watching the goings-on from a nearby branch.

When she turned the corner next to a gray and red Class A RV, she heard voices and quickened her pace. Kat, in a long tan cardigan with jeans and knee-high suede boots, stood in the RV's doorway, looking at Jayden, who had draped himself over one of the patio chairs. Tess and Chavis stood nearby.

"Put that out. Smoking will kill you and the rest of us," Chavis said to Jayden.

"A lot of other things will kill you." Jayden exhaled a blue cloud of smoke in the actor's direction. "If I'm going to go, I'm going happy. And you're not the boss of me."

Before Chavis could reply, Kat said, "Come on inside. Let's get you in the chair and out of here as soon as we can. Ashe and Derek will be here soon, and it'll get loud and crowded."

"Anything you want, Kitty Kat," Chavis purred. His grin reminded Jules of the Grinch. He wiggled his eyebrows and followed the tall stylist up the metal stairs.

"Hi, Jayden." Jules stepped closer.

He took one last puff on his cigarette and stamped it out on the cement with the toe of his biker boot.

"Hey, girl. How's life? What are you into today?"

"Taking some pictures for my website. Smile."

"Cheeeeeze!" Jayden showed all his pearly white teeth. "Here, put the camera down and give me your phone. We need to take a selfie."

Jules unlocked her phone and handed it to the lanky stylist who stood beside her. He pulled her closer and snapped several shots.

"Thanks. This has definitely been an adventure…." Before Jules could finish her sentence, a crash echoed from inside the trailer. She and Jayden jumped up. He threw open the door, and they both rushed inside.

A drawer of scissors, shears, and combs lay on the floor near Tess's station.

Chavis and Kat glared at each other. Tess's eyes glistened, and it looked like she was about to burst into tears.

"What the heck happened?" Jayden asked. "Tess, are you okay?"

"Yes," she whispered, leaning down to pick up the items and return them to the empty drawer. Jayden knelt to help.

"Are you sure you're okay?" Jayden whispered.

When all the items were back in the drawer, Tess stood and picked it up. She adjusted it and slid it back in the black cabinet at her station. "I'm fine. We were having a chat," Tess wiped her eyes with the back of her hand. She returned to her station and busied herself with rearranging towels and shampoo containers.

"Girl, you don't look fine. You wanna go for a walk?" Jayden asked.

"I'm good. Ashe will be here any minute. I've got work to do. But thanks," Tess said.

"She's fine. And, of course, Ashe will come to her rescue. He always does." Chavis said. "All I did was warn her that she's probably a suspect since they let ol' Jayden here go. He got lucky, passed Go, and collected his alibi." Chavis smirked. He sat back in Kat's chair and crossed his arms on his chest. His long legs jutted out toward Jayden.

A look of fear crossed Tess's face. "I don't know what you're talking about," she said in a voice above a whisper.

"Tess, Tess, Tessie. Of course, you do. It's so obvious. I'm surprised the police or the press haven't been all over this. Everybody knows you and Rod were a thing. You didn't even attempt to hide it. And it was a very public breakup when he dumped you at the Golden Globes for none other than the deceased Poppy, the publicist. Girl, everybody knows he prefers blonds."

Kat glared at Chavis. She pulled out a barrel brush and a curling iron to tame his messy hipster mane. She tugged and curled the top of his hair around the large barrel brush.

Chavis sat upright. "Hey, take it easy. That hurts."

Tess wiped her eyes again with her hand. "The Rod thing was over a long time ago. My life is much happier these days." She set a professional hair dryer and a can of mousse on the rolling cabinet behind her chair.

"I'd be careful if I were you. Jayden's a free bird now, so the cops are still looking for a killer. And you have a motive. You know, scorned woman and all that. It's the perfect setup for a TV drama and a murder. Everybody knows you hated Poppy." Chavis grinned as they watched Tess's countenance darken.

The petite woman frowned. "I had nothing to do with Poppy's murder. Ashe and I weren't even here. We took a drive down the Blue Ridge Parkway, and we stopped at some little inn and spent the night. We found out when we got back the next day."

Before Chavis could reply, the trailer door opened, and Ashe entered. "Morning, pretty people," he said, looking around the room.

"Ah, look, it's your alibi now," Chavis said. "You done here?" He looked up at Kat.

Kat nodded and replaced her equipment in her cabinet.

"It's been real, but I've got to run. And if you need more pictures for your newsletter thingy, come by my trailer later. I'll have some time tonight," he said, pointing to her camera.

Jules smiled, hoping that it didn't look like a grimace. "I'll try to find some time. It's been a busy week. Thanks, y'all. See ya." She backed out of the trailer and trekked toward the barn. Enough drama for this morning. But at least she picked up a few little nuggets of information.

The crew milled about moving equipment. Loud whoops resounded from the fan area. Jules turned. Chavis Ratner walked up and down the hurricane fencing, high-fiving and posing for pictures with the fans. The cheers and hollers increased as he egged on the crowd.

The noise settled down after Chavis waved to the onlookers and jogged toward the cameras. He ambled to a craft table filled with coffee urns, condiments, and gooey pastries. He filled a to-go cup and stirred in sugar and creamer. Then he pinched one of the pastries and licked his finger.

Ashe Lyons and Derek Stone approached the table, along with several crew members. Hoping to get some more information, Jules scooted closer to eavesdrop.

"Morning. How's it going?" Derek topped off his coffee.

Ashe glared at Chavis.

"Hunky dory," Chavis replied, shading his eyes from the sun's glare with his hand.

Ashe lunged forward and pushed Chavis with both hands. "Lay off Tess, will you. She doesn't need you running your mouth." Chavis's drink splashed and landed in the grass.

Chavis recovered from the push and took a step backward. The younger actor looked around the tent and straightened to his full height. "I was warning her to be careful because the police are still investigating the murders. I'm trying to help her out." Chavis wiped his hands on his jeans and put them up in the air as he faced Ashe.

"Make it right." Ashe stepped closer. Chavis took a step back.

"Sure, sure. I meant no harm. She was a tad sensitive this morning. I'll loop back with her to make sure we're okay." Chavis poured another cup of coffee without turning his back on Ashe.

"Don't be a jerk. Stay in your swim lane," Derek muttered as he turned.

Chavis pinched off part of another pastry and popped it in his mouth before heading off.

Ashe and Derek grabbed their drinks and wandered out as Jules snapped several pictures. Without any other snooping opportunities, she walked to the office to download her pictures. Tess, Rod, Chavis, Ashe. The list of possible suspects continued to grow.

Chapter Eighteen

Monday

Jules rolled out of bed and turned off the alarm. Today was her first Fern Valley Business Council meeting since Hollywood came to town, and she didn't want to be late.

After a double shot of espresso and a hot shower, she poked around her closet, looking for the right outfit for a professional event. She settled on her red blazer with a cream camisole and black dress pants. She would have preferred jeans and a sweater, but that would have to wait until later this afternoon. Jules rounded out the outfit with her a pair of low, patent leather heels.

Jules loved working on the council and coming up with ideas to bring more business to the valley, but there was a small contingent who wanted things to return to days of the past. They didn't like traffic, noise, or newcomers. Jules tried her best to address their concerns while still promoting what Fern Valley had to offer tourists.

Butterflies danced in her stomach as she went to tame her hair. Bijou sat on the bathmat as her human fluffed her bangs and put on her makeup. "Well, let's hope that's good enough," Jules said, returning the blush to her makeup bag.

She added silver earrings and her business council lapel pin. "I'm about ready. Wish me luck. Hopefully, we can stick to the agenda." Jules picked up her briefcase and purse and checked her look in the mirror one last time.

After a quick ride to town, Jules lapped the library parking lot. Not finding a space, she zipped over to the government center lot next to the sheriff's office. She hip-checked the Jeep's door and filed in the library with the other business owners.

Inside, she waved at Gail Matthews, who staffed the checkout desk with military precision. She returned the salute and pointed toward the meeting room in the back.

Jules nodded. She meandered around display tables and book racks to the conference room filled with quite a crowd, chatting in small groups or huddled around the open boxes of doughnuts from member Jocelyn Mercer's bakery, the Grateful Bread.

Secretary Cindy Johnson, owner of Johnson Motors, spotted Jules and made her way through the clumps of people. "Hey, there. Good to see you. I hope all's going well in movie land. Here's a hard copy of the agenda in case you need it. It looks like we have a full house."

"I'm glad our members are interested. I'm going to put my stuff down and get this party started," Jules said.

Cindy smiled. "I'm gonna herd them toward the seats. Get 'em, tiger." The tall woman with an arm span that would rival a basketball player started shooing people away from the food table. "Hi, all. We're going to get started in a few minutes. Take your seats." She moved through the small groups and cleared the stragglers in a matter of minutes.

Jules put her purse and briefcase on an empty chair in the front row next to diner owner Pop Riggins, and Mitch Ford, owner of Lula Belle's.

"Hey, Jules. Good to see you." Pop scooted over in his chair to make room for her things.

"Business has been record-breaking since the *Fatal Impressions* people and fans arrived. I can't tell you how excited Donna and I are about what you're doing here," Mitch said.

"It's definitely been an adventure. And I'm so glad to hear that everyone in town is benefiting." Jules pulled a folder out of her case and put the agenda inside.

Cindy made her way to the front. She tapped the microphone on the lectern. "Good morning, everybody. We're about to get started. Please grab your refreshments and a seat. We've got a lot to cover today."

Jules rose and put her folder on the lectern. She adjusted the microphone lower. She noticed J. P. Gross and his pal, Ralph Teagle, slide in the door and find seats in the back row. Jules tried not to let them rattle her. Part of his gripe was sour grapes over his loss to her in the last council election. She took a deep breath and let it out slowly to calm the nerves.

"Hello, everyone," Jules said into the mic. The dull roar in the room ceased. "I'd like to welcome you all to our fall meeting. Our secretary, Cindy Johnson, posted the minutes from the last meeting and the treasurer's report. Are there any proposed changes to either?" When no one responded, she continued, "Then do I have a motion to accept the minutes and treasurer's report?"

"Aye," Pop and Mitch said in unison.

"Thank you. Now, we'll get an update on our holiday festival plans from committee chair Elaine James."

The stout woman with the bouffant hairdo and owner of Birds and Bees Garden Shop made her way to the front with several green and red folders.

"Good morning, Fern Valley business owners. I'm so excited about our December festivities. Information has been added to our website, and we've been advertising it with Virginia tourism and social media ads. Right now, we have four Christmas musical events at local churches, the library is hosting a Dr. Seuss puppet show, and the high school is performing a concert with the music from *A Charlie Brown Christmas*. We're encouraging everyone in town to decorate. We're having contests for the best lights and decorations. If you're having a sale or special event, email me the details, and I'll get it added to our promos. Fern Valley is going to be Christmas Central this year. Oh, and I forgot to mention our big, lighted parade. We have bands from the high school, the UVA alumni pep squad, and the senior kazoo crew signed up. Fifteen floats have committed, and we've got interest from three classic car groups and a horse team. Start sharing our posts on social media."

"Thank you, Elaine. This is going to be an exciting season with lots of things for people to do to have a classic holiday, and the calendar is full from Thanksgiving to New Year's Day with events. The goal is to extend our season and keep the visitors coming," Jules said.

Hearing mumbles from the back of the room, she looked up.

J. P. Gross cleared his throat. "The goal is to increase business revenues. I'm not convinced that bringing a bunch of strangers here is what Fern Valley needs."

"Yeah," Ralph Teagle piled on. "Fern Valley is fine the way it was."

"I hear your concerns." Jules stared at the two men. "But I've worked with our county administrator and his staff to look at the numbers for Fern Valley. Without a consistent plan to grow business and take advantage of tourism dollars, Fern Valley will be like a lot of other towns with no revenue, no jobs, and high crime rates. The county has posted the results of its study on the website. It's available for you to read. We are in a much better position with a thriving downtown than a lot of other rural towns."

Mitch Hall whooped, and others joined in with clapping. "My revenue at Lula Belle's is up every season since Jules started the vintage trailer campground. And now events like this will extend the season beyond local sales. Donna and I have definitely benefited from all the hard work the council's been doing."

"Me, too," Pop added. "I'm planning a holiday menu for this year's festivities. And I'm working with Elaine and the car clubs to have a holiday cruise-in through town to look at lights. One of the stops will be a nostalgic diner stop from a bygone era. My numbers are up, too. And the movie people and their fans have spent a lot of money this fall."

"And there's been traffic and closed streets," Ralph Teagle bellowed.

"Yeah, are we paying more overtime for services because of it? And what about the two murders. Fern Valley is becoming ground zero for crime. We've had four murders in the last year. That's four more than we've had in the last ten years," J. P. Gross added with a wave of his fist in the air.

Sheriff Hobbs, who was standing in the doorway near the refreshment table, cleared his throat. "This fall, with the movie people in town, we have had no additional overtime costs to the town. Part of the negotiation of the use of town property was a fee structure to pay for electricity, police, fire, and EMT services. Ask Tom Berryman or the treasurer's office, the town actually made money on this deal."

The audience broke into applause and cheers again.

"Thanks, Sheriff, for the reminder that the town was very deliberate in its scrutiny of the film company's offerings," Jules noted.

"That still doesn't address the murders, and I think you need to bear most of the blame since they're all affiliated with that campground of yours," Gross bellowed.

Some of the audience turned to stare at him.

Jules could feel the heat creeping across her cheeks. She took a deep breath and let it out slowly.

"It's not her fault. And you can't pin that on Jules," Carleen "Red" Tucker, dressed in a black western shirt, designer jeans, and red cowgirl boots, piped up from the back of the room. The petite owner of Red's wagged her finger in J. P. Gross's direction. "And if I remember correctly, one of the bodies was found on your property. So maybe you share some of the blame." A low murmur swept through the room, and J. P. Gross looked down at his shoes.

After a pause, Carleen continued, "I've lived in these parts my entire life. Red's Honky-tonk has been in my family for over seventy-five years. And any of y'all old enough to remember the seventies and eighties may need a refresher that this town went broke a couple of times. Most of downtown was boarded up. I'm the third 'Red' to own this establishment, and I like nostalgia as much as the next gal, but I have no problem raking in money from new folks and tourists. We need people like Jules to come up with ideas to keep people spending money in our area. And for the record, I love that her resort is in town. Red's does a steady business with her guests, so J. P., you and your posse need to chill out. The alternative to progress is a dead little town with no jobs and an opioid crisis. You and your boys should be buying Jules roses for all she's done to line your pockets. And I don't see you and your cronies turning down the business from outsiders."

More cheers erupted from the audience.

"Thank you. Any other comments?" Jules asked. She paused. When no one responded, she continued, "Then the only other item for new business is our spring committee. Elaine James and Kim Lacy have volunteered to chair the planning committee. Send your ideas to them. Do y'all want to say something?"

Kim jumped to her feet and rushed to the podium. Elaine tottered down the aisle behind her.

"Thanks, Jules," Kim, owner of KnitWits, said. "Yes, we want to have events in March, April, and May to bring in folks every weekend. In March, we're having a literary festival with talks, readings, workshops, and author events. The library is going to help us with this. In April, we plan to have a craft festival. We'll have hundreds of booths that vendors will rent. On the other weekends, there will be classes, workshops, and demonstrations all around town. And then in May, we want to have a film festival centered around the Bijou Theatre. We will have films, lectures, and other special events. We're hoping this will be popular, and we can repeat it next year with a debut of the new season of *Fatal Impressions*. We're so excited. But we need your help. Elaine has sign-up sheets. Please let us know what you're interested in. We have lots of committees that need staffing."

When Kim stopped for a breath, Elaine waved two clipboards above her head. "I'm going to put these back on the food table. Make sure you sign up before you leave. Our projects only work if everyone helps."

"Thanks, Kim and Elaine. This is going to be a fun spring with lots of visitors to the area. Any other new business? Please sign up to help with holiday and spring events. Send your pictures to Elizabeth Rhoney at Between the Covers. She's updating our website and social media pages." Jules paused and scanned the room. "Okay, if there's nothing else. We're adjourned until next month's meeting. Watch your email for subcommittee meeting dates."

Jules picked up her folder and returned it to her briefcase. Pop patted her on the shoulder as he made his way to the sign-up table. "Good job. Keep it up, Jules."

Several other business owners shared the same sentiment with her. Jules appreciated the validation. It was nice to know that the council members were in this together.

Before she could revel any further in the compliments, J. P. Gross, in his shiny gray suit, sidled over to her. She steeled herself for whatever his cutting remarks would be.

"The numbers are on your side. The town is growing and thriving. Let's hope it stays that way because your resort is still linked to all those murders. And one day, your luck will run out." He turned on the heels of his scuffed black dress shoes and strode out the door.

Chapter Nineteen

Tuesday

Tired of tossing and turning, Jules gave up on trying to draw connections among Sorbonne, Poppy, Chavis, Tess, and Rod. Two espressos made the groggies go away, and now she was antsy to do something. The photographer guise had worked well in the past, so she decided to try it again to see what she could find on the set. In today's social media world, everyone snapped photos to share, so it wasn't that much of a ruse.

She patted Bijou on the head and sent Roxanne a text telling her where she was. The crisp morning air jarred her when she stepped outside. Autumn had definitely arrived. The warm days would be a thing of the past for a while. Zipping her fleece jacket, she walked toward the woods.

The chilly morning didn't deter the spectators. A steady stream of people representing all age groups made their way from the parking lot. Jules jogged around the fan area. She heard voices near the tents and made a detour.

Under one of the canopies, Topher Smythe unloaded props onto long portable tables under the watchful eye of Bradley Taylor, who marked items off his clipboard and arranged the items by scenes. The two worked meticulously to arrange hundreds of items on the tables.

Ashe Lyons strolled in and perused the items that looked like a rummage sale display.

"Your stuff is on table three. But please don't touch anything yet," Topher moved an empty wooden crate to the back of the tent.

Chavis walked by with Kat. He paused when he saw people and stepped under the tent. Jules snapped candids while he and Ashe looked at each other sideways like two cats defending their turf. Bradley and Topher continued their work unfazed.

Ashe continued to finger items on the table.

"Where's my stuff?" Chavis asked.

"Table two," Topher answered without turning around.

Chavis stepped over and perused the items assigned to him for today's filming. He picked up a metal cigarette lighter and flipped the top open and closed.

After about the tenth metal clink, Ashe glared at him. "Do you really have to do that?"

"Just checking stuff out. Making sure it all works."

"It does." Topher looked up from the crate he was unpacking.

"Looks like Bradley's outfitting special forces today." Ashe picked up a submachine gun.

"Hey, I don't have one of those?" Chavis whined. "How come I have a garbage can lid and a backpack? Oh, wait, there's a pocketknife and a .22 caliber with an ankle holster."

Ashe picked up several knives. "Maybe I'll take up juggling." He threw one in the air, and it landed in the grass without embedding itself in the ground.

Topher rushed over, wiped it off, and put it back on the table. "We're not done here. There's another two crates to unload. Do you all need anything in particular?"

Ashe shook his head and moved over to Chavis's table. He picked up the .22 and pulled it out of the holster. He clicked the release and checked the cylinder. He pulled out one of the blanks and fingered it. When Bradley looked at him, he replaced it and clicked it in place. He did several quick draws and then dropped it on the table when Topher frowned at him.

"We're not done certifying the weapons. Please step away from the tables," Topher directed.

Chavis sidled over and picked up the gun. "I would have thought the gun would have been sturdier when I read the script. I'm supposed to use this to fight off the bad guys? Don't you all have something heftier back there? Something that fits Beau Staunton's character better?"

"That's what the prop list calls for." Topher leaned into an open crate. "Talk to Rod."

Chavis rolled his eyes and did a few quick draws of his own. Then he pointed the gun at Ashe. "We don't like the way you've been talkin' to folks around here, partner. I'm going to have to teach you a lesson."

"What?" Ashe said, stepping closer to the other actor. "You're the one who's all mouth."

"I'm channeling Matt Dillon here."

"More like Wild Bill Hickok." Ashe looked around to see if anyone noticed.

Chavis raised the gun and pointed it a few feet from Ashe's thigh. He cocked the hammer and pulled the trigger. "Bang," he said right before the gun exploded.

It sounded like real gunfire to Jules. Smoke filled the tent. Jules froze.

Ashe grabbed his leg and screamed. Bradley, Topher, and other crew members ran to him. The tent filled quickly with crew members. Someone shoved Chavis to the side, and he set the gun on the nearest table.

Jules dialed 9-1-1 and stepped outside the tent. Covering her ear, she told the dispatcher what happened and asked for an ambulance. When she disconnected, she called Jake.

"What's up?"

"Ashe Lyons was shot. It was supposed to be a blank, but he's bleeding. I called the rescue squad. Could you and Lester get out to the entrance and the maintenance road and wave them over to the tents next to the barn? I don't want them to get in all that parking lot traffic."

"Gotcha. We'll take care of it," he said, disconnecting.

Jules's next call was to the sheriff. After his voicemail message, she said, "I called for an ambulance. Chavis Ratner shot Ashe Lyons. He was horsing around with one of the props." Jules pocketed her phone and stepped back under the tent.

By now, a crowd surrounded the smaller tent. Jules wormed her way to the sidelines for a better view. Topher and a guy in all black were using towels to staunch Ashe's bleeding. Tess rushed in and pushed her way to Ashe. She held his hand while the other two men applied pressure to his leg. Kat stood stoically off to the side, checking her phone.

About the time Jules heard sirens, Rod Avery and Paul Bishop rushed in.

"What happened here?" Rod bellowed.

"Chavis and Ashe were inspecting the props. Chavis pulled a gun on Ashe and shot him at close range. It looks like the casing hit him. She called an ambulance." Bradley pointed to Jules.

"Sherri, Drake, go with him to the hospital and keep me posted. And try to keep the curious onlookers to a minimum. This was a filming accident, and I'm sure Ashe will be as good as new soon. Just horseplay. Nothing to this."

Sherri nodded.

An ambulance, followed by the sheriff's cruiser, pulled off the maintenance road and ran through the grass to the edge of the tents. Several EMTs jumped out and took control of the patient.

Sheriff Hobbs and Deputy Mario Caswell circled the crowd. The deputy asked onlookers to step back and witnesses to stay.

Jules heard bird caws in the distance. Only whispered conversations bounced around the tent for what felt like an eternity.

"On three," one of the EMTs said, breaking the silence. "One, two, three." All three men shifted the actor onto a gurney and raised it. Tess ran behind, and the EMTs guided it across the grass to the ambulance.

The deputy and sheriff rounded up witnesses. Chavis sat on one of the prop tables. He had his head in his hands. No one from the cast or crew approached him.

It took over two hours for the deputy and sheriff to talk to everyone. The crowd around the tent had thinned considerably when Rod told everyone not involved to return to the set for prep and filming. Deputy Caswell interviewed Topher and Bradley near one of the prop tables, and Sheriff Hobbs approached Chavis.

Jules scooted closer to hear the actor's responses. She might as well learn something while she waited for her turn.

"What happened?" Sheriff Hobbs stared at the actor, who look like he had aged five years since this morning.

"We were goofing off," Chavis stammered. "It had blanks in it. I didn't mean to hurt him."

"Didn't your prop guy warn you that they were still dangerous?" The sheriff asked.

"Maybe. I don't remember. It seemed harmless. They weren't real bullets. I wasn't thinking. Like I said, we were goofing around. I pulled the trigger. I had no idea anything would come out of it." He paused, looked around, and continued, "It was a freak accident."

The sheriff grunted. "Were you angry with Ashe or had any reason to hurt him?"

"Uh, no. Just guy talk. We mouthed off at each other yesterday, but it was no big deal. I have no grudges. I didn't know anything would fly out of the gun."

Jules raised her eyebrows and bit her tongue.

"Anything else you want to tell me?" Sheriff Hobbs asked.

"No. I'm sorry he got hurt. I wouldn't have pulled the trigger if I knew that was going to happen."

"Don't leave the resort. I may have a few more questions for you later," Sheriff Hobbs said.

"Yes, sir," Chavis said quietly. As soon as the sheriff turned toward Jules, Chavis hightailed it out of the tent. Jules watched him scurry toward the RVs.

"Looks like you had ringside seats. What'd you see?" he asked Jules.

"Ashe and Chavis were bantering back and forth. Chavis remarked that his prop table didn't have cool weapons like Ashe's did. Chavis did some quick draws and some silly cowboy talk. Then he aimed and pulled the trigger. It sounded like a real gun to me."

"It is a real gun. The bullets are blanks, but sometimes, the force ejects the casing from the barrel. And you shouldn't shoot it at close range. People have died from accidents with blanks." The sheriff paused and looked around.

"Anything else?"

"Chavis made some snarky comment to Ashe's girlfriend Tess about her being a suspect. She's one of the makeup artists. It seems Rod Avery dumped her for Poppy."

A look of surprise crossed the sheriff's face, and he scribbled in his notebook.

"I took some pictures. I can send you those when I get back to the office."

"Thanks. This is an easy one to solve. We're going to head over to the hospital in Charlottesville and talk to Ashe. It looks like stupidity and not maliciousness, but I'll see if Ashe wants to press charges. If not, he can always file a lawsuit later. Marco, I'm going to talk to the producer. Be back in a few."

"I'll wrap it up here and meet you at the car." The deputy returned to his conversation with the prop master and his apprentice.

Jules raced to the office to download her photos. She captured the quick draws and the bloodstain on Ashe's thigh. She posted them in DropBox for the sheriff. *Wouldn't Jane the Pain like copies of these for her next freelance effort.* Jules smiled and resisted the urge to email a couple to her.

Jules heard a noise at the back door, and Bijou ran across the room and yipped. Roxanne, Jake, and Lester stormed in.

"What in tarnation happened?" Lester asked. "The scanner has been on fire. It seems the hospital in Charlottesville had to bring in police for crowd control when word got out that one of the actors was headed their way."

"Chavis Ratner shot Ashe Lyons. The bullet was a blank, but it still did some damage." Jules opened her photo collection and clicked through each image.

Roxanne wrinkled her nose at the ones with blood. "Matt texted me and said he was heading to Charlottesville. If it's not one thing, it's another. I guess I'll get to see him when this is all over."

"Chavis looked shellshocked when the sheriff finished questioning him." Jules clicked through more photos so the group huddled over her shoulder could see.

"Matt doesn't mince words," her aunt added.

"Those pictures would be pretty valuable right now to the paparazzi." Jake winked.

Images of big money flashed across Jules's thoughts for a moment. She pushed them away. "I'll keep these to myself. For now."

"Jane would definitely be interested," her aunt added. She's trying to make a name for herself with her intrepid *Fatal Impressions* reporting."

"I don't get all the hullabaloo about this. Let me know if you need me." Lester shuffled toward the door.

"I'm headed out, too," Jake said. "I'm going over to Kurt Marino's parents' place. I'm going to start constructing the tiny house on his lot since I can't get much work done in the barn. It'll probably be a late night. Dinner tomorrow?"

"That works. Have fun. I think I've had enough excitement for today. Bijou and I will probably hang out at home and catch up with what's on the DVR. I have an embroidery project that I'd like to make some progress on." But first, she had to update her notes with everything she learned today and text Pixel about the shooting.

Chapter Twenty

Wednesday

Jules heard a helicopter flying low, but her phone buzzed and distracted her.

"Hey, boss. You may want to check the morning news and then head over to the office. This Ashe/Chavis thing took on a life of its own. Drake said that they've already had drones and news helicopters over the property this morning," Lester said.

"Be there in a few. Thanks for the update." She sighed and disconnected the call.

Jules flipped on the TV. Overhead pictures of her resort flashed on CNN. The shots switched to a reporter at her front gate talking about the horrible accident that injured actor, Ashe Lyons. Then a local reporter outside of the hospital provided the latest update on the actor, who had surgery last night. The prognosis was good, and he should return to work in the next few days, though probably on crutches.

"Let's go, Bijou. It sounds like it's going to be a busy morning." She snapped the leash in place, and they walked across the field. A line of cars waited to get through the main entrance to the almost full parking lot. *Word traveled fast.*

Jules barely had time to unhook Bijou before her aunt swooped into the office. "The shooting is trending on Twitter. There are pictures of the resort everywhere. I even saw a clip on *Entertainment Tonight* about Ashe's maiming. Free advertising. This is so exciting…Well, for us. I'm sure he's going to be in pain for a while."

Jake sauntered in behind her. "Any word on Ashe?"

Jules chose the strongest coffee pod she could find and put her mug under the spout.

"Matt said he was going to be okay. He was out of surgery and talking last night. He's going to be sore for a while. But he'll be released either today or tomorrow," Roxanne said.

"There's a crowd out front and one at the hospital. Poppy would have loved this," Jules said. The coffee maker sputtered and let out a puff of steam. Jules stirred in sugar and extra cream.

"They released a statement yesterday that it was a tragic accident, and their thoughts and prayers were with Ashe. Matt said that Ashe hasn't decided whether he wants to press charges or not." Roxanne cocked an eyebrow and smirked.

"Chavis must be a bundle of nerves. He didn't look too good yesterday when it happened. He's usually Mr. Cool." Jules picked up her mug and settled in at her desk. She scanned through some online news sites and saved copies of the stories.

"Drake's guys are taking care of crowd control. I'm going to head to the entrance and check on the traffic. I've got my phone if you need me." Jake disappeared through the front door as Roxanne settled behind the front counter.

"It really is all over social media," Roxanne said, scrolling through sites on her phone.

Jules leaned on the door jamb. "I'm curious to see what Ashe will do. Chavis made a nasty comment that Tess should be worried because she's now a suspect. Then Ashe and Chavis had a little confrontation with some pushing and shoving."

"Who's Tess?" A slight frown crossed Roxanne's face.

"She's one of the makeup artists. She and Rod Avery were an item until he dumped her for Poppy."

Roxanne's eyes widened.

"Tess is seeing Ashe now," Jules added.

"You sound like Emily with all these Hollywood romances and fan stories." Roxanne rolled her eyes and returned to scrolling through Instagram posts on her phone.

The door creaked open. A gangly man dressed in an olive-green trench coat wearing thick black gloves entered. It took him several seconds to pull off his gloves and stuff them in his pockets. "Sorry to burst in on you like this, but I need to talk to someone in charge of the filming. I'm Sam Arnold."

"Good morning," Jules said. "Who did you need to speak with?"

Roxanne set her phone down and looked the man over from head to toe.

"I need to talk to whoever's in charge. I have some information that he needs about a feud between his actors." His glance darted around the room. "And the murder," he said, lowering his voice to above a whisper.

"Which murder?" Roxanne asked, leaning forward over the counter like she was waiting for the man to tell her a secret.

"The murder in town of that gal." Sam's brow furrowed. "I'm kinda in a hurry. I drove a long way to get here, and I need to talk to someone."

"Have you talked to the police?" Jules asked.

"No, not yet. I need to see someone in charge of the TV show first," he sputtered.

"Mr. Arnold, the *Fatal Impressions* folks have already started filming this morning. You'll have to contact the staff through the show's website if you need an appointment," Jules said. "But if your information is important, you should swing through town and see the sheriff."

"That won't do. I drove like crazy to get here. All the way from Ohio." His face darkened, and his glance continued to dart around the room.

"Do you want to leave a note or a business card? I can make sure that the production folks get it."

Sam paused and blinked. "Well, if that's the best you can do. But I really need to talk to someone today." He looked around the store and shoved both hands in his coat pockets. "Do you have any paper?"

Roxanne rummaged around the front desk and handed him several sheets of copy paper and a pen. Sam leaned down and started writing. He covered his paper like it was a seventh-grade math test, and Roxanne and Jules were trying to copy his answers. When he finished, he signed it with the flourish of John Hancock and folded the paper several times. "Here. Make sure someone important gets this. It may be key to everything that's going on." He scanned the room like he was looking for someone. "Are you sure you can't take me to see the director or somebody who can help me?"

"No, I'm sorry. The film crew has security. They've blocked access to the filming. If it's something related to public safety, you could talk to the town sheriff," Jules said.

"Nah, it's not police-related. I'll let the film people take care of it." He wiped his eye and pushed a stray lock of dark hair from his forehead.

"There is a fan area if you want to see what's going on," Roxanne added.

"Okay. Maybe I'll do that. Please make sure that someone gets my note. I added my cell number. It's really important." He shoved both hands in his pockets and turned. "Are you going to take it to the head honcho now?"

Jules nodded, and he shuffled out.

"That was interesting," Roxanne said as the door closed. She pulled out an emery board and touched up one of her pearly pink nails.

Jules unfolded his note. The handwriting was hard to read, but the gist was he saw some tweets on Twitter from Chavis Ratner, and he felt that the actors were in danger."

"Anything worthwhile?" Roxanne asked.

"No. It's hard to read. It's a warning that the actors could be in danger. I'll be back in a minute. I want to see where he goes." She snapped a picture of the note and slid the paper into her back pocket.

"I'll give Jake and Lester a heads up. You never know when you'll need backup," Roxanne yelled.

Jules slid out the front door and stood on the porch for a few seconds. She spotted the man loping across the grass. Ignoring the chill in the air, Jules rushed after him. She had to dodge fans who lined the sidewalks and the spectator area that looked to be at capacity.

Jules followed Sam Arnold as he meandered around people and pushed his way to the edge of the viewing area. He paused for a few moments at the orange plastic fence. Jules stood a few feet behind him, using people in the crowd as cover.

The morning chill cut through her turtleneck and sweater. Wishing she had grabbed her coat, she bounced on her toes and rubbed her hands together to get some feeling back in her digits.

Her phone beeped with a text from Jake. **Traffic's at a standstill. Let me know if you need me.**

Always need you. Things are OK here. Call Bubba if you need help with the jam, she tapped into her phone. By the time she looked up, Sam Arnold had disappeared. Jules made her way to the edge and searched the area for the odd visitor.

No sign of him near the parking lot. When Jules cleared the fan area, she doubled back to the barn. Topher and Bradley moved a large silver cart while Drake, Rod, and Sherri stood off to the side, chatting.

"Good morning." Jules paused to catch her breath. "We had an interesting visitor in the office this morning. He's a lanky guy in a green trench coat. He said he had information that your actors were in danger. Here's the note he left for you."

"Your aunt texted me," Drake said. "We get a bunch of fans who border on kooky. I wouldn't worry too much about it." Drake took the folded paper she offered.

"I followed him to the fan viewing area, but I lost him."

"It happens all the time. People try to figure out ways to get access. They send things and pretend to be delivery drivers and singing telegrams. Some of them are pretty creative. It keeps my guys busy. Anything else going on?"

Jules shook her head. "How is Ashe doing?"

"Fine," Rod said, looking up from his black binder. "He'll be back here this afternoon. And if I know him, he'll be antsy to get back to work."

Jules had a puzzled look on her face.

"We'll write something in the script if he looks injured. We do it all the time," Sherri added.

"Good to know." Jules scanned the crowd, looking for Sam.

"My guys said the hospital was swamped. They had to close off part of the wing because people kept trying to sneak in to see Ashe. People are crazy," Drake said.

"Everyone wants a selfie." Sherri took a sip of her coffee.

A loud whoop emanated from the fan area, and it turned into cheers and whistles. Rod and Sherri looked around.

"What's up? None of the actors are on set yet." Drake scanned the fenced-in area.

A golf cart sped across the grass toward the barn. The driver had his dark head down, focused on the bumpy path ahead of him. His trench coat blew behind him like an olive-colored cape.

Jules sighed. Her staff usually left the keys in the carts and ATVs. Sam Arnold had found an opportunity.

The cart dodged the temporary fencing and skidded to a stop near the cameras. Sam jumped out and looked around. Spotting Jules, he jogged over to where she huddled with Rod's team.

Panting, the man raised his arms. "I'm glad you brought my note over so fast. I need to talk to you. This is an urgent matter."

Drake tapped something in his phone and stepped forward. "Right this way, sir. We can talk as we walk."

"Uh, no. I need to talk to whoever is in charge. Your actors have been having a tweet war, and something's going to happen. You've got to stop it before it's too late," Sam Arnold whined. "I had a dream, and a traveler from another dimension told me that it was my destiny to warn you."

Drake grabbed his arm and shuffled the man toward the tents. Two of his guards, in matching black outfits, stood at the end of the walkway. The three circled Sam and escorted him toward one of the RVs.

Jules wondered if she should let the sheriff know. He probably had enough on his plate without an excited fan with a space alien tale.

"It happens all the time," Sherri said, returning to the papers on her clipboard.

Jules raised an eyebrow. "I'll get this out of your way. It looks like Drake has everything under control."

"Drake's got it. You won't see the guy again," Rod said without looking up.

Jules hopped in the golf cart and turned it around for a quick trip to the office. When she passed the fan area, the whoops and cheers started again. She waved and enjoyed her fleeting moment of celebrity.

Chapter Twenty-One

.

Jules and Bijou had settled on her couch under a fuzzy blanket to binge-watch the latest season of *Father Brown* when Jake's ringtone interrupted life in Kembleford.

"What's up?" she asked.

"Put your dancing shoes on and get ready to snoop."

"Huh," she said, glancing over at the clock on the DVR. 9:38 p.m.

"I got a call from Gabe Howerton. Some of the cast and crew are holding court at Red's. A perfect chance to learn stuff," Jake said.

Jules hoped he didn't hear her sigh. "I'm in my jammies."

"I'll be there in ten minutes." Jake disconnected.

"He didn't even ask." Jules fussed as she headed for her closet. She pulled on a pair of jeans and layered a black T-shirt with a royal purple tunic.

She stared at the hot mess that looked back at her in the bathroom mirror. Heating her curling iron, she pulled the scrunchie out of her hair and dabbed on makeup while she waited. A couple of squeezes of stiffening gel and the hot curls helped the hair. "Bijou, this is as good as it gets with ten minutes' notice."

The dog cocked her head and wandered back to the living room to claim her space on the blanket.

Jules checked her look one more time in the mirror and unplugged the curling iron. Time to find her black lace-up boots.

A knock at the cabin's front door sent Bijou into a barking jag. She calmed down when she saw Jake through the window.

"Lookin' good. I like purple." He stepped into the front room. "Gabe said that Chavis, Kat, and a bunch of the crew arrived, and the locals were going crazy."

"Hollywood takes over Fern Valley." Jules picked up her coat and followed Jake outside.

His Mustang made the ride to Red's Honky-tonk seem shorter than normal until the traffic came to a complete standstill as a line of cars inched forward toward the gravel lot. Word of celebrity sightings in Fern Valley spread faster than free stuff at a grand opening.

After beeping and creeping along in traffic, Jake made a spot in the grass near the edge of the lot near an oak tree. Jules grabbed her ID and phone and pushed her purse under the front seat. She wiggled out of her coat and left it in the car.

Jake reached for her hand as they walked through the semi-lit parking lot. He looked at the line that snaked around the front porch and led her to the bouncer at the door who nodded and stepped aside for them to enter. Every inch of floor space was covered in wall-to-wall people, three deep at the bar.

Jake and Jules squeezed in at the edge of the bar. When Jake finally made eye contact with the bartender, he yelled their order, and it took a few minutes to get the drinks. Jules picked up her Coke, and they moved to the railing overlooking the dance floor. Chavis, Kat, Topher, Jayden, and four other guys sat around a rectangular table in the corner. One of Drake's guards, sporting a menacing look, stood nearby. A plate of half-eaten nachos sat on the table, surrounded by empty mugs and wine glasses.

The noise level made it hard to catch any snippets of the conversation. Jules watched the crowd.

Every once in a while, a local would sidle up to the table either alone or with a friend to get a photo or an autograph, and Drake's guy would keep them at bay.

Jules's legs started to twinge. "Let's shake this up. We're not getting any new information from this vantage point."

Jake nodded and followed her through the crowd, down the steps, and around the dance floor. They stopped a few inches from the bodyguard. Jules yelled, "Hi, Kat. Hey, Jayden." She waved with her free hand.

The security guard stepped forward with his hands raised. Jules wasn't sure if this was C. J. or Titus. They could easily pass for brothers. "Hi, I'm Jules Keene from the resort. Drake introduced us."

The mountain of a man looked at Jules and then at the group.

Jayden piped up with, "C. J., she's cool. That's Jules and Jake. They take good care of us on the set." He slid over on the bench and patted the empty spot beside him. "Come and join us."

C. J.'s facial expression never changed, but he did move slightly so the pair could get to the table.

"This is my boyfriend, Jake," Jules said as he straddled the bench behind her.

"Oh, we know Jake," Kat cooed. She sipped her wine and had a grin that looked like her namesake with the proverbial canary. Chavis glared at her but remained silent.

Jake squeezed Jules's shoulder as he spoke, "How are you all doing? The place is hopping tonight."

Chavis put his hand atop Kat's and leaned in to whisper something. She pulled her hand away and turned to face Topher. Chavis scooted back, fluffed his hair, and leaned back in his chair. He made eye contact with two girls at a nearby table. Within minutes, he rose and zeroed in on the peroxide pair.

"We're waiting for the bewitching karaoke hour. There's a hundred-dollar prize and free beer for the best group rendition. If I can get a few more drinks in this bunch, we're going to be amazing. Wanna join us?" Jayden asked.

"Uh, no," Jules said, leaning closer to the stylist. "I'm better at being the audience."

The waitress appeared with another tray of appetizers and two pitchers of beer. "Let me know if you all need anything else. And here's a ginger ale for you, big boy, since I know you're on duty," she said with a half-smile. C.

J. took the can she offered.

The song finished, and no other one followed. The throngs on the dance floor looked around, anticipating more music. A large bald man in black with a reddish beard tapped a microphone. The thunks echoed through the speakers across the bar.

"Howdy, folks. I'm Ray Dawson from Galaxy Entertainment. Who's ready for our Thursday Night Karaoke Roundup? Let me explain how this works. I've got the sign-up list right here in my paw, and I'm going to call the groups one by one. If your team hasn't signed up, it's not too late. Come up here, grab a slot, and pick your song. My partner, Mandy, will help you out." A petite blond in a sequined cowgirl hat waved at the crowd. "After each group sings, we'll gauge the audience's applause. Then around elevenish, we'll have a second round if it's close between the groups. Y'all ready?"

The cheers and whistles made Jules's ears ring.

"Alrighty then," the large man said. "Let's get this party started with June Bug and her posse." His heavy breaths after every few words echoed through the speakers.

June Bug and two other women decked out in skinny jeans took the stage. Their big hair reminded Jules of the '80s. The music blared, and the women belted out their rendition of "Girls Just Wanna Have Fun." *Appropriate song choice.*

Three other groups followed the first act. Each sang either a rock or country blast from the past.

Chavis spent his time posing for pictures with the two women and with several others in the crowd before he made his way back to his original seat. Jules stole a glimpse at Kat to see if there was any reaction. She didn't seem to notice Chavis's exit or reappearance.

After "Bohemian Rhapsody" ended, Ray grabbed the mic from one of the cowboys from the quartet. "Now, ladies and gentlemen, we have the Hollywood Crew singing "Let's Go Crazy."

"That's us," Jayden yelled. "Come on. Let's make some magic. Jules, Jake, you sure you're not in?"

Jules shook her head. Jake smiled and rose. He followed Kat, Jayden,

Topher, and Chavis to the stage. The crowd went wild. Chavis and Topher egged the audience on with gestures for them to scream louder.

"Okay, okay," Ray said. "They haven't even sung yet. Let's see what they got."

The singers found places on the small stage and took a bow. The audience went wild again. It was hard for Jules to hear the first part of the song. The noise level subsided to a dull roar, and the crew belted out the Prince classic with a few dance moves that almost looked rehearsed. Jake sounded good, singing backup for Jayden.

When the last notes sounded, the crowd roared again. The gang took several bows and made it back to their seats. Phone cameras flashed from all sides.

C. J. dissuaded anyone from approaching the table.

Three more groups performed classic country songs, and then a group of guys belted out "YMCA." After the timeless tune by the Village People, Ray corralled the microphone. "Everyone did a great job tonight. Thanks for the laughs and the entertainment. I don't think this one is even close." Someone in the back let out a wolf whistle. "I'm going to make an executive decision. Tonight's winner is the Hollywood Crew. Come on back down here to git your winnin's."

The group filed back to the stage. While the audience applauded and screamed, Ray handed Jayden an envelope. "Get your round of beer from the waitress later." Then turning to the audience, he said, "Hey, y'all. Do you want to hear one more from tonight's winners? Come on, let's give 'em some encouragement. They can't say no to so many fans."

When the noise died down, Ray looked at the group, "What'll it be?"

Jayden, Chavis, and Topher huddled together, and Chavis grabbed the microphone. "Love Shack," he said.

And the crowd went wild again. Everyone grabbed a microphone, and Chavis led the group in singing the B-52s classic. This time, the entire bar joined in. Chavis waved his arms and spun around. He missed a step and tripped off the small risers.

The crowd gasped.

Chavis rose and fist-pumped the air. He jumped on the stage and back into the song.

After the last few bars, the group took several bows, and the applause didn't completely die down until the group made their way back to the table.

The waitress met the group with three pitchers and a plate of appetizers.

Jayden handed her the envelope. "This is for you for putting up with all of us slobs all night."

The young woman opened the envelope, and her eyes widened. "Thank you." She shoved the envelope in the pocket of her black apron and returned to the bar.

Jules patted Jake on the back. "Awesome job. You have all kinds of skills that I don't know about."

Jake's smile highlighted his dimples and perfect pearly whites. "Oh, there's plenty of time for you to learn all kinds of stuff."

"You never cease to amaze me. Is there anything you can't do?" she asked.

Jake winked at her but didn't reply.

"Hey, I'll be right back." Jules scooted around him and headed to the restrooms behind the pool tables. After an unusually long wait, she washed her hands and made her way back down the narrow hallway. The line for the bathroom snaked down the hall and around to the side of the bar. She had to wiggle around people blocking the path.

As she made her way through the throngs at the bar, someone grabbed her shoulder and jerked it backward. Wedged in between people in the crowd, Jules couldn't turn around. *Just a crowd bump?* Then someone clutched her shoulder and whispered, "Stop nosing around. You're going to get hurt." She thought it was a guy's voice, but she couldn't be sure. The noise around her made it hard to discern details.

Jules's heart raced, and she managed to turn sideways slightly. No one was moving away or making eye contact. It's like the voice vanished. Nobody but party-goers with drinks or those trying to get refills. *Think, Jules. Did you recognize the voice? Someone from town?* It happened too quickly, and Jules wasn't expecting an ominous warning. *Was it a guy, or could it have been a woman?*

She replayed the encounter in her head several times as she made her way across the room to the table that now had two empty seats. "Where's everybody?" she asked Jayden.

"The not-fun people decided to leave. Kat and Chavis had words earlier, but from the kissy faces they were making, I think they made up and were planning a rendezvous of their own, but you didn't hear it from me." He started humming "Love Shack."

"Nope. I don't know a thing." Jules winked. "We're going to have to head home soon. Does anyone need a ride back?"

The men around the table shook their heads.

"We were smarter this time." Jayden said, "We brought two cars. Who knew there was a place with no car service? Somebody needs to become an Uber driver around here. Maybe I'll give up LaLa land and set up my own business. Makeup artist by day, Uber driver at night. Doesn't sound like a bad life. You could use another stylist in this town."

"I'll be your first customer," Jules said. "But I'm pretty sure the social life isn't what you're used to."

Jayden laughed and gave her a thumbs up. "You all must not watch the news either. No one seemed to notice me when I got released. I thought I would have gotten some media attention."

Jules patted his shoulder. "I can call a reporter if you want."

"Let me think on it. Maybe I should lay low for a while." Jayden waved his hand in front of his face like it was a fan.

Jake leaned over. "About ready?" Jules nodded, and he continued, "Thanks for letting me join you guys. See you back at the resort."

The blast of cold air that greeted them when they exited was a relief compared to the stale air inside the honky-tonk. Jules had had enough of humanity for one evening. The ominous message from the stranger still bothered her. She played the incident over and over in her head.

She snapped her seat belt shut when Jake started the car's engine and navigated through the traffic in the graveled lot. "Learn anything interesting tonight? Other than Kat was angry, and Chavis was, well, Chavis," she said.

"Not really. They bellyached about not having any privacy and people always wanting to talk to them. Even the crew had celebrity status tonight. What about you?"

"They do kinda act like the ordinary people bother them. It doesn't faze me, but I can see where folks in town get a little miffed. I didn't learn much about them, but I found out what a good singer you are. Did you see anyone unusual around when I went to the ladies' room?"

"No, why?" he asked.

"When I was walking back by the bar, someone whispered in my ear and told me to stop poking around."

"See who it was?" Jake squeezed her hand and stared at her for several beats.

"Nope," Jules said. "I couldn't even tell if it was a guy or girl."

"You sure it was about the murders? You wanna go back inside?"

"No. It all happened so quick. It didn't quite register until it was over. What else could it be? The only other thing going on is the planning for Fern Valley's Christmas festival in December. I hardly think it was that. I didn't think it sounded that dire. It was loud in there, too, so I may have misheard."

"Maybe the warning's a good sign," he said.

"Huh?"

"You're close enough to make someone uncomfortable," Jake said.

"That's the puzzling part. I have no idea what it could be."

The traffic thinned out as they drove away from town.

Jake stopped in front of Jules's cabin, and his tires squealed. She pulled her purse out from under the seat as he jumped out and held the door for her. He kissed her under the porch light while Bijou gawked from the living room window.

"Night. Thanks for an entertaining evening," she said.

After a long pause, he added, "Make sure your door's locked."

"Yes, sir. Night," she said, closing the door.

Jules's thoughts about the warning raced around in her head. Maybe C. J. saw something odd at Red's. He was awfully quiet. He had to be watching somebody.

Chapter Twenty-Two

Friday

Jules slipped into the lodge through the big oak doors and blended in with the crew in front of the table laden with urns for coffee, organic teas, and three kinds of hot chocolate. She filled a to-go cup with a blend called "Jamaica me Happy," stirred in creamer, and plopped on the plastic top.

Scanning the crowds surrounding the food tables around the perimeter of the room, she spotted Titus and C. J. at a small table near the wall of windows that incorporated the view of the Blue Ridge Mountains. Jules wended her way around tables and dodged crew members with food-laden plates.

"Good morning." Jules approached the two men.

Both guys, who must have played football or rugby in their earlier days, looked up without saying anything.

"I'm sorry to bother you on your time off, but I wanted to know if you'd help me with something."

C. J. stirred his drink and stared.

Titus said, "Sure. Have a seat. What's up?"

"When I was at Red's last night near the bar, someone whispered a warning in my ear. I was wondering if you noticed anything unusual last night, or anytime you were out with the crew."

"Define unusual. We've had a woman in a bikini and a fur coat try to sneak into Derek's Stone's trailer. I've lost count of the number of drones that keep hovering over the set, and some guy tried to disguise himself as a flower delivery guy to get close to Kayleigh. Oh, and I didn't even mention the two murders." C. J. raised one eyebrow.

Titus almost cracked a smile. "You forgot the alien prophet from the other day. It's never a dull moment with this bunch. Some days, the kooks outnumber the normal people. Everybody thinks they have a new idea to sneak on the set."

"I didn't see anything crazy last night. I was trying to keep the locals from getting close to the actors and crew. They want to be near anything affiliated with the show. What did the person look like who warned you?" C. J. scooped up a huge bite of scrambled eggs and cheese mixed with hash browns.

"I felt a tap on my shoulder in the crowd, and someone whispered in my ear. I have no idea who it was."

C. J. swallowed and stared out the window for a moment. "Nothing unusual happened last night. Kat and Chavis left early, right before you did. The rest of the group headed back to the resort when the bar closed."

"I was with the group the night that Poppy was killed. It was like C. J. said. Lots of people wanted to get close to the actors. That night the A-listers were Derek, Chavis, and Ashe. Kat and Tess were there, too. All night, mostly women tried to get photos and autographs. And some wanted a dance or karaoke partner." Titus wiped his mouth and refolded the paper napkin.

"Did Poppy say she was leaving that night?" Jules asked.

"She didn't tell me," Titus said. "She went outside with Kat and Chavis. And maybe Derek. I remember Derek came back to the table and bought a round of shots for the group. Later, I drove the van back to the resort. Everybody was there except Poppy, Kat, and Chavis. I saw Chavis leave with two locals. Not sure what happened to Kat."

"She was luckier than Poppy," C. J. muttered, taking a bite of a piece of buttered toast.

Jules raised her eyebrows. *Kat hadn't mentioned anything about catching a ride back to the resort.* "If you remember anything else, let me know." She rose and glanced around the room.

Jules walked through a maze of tables and chairs, disappointed that she didn't learn anything new. Near the front door, Tess and Jayden leaned in close at a four-top. "Hi, y'all. Thanks for a fun night last night. We really enjoyed it," Jules said.

Jayden looked up, and a megawatt smile broke across his face. "Hey, Jules. Pull up a chair. Karaoke is always fun with this bunch. I was telling Tess about everything she missed. She's in love and would rather hang out with her new beau than with us."

The petite woman blushed and giggled. "He is something else. And I met him at the perfect time. He is so supportive, not like a lot of other show biz types. I guess I had to learn the hard way."

"How long have you been in this business?" Jules plunked down in one of the empty seats next to Tess.

"Oh, since high school. I did an apprenticeship with one of the studios. I love being a part of the collective pop culture."

"She did hair on *Friends* and *Modern Family*," Jayden added, twirling his finger in the air.

Tess smiled. "I've been fortunate. I've always been able to work."

"And she's picked up quite a few hot boyfriends through the years." Jayden gave Tess an exaggerated wink.

The woman's face flushed. "There weren't that many."

"She's done quite well for herself with Ashe, and if I do say so myself, I think it's an upgrade from the last one." Jayden winked again and patted the other stylist's hand.

Jules looked at Tess's petite features. The fine creases around her eyes and mouth gave away her true age. Jules did some quick calculations, and her guess was that Ashe was a few years younger than the stylist. "You missed some fun last night."

"We'll be sure to make it next time. Ashe always likes a good party." Tess added creamer and stirred figure eights around the mug.

"It was kinda subdued. Almost mellow. Not implying anything because you and your boyfriend were there. Chavis and Kat didn't seem to bring their A-game." Jayden waved both hands around as he spoke.

"The place was packed," Jules said. "It took us a while to find a parking space. I think word spread quickly that you all were in the house."

A look of concern crossed Tess's face. "I hope Chavis is still feeling guilty about what he did. He apologized, but I'm still furious with him about his stupid behavior. Ashe had to have surgery because of him."

"Your boy's going to be okay. I know lots of guys who've survived being shot with real bullets. He's up and around already. He and Chavis will kiss and make up. They've been friends way too long to stay mad at each other. It was a dumb accident."

"I don't know. Ashe was pretty upset with him. He was even talking to his agent about suing him."

Jayden rolled his eyes. "You and I both know that's a threat. They're stirring up the stink to keep it in the news. They both love being in the headlines. I bet he gets a book deal out of this. And at minimum, all the talk shows will want him."

Tess shrugged her shoulders. "We'll see. I need to get back. I want to check on Ashe before I have to prep for today. See ya." Tess rose and disappeared in the crowd near the front door.

Jayden scrunched his face like he had tasted spoiled milk. "Like I said before, Kat was in a mood yesterday. She's mad at Chavis for something. And he's trying his darndest to get back in her good graces. He follows her around like a lost puppy lately. Clingy. Clingy. I'll see what I can get out of her today. I'm dying to know the details."

"They did seem out of sorts last night," Jules mused.

"I'll figure out what it is. Give me your number in case it's juicy." Jayden handed her his phone, and she tapped in her contact. "He kept trying to get kissy with her, and she rebuffed him last night. And the little boy has such a fragile ego."

"But they left together?"

"Who knows. Maybe they kissed and made up, too. I'll find out. I need to get a move on. See ya around." Jayden air-kissed Jules and headed out, leaving his chair out in the aisle.

Jules rose and pushed the chair in. She started to clear the table and then remembered the caterers. She put the plates back on the table.

Not in the mood to work, Jules swung by the office and grabbed her camera. Her first stop, tent city.

Most of the crew stood at the edge of the woods. Jules started her snooping around the tents. When she rounded the corner, she heard a loud shriek and a high-pitched, "Stay out of my stuff! How many times do I have to tell you?" Kat stood with her hands on her hips, facing Jayden, who was rooting around boxes and bags at the next table.

"I was looking for my set of picks," Jayden said. "They aren't in this bag, and I thought they might have gotten mixed up in your stuff. You could have packed them in your bag by mistake."

"No, they're not in with my stuff," Kat sneered. "I'm careful with my tools and don't leave them lying around like some people." She slammed a bag on the table. The force made the card table wobble. The tall woman turned on her stiletto-heeled boots and stepped outside the tent.

Tess, with a deer-in-the-headlights look, stood quietly behind a stylist chair.

"Someone's in a mood," Jayden whispered to Jules. "Obviously, her evening with Chavis wasn't picture perfect."

"What did you say?" Kat demanded as she stormed back into the tent.

Tess made herself smaller behind the chair and pretended to unload her equipment.

"Nothing. Nothing at all." Jayden focused on the black vinyl bags in front of him.

"Today's not the day for goofing. We've got a packed schedule. Ashe, Derek, and Kayleigh will be here any minute. I don't want Rod screaming at us for holding things up." Kat slid the empty bags under the table and straightened the items near her station. Then she stepped outside again with her e-cigarette.

"And don't forget Chaaa-vis," Jayden whispered, making a face at Kat's back.

Tess stifled a giggle.

Jules patted Jayden on the arm. "Good luck today. Text me if you hear anything."

"You know it, girl." Jayden's voice trailed off as a red golf cart with *Fatal Impressions* emblazoned on the side pulled up and stopped in the grass outside. Titus hopped out and handed Ashe a pair of crutches.

Tess jumped into mama bear mode and helped him hobble to her chair. She fussed over the actor and sent Titus to get him a soy vanilla latte.

Jules hesitated. There was no need to rush off when all the drama seemed to be right here. She focused her camera and snapped shots of Tess and Ashe giggling in the corner. They didn't seem to notice that anyone else was around. She took a few photos of Jayden, who posed with his shears and blow dryer. Kat stormed back under the tent, and a fruity smell trailed after her. She looked around, glared at her coworkers, and busied herself with rearranging items at her station while Tess and Ashe continued their hushed conversation.

Jayden pulled a pack of cigarettes out of his bag and stepped outside the tent as Chavis Ratner strolled in. The pair high-fived and did some sort of secret handshake from middle school.

"Good morning, people. Let's get our groove on," Chavis announced, waving both arms around above his head. "Chavis is here."

Ashe muttered something, and Chavis's head jerked toward the actor. "I hope you're feeling better this morning. You seem to be on the mend. Anything I can get you?"

"Nope. We're good," Tess replied.

"I've heard you're good, but I wasn't talking to you," Chavis said, glaring at Ashe. "Bro, you doin' okay?"

Ashe glared at him until Tess spun the chair around to work on the front of his hair.

"Okay, good then," Chavis added. "Kitty Kat, is this your lucky day?"

"All my days are lucky," Kat mumbled. "Have a seat, and I'll have you out of here in a jiff." She draped a plastic cape around his shoulders and fastened it at the neck.

"Ouch. Not so tight." Chavis wiggled and pulled on the cape's collar.

CHAPTER TWENTY-TWO

Kat flipped through pages on a clipboard and then chose Chavis's makeup.

"What's wrong, Kitty Kat? Did you stay up too late last night? You're not getting old on me, are you?"

"Maybe I found a new pastime." Kat added blush with an oversized brush and then outlined his eyelids and brows with a brown liner. "Sit still. You're too squirmy this morning."

"It thought you liked my moves?" Chavis looked up at Kat with his best puppy eyes.

Ignoring the actor, she ran a hot comb through the top of his locks and fluffed it with a pick. "Okay, we're almost done here. Don't want to keep you from your busy day."

"New hobbies, huh? Hey, Jules, what do people do for fun around here since the nightlife is basically non-existent?" Chavis asked.

"There's lots to do," Jules said, pointing her camera at the actor. "I'll have some brochures dropped off at your trailer."

"Can't wait. And Kat, what kind of special treatment is this? This is not your usual customer service or your style, girlfriend," he said, grabbing her by the waist and pulling her into the chair.

Kat stumbled and stood. "Not a bright idea when I'm holding a hot instrument. We're done here. I'll see you later." Kat turned her back and unplugged the hot comb.

"You're no fun today. Hope you're in a better mood later. I could help with that." Chavis stood and looked around the tent. When he realized he wasn't the center of attention, he announced his departure loudly. "See you lovely peeps later." The actor lightly boxed Jayden on the shoulder as they passed under the canopy.

Jules watched for a while as Kat and Jayden transformed the actors and extras into something that looked like zombie apocalypse victims. Kat gelled her person's hair to stand up on the ends, and Jayden covered his person's face, hands, and arms in grayish makeup.

"Do you all do the horror makeup, too?" Jules asked, fascinated at the transformation of the two actors in just minutes.

"We do regular makeup and hair," Kat said. "There's a guy in costumes that does the special stuff like cuts and blood. He makes the monsters and the corpses."

"And the effects people use CGI to do a lot of the scenery and scary stuff," Jayden added. "You should go over and see Toye and Dez. They're usually in a couple of RVs near where they're filming."

"I don't think I've met them yet." Jules looked around the tent.

"They're always busy behind the scenes. Toye is the costume manager. She can make anything, and Dez was that kid who doodled in class all the time. His Halloween costumes must have been epic," Jayden said.

Jules snapped more pictures. She couldn't wait to update her website and brochures with the Hollywood magic. Maybe Roxanne was right about using the filming as marketing for the resort.

Jayden spun the young woman around in the chair. "Just a few more spots on your face and neck, and I'll be done here. Let me add some smeared lipstick too. It's perfect for the hot mess look."

The young woman, who looked like she'd been in a fire or chased by wild animals, admired her frightful look in the mirror. "Looks good, as usual. Thanks for getting me in and out of here so quickly. Now I have time to grab food before I wander through the woods all day."

"Grrr," Jayden said to her, making a snarly face and claw hands in her direction. "See ya tomorrow."

"I'm going to head out too. I want to see the cool costumes," Jules said.

"Look for the RVs near the woods. If not, ask anyone. Everybody knows Toye and Dez," Jayden yelled.

Jules walked toward the woods, stopping every few feet to snap pictures. She wanted to make sure she had photos that captured all the adventures the crew brought to the resort.

Sherri, involved in a conversation with Rod and several other crew members, stood near the edge of the action. When the discussion broke up, and the men moved on, she spoke, "Hi, Jules. What can I do for you?"

"I'm trying to get pictures for our website and newsletter. Jayden said I needed to meet the costume and special makeup folks. He went on and on about their amazing skills. Can you tell me where they are today?"

"Toye and Dez are over there in those two RVs that are gray and red." Sherri pointed over her shoulder at the two mobile homes parked closest to the tree line.

"I appreciate it. Everything going okay?"

"Yep. We roll with whatever comes our way. Right now, it's trying to rearrange Ashe's shots so he doesn't have to stand long without his crutches." Sherri pushed the sleeves up on her flannel shirt and checked her phone. "It's never a dull moment on the set."

"I'm sure that nobody watching will ever know he was injured," Jules said.

Sherri nodded and tapped something on her phone's screen.

Jules waited for the camera operators to move a boom and its cart to the wood's edge. Another two guys parked a second camera directly opposite it. Someone blew a whistle, and the crew and extras moved toward the trees. Jules snapped a few more pictures and wandered over to the RVs.

A guy in jeans sat across from an actor under the trailer's awning. The two men made the patio table look kiddie-sized. The man in jeans hunched over the actor's arm and painted bloodstains around a festering open wound. Another oozing sore was drying on his neck.

"Wow," Jules said as she neared the table. "That looks so lifelike." She tried to stifle a shudder.

Both guys looked up and stared at her.

"Hi, I'm Jules Keene, owner of the resort. Jayden sent me over to see your handiwork. He raved about your designs."

"Thanks. I'm Dez," the man in jeans with the bushy black beard said. "This is Pete. He plays one of the woodland victims. The wolves gnawed on his arm here."

"Do you mind if I take some pictures? This is so amazing."

Dez shook his head. "Help yourself. I'm about done here. Pete, let that dry for a few minutes, and you'll be good to go."

"How long have you been with *Fatal Impressions*?" Jules asked.

"This is my first season. I'm a victim of the wolf attacks in town. Dez has crazy, mad skills."

"I was an art major in school, but I've been around films all my life. I grew up on movie sets." Dez stood. "I'll be right back."

Before Jules could respond, Dez disappeared in the RV and returned a few seconds later with a photo album. "Here's my recent stuff."

Jules flipped through pages and pages of tattoos, scars, wounds, and bullet holes. "You are amazing. I didn't realize all this was done with makeup. I am learning so much about filming."

"It's like living in the land of make-believe all the time. Do you have a minute? I wanna take you over to meet Mom. The costumes are pretty cool, too. This show is set in modern times, so there's not a lot of creativity except for the wolves and werewolves. She's had a ball working on their costumes. Wait 'til you see the show after all the editing. Pete, you're good to go,"

"Thanks, man." Pete rose and ambled out.

Jules followed Dez over to the RV parked perpendicular to his. He pulled open the door and stepped inside. "Mom, hey, Mom."

"I'm back here," a voice called from within.

Jules stepped inside behind Dez. The walls, lined with racks that hung at three different levels from the ceiling, looked like one giant, rolling closet.

"I'm pulling stuff out to get ready for tomorrow's shoot," said the plump woman with platinum blond hair combed straight up and out in all directions. Her do reminded Jules of a cross between Andy Warhol and Dr. Emmett Brown from *Back to the Future*. Her reading glasses dangled from a rainbow chain.

"This is Jules. She runs the resort. Jayden sent her over to check out what we do."

"It's so nice to meet you." Toye shook Jules's hand with both of hers.

"Wow!" Jules stared at the racks and racks of clothes.

"Oh, this is only a smidge of what we have. There are three or four shipping containers and a semi full of costumes. We have about any outfit you'd want. And if it's a main character, we have multiples."

"Mom's always sewing, mending, or creating something," Dez said.

"I am in awe of what you all do. Do you mind if I get some photos?" Jules asked.

Toye and Dez posed for several shots, and Jules made sure to get the racks and racks of clothing in as the background. Toye returned to her sewing machine on a small table near the door. She used a seam ripper to pull out some of the stitching in a red dress. "What? I have to make these a little bigger for Kayleigh." The older woman winked and returned to her task.

"Thanks so much for taking the time to talk with me. This is so cool. I can't wait to watch the new season." Jules followed Dez down the RV's narrow stairs. "Thanks for the tour. I enjoyed it."

"Come back anytime. We're always doing something new. The writers come up with some crazy monsters that we bring to life."

Jules pasted a half-smile on her face. Scary as they were, these monsters paled in comparison to the flesh-and-blood kind lurking around Fern Valley lately.

Chapter Twenty-Three

Saturday

Jules's phone buzzed as she tried to organize all of her behind-the-scenes photos from the last few days. "Hello, Drake. What can I help you with?"

"Hey. We're in town filming around the courthouse. I hate to ask you to do this, but my entire crew is here, and I don't have anyone to send back to your place. It seems Chavis tied one on last night, and nobody's seen him. And he hasn't shown up for today's shoot. Could you and your guys see if you can locate him?

"Sure, that's not a problem. I'll let you know what we find." Jules disconnected the call and texted Lester and Jake.

While she waited for the guys, she checked to see which trailer had been assigned to Chavis. As Lester and Jake stomped up the back steps, she grabbed the extra key to the 1964 Airstream that she nicknamed "8 Days a Week" in honor of the Beatles' first visit to the United States.

"Sorry to interrupt what you were doing, but Drake called. He said Chavis was out partying last night and didn't show up at the set today in town. He wanted to know if we could locate him and drag him out of bed."

Jake snickered. "Nothing like being den mother. Hey, Lester, why don't you get the golf cart and take Jules to the trailer. If he's not there, check out the grounds from the barn to the property line. I'll go get the ATV and cover everything west of that and let me know what you find."

"Sounds good. Come on, Jules. Let's see if we can round him up."

Jules hoped the actor was sleeping it off in his own bed, and she could get him to town with little fuss. It was already 11:35 a.m.

Lester stopped near the patio of the Beatles-themed trailer. Jules hopped out and banged on the door. After what seemed to her like forever, she banged again.

Still no answer. She banged a third time and yelled, "Housekeeping."

When there was no response, she fished the key out of her pocket and opened the door. Piles of discarded clothes covered every surface. Jules was pretty sure it hadn't been ransacked, but it was hard to tell. She searched the entire trailer. No Chavis. No phone and no indication of the last time he'd been there.

She backed out of the trailer and locked the door. "No sign of him. Let's take a ride."

"I walked around the perimeter while you were inside. I didn't see anything out of place," Lester said, climbing back into the golf cart.

Lester mashed the accelerator and looped around the vintage trailers. She wondered if he had stayed with Kat. She texted Drake. **Is Kat on set?**

Yes. Came his speedy reply.

Wondering if she knew his location.

She said she left the party before he did, Drake replied.

Jules pocketed her phone. "I thought he might be in a friend's trailer, but she's said she wasn't with him. Where else should we check?"

"We'll move that way." He pointed toward the barn, and they rode slowly up and down the rows of all the vintage trailers. No signs of life.

After they tooled around the barn, Lester parked at the spot where the tents had been. The big party tent stood alone and empty.

"It looks like a ghost town," Lester muttered.

Having no luck on the Chavis front, they cruised over to the RVs. Only faded grass stood where makeup, props, and costume trailers had been parked. They drove around the storage containers. Lester even cruised around the parking lot to the edge of the main road. No sign of Chavis anywhere.

Any luck? Jake texted.

Nope. Headed to the Lodge, Jules tapped on her phone.

When Lester and Jules pulled in front of the dining hall, Jake sat with his head resting on his arms on the ATV's handlebars. "I didn't have any luck either."

"I have no idea where he could be. I'm going to try his trailer once more, and then I'll call Drake." Jules pushed a stray curl out of her eyes. "Should we check inside here?"

"Front and back doors are locked. No one was inside," Jake said.

"Hop on. I'll give you a lift," Jake said. "And if you're nice, I'll buy you lunch."

Jules winked at Jake. "Thanks, Lester. I appreciate all your help."

"No problemo. I'm headed back to get some mowing done while all those Hollywood folks are gone. The grass is getting a little high in places. If I see Chavis, I'll let you know."

Jules climbed on the back of the ATV, and Jake revved the engine. They zoomed toward the vintage trailers. "Which one is it?" he yelled over the roar.

"The Beatles one," she yelled in his ear.

When they reached the refurbished Airstream, Jules repeated her routine of banging on the door. When no one answered, she opened the door and checked inside the trailer again.

"No luck," she said, relocking the door. "We didn't check the tiny houses. Let's take a quick loop over there, and then I'll call Drake."

Only a squirrel and a couple of birds hopped around the tiny neighborhood.

"I'm going to drop you at the office and lock this up. Wanna go into town for lunch?" he asked. She nodded, and he continued, "How about Nacho Mama's? It's not too terribly cold. We could sit out on the patio if you want. Do you know where in town they're filming? Just curious if they've blocked off key streets."

"I'm sure it won't be that hard to find. I'll see what the Twitter fans are saying. See you in a few."

Jules had enough time to scour the internet for chatter about the filming, put the trailer keys away, and text Drake that they'd had no luck with finding Chavis. When she heard the Mustang's roar, she grabbed her purse and locked the door behind her.

"According to the buzz on social media, they're filming near the library today," she said, climbing in the passenger seat.

"That's far enough away that we should still be able to find a place to park. We can swing by the filming afterward if you want."

The ride to town flew by until traffic snarled near Main Street. Deputies directed traffic to the Baptist church parking lot, where Jake found an empty spot in the grass near the social hall. They walked hand in hand to the town's center.

It was nice to see lots of people in town on a Saturday. Jules hoped they were spending money at the local businesses. The lines at Nacho Mama's and the Good Thyme Bistro confirmed they were.

"You wanna wait in line? It looks like it might be a while, or do you want to try for takeout boxes at Lula Belle's?"

"Let's see what the line looks like there. We can always come back. I have no plans for the afternoon."

"It might be dinner before we get fed here," Jake said.

The couple walked down the street and around the corner to the lunch counter. The line spilled out from the front door and down the sidewalk in front of the two businesses next door.

"Let's try it," she said. "It looks shorter than the other places."

They waited for the line to crawl slowly to the counter. *Hopefully, the Halls won't run out of food before it's our turn.*

Almost thirty minutes later, Jules and Jake inched toward the front. Mitch Hall and one of their part-timers worked the counter as Donna zoomed in and out of the back.

"Hey, guys," Mitch said when they made it to the counter. "What can I get you?"

"Two boxes. I'll have the ham and swiss one with an iced tea. What about you?" Jake asked.

"I'll have the pimento cheese with a strawberry lemonade."

The young helper grabbed the to-go cups, and Mitch bagged the boxes as Jake handed over his debit card.

"There you go. Enjoy. I threw in some extra dessert. Thanks for keeping the town open on weekends." Mitch winked and moved on to the next order.

"It's hopping around here. Word has gotten out about Lula Belle's," Jules said as Jake picked up the bag. The line outside had doubled in size.

"Wanna check out the filming? Maybe we can find a place to sit near the sheriff's office," Jake said.

The pair walked in silence toward the government center. Thoughts bounced around like pinballs in her head. *What happened to Chavis? Drake hadn't said where the party was. Did Chavis stay in town with someone?*

The crowd grew as they got closer. People stood in the grass and on the sidewalks. She and Jake found a spot under an oak tree out of the prime viewing area. They sat on the tree's exposed roots and enjoyed sandwiches on crusty homemade bread with sides of pasta salad, purple grapes, and gooey brownies. They each had a key lime pie parfait as a Lula Belle bonus.

"You look lost in thought," he said, finishing his brownie.

"Thinking about Chavis and that warning at the bar. It could have been anyone." She watched people walk back and forth on the sidewalk.

"You worried?" His smile faded.

"No, it didn't feel ominous or scary at the time. I'm more curious about who it was. I've played it over and over in my mind. It could have been a woman's voice, but I have no clue who would've warned me."

"Make sure the sheriff knows about it. He may be more concerned than you are. Maybe we use the buddy system when we go out until this is over."

"I have cameras and a crack security team. I'll be fine. I'll be careful."

"'Bout done?" he asked, helping her up.

"Let's see what we can see." Jules took one last slurp of her strawberry lemonade.

He put one arm around her, and they walked the perimeter of the crowd. It was hard to tell what anyone was watching. All Jules could see were the backs of hundreds of heads. They navigated around the edge of the crowd, easing closer to the front on the far perimeter. She caught sight of the sound crew and one camera rig as Jake found a trash can for their lunch remnants.

"Come on." Jules tugged Jake's sleeve. He looked puzzled as she dodged viewers to get near the hurricane fencing that blocked the viewers from the crew. "Drake," she yelled and waved both arms.

The large man looked up and moved toward the couple.

"Hey. Did Chavis ever show up on set?"

"Nope." Drake shook his head and scanned the crowd. It was hard to tell his facial expression behind the large, mirrored sunglasses. "Any casinos nearby?" he asked.

"No. Not unless there's a backroom poker game somewhere," Jake said.

"That's probably where he was, and now he's sleeping it off," Drake said. "Rod and Paul are furious. He better be half-dead with a really good excuse if he wants to save his job. Text me if you see him."

"Will do." Jules waved as the director of security stepped back and returned to watching the crowds.

"That's interesting." Jules stood on her tiptoes to whisper in Jake's ear. "I heard Rod say to him once that if he screwed up again that he would put Chavis's character in a coma for the rest of the season."

Jake snickered. "That's one way to keep him quiet. Anything else you want to see here?"

"No. Let's take one more look around the resort. I need to let Bijou out. I owe her a really good walk."

When Jake pulled up in her driveway, she said, "Thanks for lunch. I forgot to ask you how Kurt's tiny house is coming along."

Jake pulled out his phone and scrolled through pictures. "He's providing some of the labor to keep the cost down. We're done with the framing and roof. We'll be working on the inside tomorrow. I'm guessing we've got about another two weeks of work left."

"It's beautiful. I can't wait to see it when it's finished." She leaned over and kissed him.

Jake opened the car door for her and waited until she unlocked the cabin door. Bijou ran out to greet him, and he got a few puppy kisses before he left.

"Come on, Bijou. Let's find your leash," Jules said as Jake departed down the maintenance road.

A few minutes later, Bijou led the way to the tiny houses. Not seeing anything stir there, they walked through the crew's RVs. All quiet.

On a whim, Jules circled back to Chavis's trailer. She banged on the door twice. When there was no answer, she walked around the outside. Satisfied that it was still empty, Jules led Bijou home to snuggle up with a hot cup of tea and a good book.

But thoughts of Chavis and the murders kept distracting her. She pulled out her folder and looked at her drawing of all the people and their connections. She added some notes next to Ashe, Tess, and Chavis. She retraced the lines to all players and doodled on the edges. Chavis was the one common denominator to all the recent incidents. Where could he have disappeared to? Did he flee the scene, or was he lying low somewhere?

Chapter Twenty-Four

Sunday

J ules refilled her travel mug with a second espresso and grabbed her keys. "You guard the cabin while I'm gone. I want to check on a few things."

Bijou yipped and returned to her favorite spot of sun on the couch.

The cool air nipped at Jules's cheeks and fingers. She rubbed her hands together and picked up her pace. Fall was slowly replacing summer as Jules's favorite season. The Blue Ridge Mountains were the place to be when the leaves turned.

A piercing scream jolted Jules from her daydream. Before she could quite determine its source, she heard another scream, longer and louder. Jules ran toward the RVs.

She dodged the parked vehicles and stopped suddenly in front of the large metal containers. A pale Toye Thomas, dressed in a hot pink tracksuit, stood at the mouth of one of the shipping containers. Both doors were open, and her hand covered her mouth.

"Toye, are you okay?"

"I am," she whispered. "But he's not." The woman pointed inside.

"Holy crap." Jules rushed toward the prone figure. She rolled the figure toward her and checked for a pulse. She punched 9-1-1 into her phone. "Yes, this is Jules Keene at the Fern Valley Luxury Camping Resort. I have an unconscious person in one of the shipping containers that the film crew is using. I need an ambulance immediately. There is a slight pulse. And he's breathing."

"No. I'm not sure how long he's been here. You may want to send the police, too. No, I don't see any signs of blood. But it's dark where we found him…."

Jules disconnected and called Jake. "I'm sorry to bother you so early on a Sunday. Are you at the resort?"

"Good morning. I was getting ready to head out to Kurt's place. What's up?"

"I had to call an ambulance. The costume manager found Chavis in one of the storage units. He's got a faint pulse. Before you leave, could you direct the ambulance over here?"

"Sure, Boss. See you in a few."

Jules called Drake. When his voicemail message ended, she said, "Drake. It's Jules. Toye and I found Chavis in a shipping container. The ambulance is on its way."

Jules pushed the red button and pocketed her phone. She stepped outside and put her arm around Toye. "Help is on its way. What happened?"

"I was getting costumes ready for this week's filming, and I needed some items in storage. When I opened the doors and stepped in, I tripped over something, and it was him." The woman wiped her eye to keep a tear from escaping.

"It'll be okay. The EMTs will know what to do."

Minutes ticked by, and sirens echoed in the distance, and they got louder by the second. An ambulance, followed by two police cruisers, sped off the maintenance road and bumped across the grass near where the women were standing. Jules waved to get their attention.

The ambulance had barely stopped before the EMTs jumped out. Jules pointed inside the container, and three men with what looked like plastic tackle boxes rushed in.

Sheriff Hobbs parked next to the ambulance a few seconds before another cruiser pulled in behind him. When Deputy Dempsey exited his vehicle, the sheriff said, "Charles, please secure the perimeter."

"Will do." Deputy Dempsey hiked up his pants and adjusted his thick gun belt.

"Hey, Jules. What's going on?" The sheriff asked after checking on the EMTs.

"Morning. I heard a scream, and I found Toye here by the open door." She paused to catch her breath. "She tripped over Chavis Ratner. This is Toye Thomas. She's in charge of the costumes."

Toye nodded. "That's right. I went to get some things out of storage. I thought he was dead."

"When I checked on him, he was breathing, but unresponsive," Jules added.

"Anything else stand out as odd to either of you?" he asked, writing in a small notebook.

"No, sorry. It was kinda dark in there. I rolled him over and checked his neck. I don't remember seeing anything near him," Jules said.

"Y'all stay around here." He tapped on his phone and stepped aside to give instructions to someone on the phone.

Deputy Dempsey looped yellow crime scene tape around the shipping container as the EMTs surrounded Chavis.

Jules pulled her jacket around her to ward off the chill. *How long had Chavis been in there?*

The minutes ticked by in slow motion for Jules until the EMTs removed Chavis on a gurney. The sheet didn't cover his head, so that offered a slight relief. As the medics were leaving, the forensics team descended on the shipping crate and set up a small generator and LED lights. With the area flooded with light, Jules could see a small stain on the floor. She wondered what kind of wound Chavis had.

The sheriff ambled over to where Toye and Jules stood, staring into the shipping container. "Anything else either of you remember?"

Toye shook her head. "I didn't expect to see anything like that early on a Sunday morning."

"You may want to talk to Rod Avery or Drake Kelly. Drake called me yesterday. Chavis didn't show up to the set. I checked his trailer, and Lester, Jake, and I looked around the resort, but we couldn't find him." Jules twisted the button on her shirt.

"Okay. I need to get the key from you for his trailer. I'll have the forensic folks go over it when they're done here." The sheriff pocketed his notebook and pen.

"I'll go get it. Toye, are you going to be okay? Do you want me to walk you back to your RV?"

"Oh, honey, I'm fine. Just getting over the surprise. I've got work to do. If you all need me, I'll be in the costume trailer." She pointed to the row of RVs behind her.

Jules nodded and made a quick round trip to retrieve the key to Chavis's Airstream.

When she returned, Deputy Dempsey shooed crew members back with both arms extended like some kind of crazed bird. "Stay behind the line, please. The sheriff will release a statement later this afternoon."

Jane the Pain, Fern Valley's intrepid reporter, stood at the edge of the growing crowd with her phone and camera in hand.

"Do you need me for anything else?" Jules asked the sheriff.

"No, I'll get the key back to you when my guys are done. Thanks for all your help."

Before Jules got to the coffee maker in the office, Lester and Jake strolled in through the back.

"The scanner's been buzzing this morning, and I heard the sirens." Lester pulled up a chair at the small table in the kitchen area. "We know you'd have a bead on what was going on."

"Looks like you found Chavis," Jake said, pulling out a clean mug.

"The costume lady found him in one of her shipping containers this morning," Jules said.

"Wow. It's like this film crew is jinxed," Lester muttered.

When Jake's coffee finished brewing, he looked at Lester. "Wanna cup?"

"No, that's okay. I've had breakfast. I'm going to go check out the goings-on, and then I'll be back in my cabin. Let me know if you need anything." The older man rose and made his way out the back.

Before anyone could comment, they heard a knock on the store door.

Jules jogged to the front and let Sheriff Hobbs in.

"Here's the key," he said. "The guys will pull the door shut and make sure it's locked before they leave."

"Come on in. Can I get you some coffee?"

The sheriff nodded, took off his hat, and followed her to the office.

While his drink brewed, Jules asked, "Any word on Chavis?"

"Not much," he replied, settling down in the chair Lester had vacated. "They're taking him to Charlottesville. He's breathing. Any ideas on how he got in the container?"

Jules and Jake shook their heads.

"Drake asked us to look for him yesterday morning about eleven. Drake also wanted to know if there were any gambling parlors in the area. I don't know if that helps or not."

The sheriff raised an eyebrow. "If you think of anything else, let me know." The sheriff took a swig of his coffee. "Keep your eyes open for any odd behavior."

"Will do," Jules replied. *A lot of the Hollywood behavior is odd.*

"That's the first I heard of the gambling. We knew he had a lot of, uh, friends," the sheriff said. "Where did you all look for him?"

"We split up and checked all the main areas," Jake said.

"I went in his trailer twice to check on him. It was on the messy side, but it didn't look like there was a struggle. I couldn't tell if the place had been slept in or not."

"Thanks. We'll know more later. I'm hoping after he's stabilized he'll be able to provide us with some key details. Thanks for the coffee. I need to get on the road."

As the sheriff exited through the back door, Jules asked Jake, "So, what's next?"

"If you don't need me here, I'm going to head over to work on the tiny house."

"I'll call you if anything interesting pops up."

Jake kissed her on the top of the head and rubbed her shoulders. "Not sure when I'll be back tonight. It might be late. Maybe we could do dinner tomorrow?"

"Sounds like a plan." Jules pulled out her *Fatal Impressions* folder and made some Chavis notes. So far, she had more question marks than answers. She poked around the show's social media and fan sites for a while. Word had leaked about Chavis being transported to the hospital, but she couldn't find any more details. She flipped through several online news sites without any avail.

Feeling slightly frustrated, she grabbed her phone and tapped in a message for Pixel. **Chavis sent to UVA hosp. Can you find any news?**

I'm on it. Pixel texted back with a series of surprised smiley face emojis.

Jules tapped her fingers on the desk. Sheriff Hobbs was busy, and she probably couldn't sneak into the hospital with the other hundreds of screaming fans. That left the film people who were in town today. Jules pulled out her phone and checked Sherri's last update. They were filming today at the tri-county high school. Guessing that would be her best shot for information, Jules made sure the lights were off. She took Bijou for an abbreviated walk and jumped in the Jeep, and headed for town.

A deputy directed traffic toward an empty field across the street from the school, and her Jeep bounced across the rutted terrain to a spot next to a minivan. Jules mixed in with other spectators and crossed the road. Hundreds of people stood on the track and behind one of the endzones in the football stadium.

Jules milled around for a while, not seeing much filming. She picked up some snippets of conversation around her that the crew was inside the school. Someone guessed they would be outside later because of all the equipment near the stands on the press box side.

She stood for what felt like hours. Two men in black walked out of one of the exits, and the crowd roared. One waved as he made his way to a cart. Jules's legs began to ache from standing. She stretched as more crew came outside and shifted equipment.

Sherri exited and leaned against the brick wall with her clipboard. Jules made her way through the crowd to get as close as she could. Waving and calling the production assistant's name didn't get her attention, so Jules typed a quick text to her.

Sherri seemed preoccupied with the notes on her clipboard. At about the time Jules had decided to head back to the resort, Titus from security ambled across the track toward the fence.

"Hey, Titus," Jules said, inching closer to the large man in his standard black outfit and Raybans.

"Whatcha doing here?" he asked, staring at the crowd.

"I stopped by to see how filming was going. Any word on Chavis?" she asked.

"Come around here," he said, waving her to the other side of the aluminum fencing. When she got closer to him, he continued, "I heard he was stable. They had to move him to another room with more security because fans and staff keep trying to sneak in to see him and take pictures. Drake is trying to calm things down there with the new publicist they brought in. He said there were reporters from everywhere."

"I guess it's a matter of time before they show up in Fern Valley. Any news on the prognosis?" She shielded her eyes with her hand, wishing she had brought her sunglasses with her.

"Drake said that he had a major concussion and was dehydrated. The doctors want to keep an eye on him, but Rod was hopeful that he'd be back to work soon." He laughed. "Or Rod said they would write a coma into the script and do some shots at the hospital."

Jules raised her eyebrows but didn't comment. That's the second time she's heard Rod refer to putting Chavis's character in a coma. "Any idea how he got to where Toye found him?"

Titus made a harrumphing sound.

"It can be a good theory or hunch." Jules egged him on, hoping to get any information.

"A bunch of the crew was in one of the RVs playing poker and drinking. They said that Chavis got up several times, usually when he was losing. Then after an altercation with one of the sound guys about cheating, Chavis threw a tantrum and stormed out. That's the last the gang saw of him."

"Could he have gone to meet someone?"

"Maybe. He has lots of different dance partners." Titus continued to check out the crowds.

When he didn't continue, Jules said, "That probably caused some drama."

"We had the occasional catfight over him. When they got clingy or wanted a relationship, he usually dumped them and moved on to someone else."

"Any major issues?"

Titus pursed his lips and gave a half-smile. "No more than you would expect or that the publicist or his agent couldn't handle. There were dustups and outbursts, but most were spun as crazy fan stories."

"And would he have left a poker game to go meet someone?"

This time, Titus did smile. "Uh, yeah. Especially since he was losing."

"It looks like you all have your hands full here. Let me know if you hear anything else about Chavis."

"All in a day's work. See you around." Titus returned to watching the surroundings, and Jules picked her way around the fence line. She felt like she was swimming upstream with the throngs of people passing her in the opposite direction as she headed back to where she parked.

Twenty minutes later, she found the Jeep and inched it closer to the exit. Traffic snarled in both directions. Her phone dinged before the deputy waved her line of traffic forward.

She glanced at her phone. Pixel had texted, **Found stuff. Wanna meet? Late lunch?** Jules tapped quickly before the car in front of her moved. **Pop's? Starving!**

Jules texted a smiley emoji. **Headed there now.**

Be there in 20. Save me a seat, Pixel responded.

Jules dropped her phone in her purse and inched forward until she made it to the main road.

It took longer than expected, but she found a spot behind the restaurant and put her name on the waiting list before Pixel arrived.

"Keene, party of two," the hostess called as Pixel walked through the diner's doors.

"Good timing," Jules said, hugging her friend.

The hostess motioned for them to follow her.

Marsha, with her pink bouffant hairdo, swooped in with menus and two glasses of water as the pair settled in a booth in the restaurant's section dedicated to honoring the Motown greats. "Hey, y'all. Whatcha feel like today?"

"Hi, Marsha. I'll have the Coney dog with mustard, fries, and an unsweetened tea," Jules said.

"I'll have the veggie dog with everything, including jalapeños. Can I have lime for my water?" Pixel handed Marsha the menu.

"Be back as soon as I can." The waitress turned on her soft-soled shoes and ambled toward the kitchen.

"So, what did you find?" Jules asked.

Pixel pulled out her phone. "Okay. The Chavis fan sites, including the dark underground ones, have recent stories about an attempted murder, a love triangle gone bad, a robbery, and an alien abduction."

"The head of security called me yesterday and asked my guys to check the resort for him when he didn't show up for filming. I talked to one of the guys today, and he said that Chavis was at a poker game in one of the RVs the last time anyone saw him."

"I'm discounting most of these stories, but there was something interesting in the love triangle one. It caught my eye because the person who posted hinted that he or she was on set and knew things. Take it for what it's worth. The person claims that Chavis was involved with the head writer to keep his character alive and viable on the show. He was also dallying with the publicist. Then the author goes on to list fifteen or twenty other Chavis hookups from the past two months, without names, of course. One of them was a makeup artist."

"That's Kat. I've seen her with Chavis a couple of times," Jules said.

"I've sent you the link to this, but you'll need a deep web browser like Tor to get to it. In the last couple of paragraphs, the writer hints that Chavis's shooting of Ashe Lyons wasn't an accident like the production company claims and that someone is trying to neutralize Chavis because he knows too much about the murders. Think there's any truth to it?" Pixel asked, looking up from her phone.

Marsha interrupted when she set down their plates. "Let me know if you all need anything else."

"Thanks, it looks good," Pixel said. She squeezed the flatbread around her veggie dog to keep in all the toppings and took a bite. After wiping her chin with the paper napkin, she continued, "Whatcha think? You've been around a lot of the players lately."

"A lot of that article is true. I don't know about the Ashe part. I think that was horseplay. But Chavis did warn Ashe's girlfriend Tess, who is also a makeup artist, that she was a suspect in Poppy's death because of her link to Rod Avery. Not sure if he was really warning her or deflecting attention from himself. Any idea who wrote the post? If they're in town, it would be interesting to have a chat."

Pixel said, "I'll need to poke around some. I may be able to trace it to someone. I'm saying it's a guy. I don't really know. The handle is WYSIWYG."

"That doesn't trigger anything. See what you can find. I do think Chavis is key to this whole thing. Thanks for all your digging. Every bit gets us closer to an answer."

"So, what else are you doing?" Pixel asked, taking a bite of her pasta salad.

"The business council is working on plans for a big holiday celebration in town with a parade, lights, concerts, you name it. I'll be pretty busy with that in the next few weeks. Plus, they want to do some events in the spring to bring folks to town. What about you?"

"I'm still teaching my class at UVA, and work is always something new. I did get an interesting call last week from that FBI agent you worked with last summer." Pixel's eyes sparkled.

"Will Stafford?" Jules tried not to look surprised. She dipped several fries in ketchup and popped them in her mouth. Jules hadn't seen the handsome FBI agent since he closed the case on her murdered guest.

"The one and only."

"What did he want?" The special agent came to the resort as part of a task force investigating a blackmailing scheme that involved one of her guests who ended up dead in the woods.

"He wanted to see if I was interested in a job." Pixel whispered.

"That's fabulous. You were the one to crack that encrypted file and figure out what Ira Perkins had left on that secret thumb drive."

"I haven't committed to anything yet, but I am driving to Richmond next week to talk to him and his supervisor."

Jules squealed, and the couple at the table across the aisle stared. "Oh, Pixel. That is so awesome! My friend and former college roommate an FBI agent!"

"Not yet. I don't even know all the details of the job, but it did make me curious. We'll see. Keep your fingers crossed. I love what I do but working for the Feds is a whole new world. They have access to some really cool stuff. I'll listen to what they have to say. Let 'em make me an offer."

Jules smiled. What an opportunity for her friend. Jules polished off her hot dog and drained her iced tea.

"Here are some refills on your drinks." Marsha's poodle skirt swished against her crinolines as she walked to the table and set the glasses down. "Anybody save room for dessert?"

Both women shook their heads.

"Then here's the check. There's no rush. And thanks, Jules, for sending those movie folks over here. I got to meet Derek Stone and Kayleigh Bell. The highlight of my week." The fifty-something waitress fanned herself with her order book.

"It's been fun to have them at the resort," Jules said.

"You bring that Chavis Ratner over here. Send him my love and hugs for a speedy recovery. It was so terrible that he got hurt, too. Movie making must be a tough business." Marsha grimaced and moved on to the next table.

Word travels fast in Fern Valley. Jules reached for the bill and put cash in the black vinyl folder.

"Let me at least pay for mine," Pixel protested.

"Nope, we're celebrating your good news." Jules handed the folder to Marsha, who walked by on her way to the kitchen.

"Okay, but next time it's my treat."

Jules rose to hug her friend. "Good luck with the FBI discussion."

Pixel grinned. "At least it's not an interrogation about my forays into the dark web."

The friends parted at the front door, and Jules headed to the resort. With Jake at his tiny house project and the film crew on location, it looked like she had the afternoon to herself. She decided to get Bijou and go for a hike in the woods. Maybe the crisp mountain air and the exercise would help her clear her head and piece together what happened to Chavis. It was unnerving to think a murderer was running around right under her nose. She shivered and made a mental note to put her econo-size can of pepper spray in her pocket.

Chapter Twenty-Five

Monday

Jules felt great after yesterday's long walk, but it did little to clear her head today. She only came up with more questions about Chavis and his paramours, and the thoughts kept her awake most of the night. She took advantage of being wide awake to settle in the office to catch up on emails and organize her *Fatal Impressions* photos. Bijou had no trouble sleeping. She snored loudly in the corner in her puffy bed.

Somewhere around Jules's second coffee to ward off the foggy-headedness, Roxanne breezed in and dropped her black Michael Kors purse and a Between the Covers shopping bag on her desk. She left her sunglasses on and headed for the back counter. After the coffee maker started chugging and emitting steam, her aunt said, "Good morning, Jules. How're things?"

"Rough night?"

"No, just a late one. I waited up for Matt to call me, and it was close to one-thirty before he left work. It's nothing a little concealer and caffeine won't fix for me. He, on the other hand, needs to solve these murders and get some sleep. He's like the walking dead."

"Learn anything new?" Jules asked.

Roxanne added sugar and creamer to her mug and settled in at her desk. "Let's see. You already know that Sorbonne's cause of death was asphyxiation. The stab wounds happened after she was already dead. Poppy was also strangled. Sheriff thinks both were choked and that their scarves were used to kill them."

"Eww. What a horrible way to go," Jules said.

"I know. Let's see. What else? He thinks the Ashe shooting was horseplay and not criminal. And then there's the whole Chavis thing. The good news is that he may be released either today or tomorrow." Her aunt took several sips of her coffee. "The investigators are a little frustrated with Chavis. It seems someone konked him on the head with something heavy, and then he woke up in the hospital. He doesn't remember anything else. The doctors cautioned Matt to give it some time. They're saying he has amnesia and a concussion. He also got a few stitches to close up that head wound. He'll have to take it easy for a while. Just between us, I think the cops think he's being uncooperative."

"I poked around some fan pages. His unfortunate incident has done wonders for his trending on social media sites with all the posts from sympathetic fans," Jules remarked.

"And in person. The hospital staff had to move him because of all the attention. It was bothering the other patients in the main ward. I'm sure we'll get to hear all about it when he returns. Though Matt did tell me an interesting little tidbit."

"What?" Jules leaned forward in her chair.

"Since they don't know how long Chavis won't be available, they changed this season's script to put him in a coma. He said the hospital staff was thrilled that they were doing some filming there before they released the actor. The staff got to be extras."

"Interesting. Rod did say he was going to write in a coma scene."

"Huh?" Roxanne sipped her drink.

"I overheard a couple of their conversations. Chavis was bothering the writers. Rod told him no script changes, or he would put his character in a coma for the rest of the season."

"Don't let what I told you leak out. Matt will kill me or, at the very least, never tell me anything again about one of his investigations." Roxanne's eyes widened.

Jules mimicked locking her lips. "Not a peep out of me. Oh, I had lunch with Pixel yesterday, and that FBI agent set up a meeting with her in Richmond to talk about offering her a job."

"Cute Agent Stafford? He should. She broke open those files way before anyone from law enforcement did. How exciting! Special Agent Pixel."

Her aunt booted up her laptop and settled in at her desk. When she opened the drawer, Bijou ran over for a treat from Roxanne's secret stash. She picked up Bijou, and they cuddled in the chair while the terrier scarfed down the peanut butter snack.

Jules pulled out her folder on the cast and crew and added notes from what she learned from Pixel and Roxanne.

Her phone's text alert jarred her from her thoughts.

Figured it out, Pixel texted.

Jules picked up her phone and selected Pixel's contact. After two rings, Jules blurted, "What'd you find?"

"Good morning, and how are you?"

"Sorry. I got excited when I saw your text. Good morning."

"You dialed faster than I can text. That rarely happens," Pixel said. "I did some serious Nancy Drew work last night and found out that the writer of those posts is a Trevor Desmond Thomas from Los Angeles."

Jules paused until it clicked. "Dez," she said aloud.

"Who?"

"He goes by Dez. That makes sense. His mom was the one who found Chavis. He's a special effects makeup artist for the show." Jules found it interesting that all the cool Hollywood types had a regular name and life before they remade themselves into new personas with hipper dossiers.

"That would make sense. His other posts and memes are all decorated with artwork."

"I think I have a picture here of him. I'll send it over in a sec." Jules tapped on her laptop's keyboard and located the photos of Dez at the RV. "You should have them soon. He's the tall one with the bushy, black beard. Thanks for checking into this. I'm going to go pay him a visit."

"No problem. See you soon. Let me know what he says."

"Good luck with your interview," Jules said as she disconnected. "Interesting. Very interesting." Jules tapped her pen on the desk."

"What's interesting?" Roxanne breezed in from the store.

"Pixel found an online article about what happened to Chavis. It tied him to both murders and hinted that someone was trying to keep the actor quiet. She was able to trace it back to Dez, the special makeup guy." Jules checked her phone to see where the filming was scheduled today. "Good. They're back here at the resort for a few days."

"I'm sure the sheriff will be interested in what you find out. From his Eeyore attitude yesterday, his team could probably use all the help they can get."

"Bijou, stay here with Aunt Roxanne. I'll be back soon, and then we can think about lunch."

"We'll keep everything running here. Go get 'em, Miss Marple."

Jules slid into her jacket and picked up her phone. Deciding against taking the golf cart, she chose to get some steps in with a quick walk. She bypassed the fan area and cut through the vintage trailers on her way to the RVs. Near Dez's trailer, she heard voices. Jules climbed the steps and poked her head in. Dez sat at a table with an attached magnifier light. He leaned over an extra's arm, adding blood coloring to an open gash. Both men looked up.

"Sorry. I didn't mean to interrupt. Do you mind if I watch? This is so fascinating."

"No problem. Pull up a seat," Dez said. "This is Ian."

The other man looked up from his phone and nodded.

"This looks so realistic. How did you learn to do this?" Jules asked.

"I was one of those kids who doodled and drew constantly. And I read every horror and Sci-Fi book I could get my hands on. My mom's connection to the movie business helped, too, and I was able to parlay my art into a job. I mean it's every twelve-year-old boy's dream to get paid to create scars, wounds, and animal bites for a living."

Ian laughed and held up his arm. "Dez is one of the best around."

"I'm almost done here. I'm going to spray this with a little bit of hairspray to give it a sheen. Let it dry, and you're ready to go battle some more wolves."

"What's your favorite project?" Jules asked.

"*Fatal Impressions* has been great. I've been able to do lots of different things over the years on this show. Everything from killer bacteria and alien abductions to animal attacks and zombie invasions. One of the best times was when I did a plane crash. It was one of my first gigs for a movie. That was fun...Ian, I think you're dry now," Dez said, wiping his hands on a towel covered in paint and makeup splotches.

Ian picked up his phone and charged down the RV steps.

"I'm fascinated with what you do. It looks so real on the screen," Jules said.

Dez cleared his workstation and wiped down the surface with a damp towel.

When he didn't reply, she continued, "I need to ask you something about one of your blog posts," Jules said.

Dez looked up. A puzzled look crossed his countenance. "What exactly?"

"My friend found a post about the murders and Chavis's accident."

"I don't remember using my name on any posts." Dez picked up several brushes and dropped them in a red stadium cup.

"My friend traced it to you. I wanted to talk to you about what you wrote if you have a few minutes."

The large man sighed. "If you'll keep it to yourself, I have a few before my next victim arrives. What do you want to know?"

"I know that Chavis was involved with Sorbonne and Poppy."

"And Kat, and Tess, and probably a whole slew of the extras and fans," Dez added.

"What do you know about the Ashe shooting?"

"The higher-ups wanted it to be characterized as horseplay or a stupid accident," he said.

"And you think it's not?" she asked.

"Like the old saying, there's a lot of truth in jest. I think Chavis was mad at Ashe, and he reacted. It may not have been premeditated, but I think there was some anger and jealousy going on."

"How do you think Chavis ended up in that container?"

"I have no idea. He scared the crap out of Mom when she opened the door. He was at a poker game the night before. When one of the crew accused him of cheating, there was a dustup. Chavis gave the guy the rest of his chips and took off."

"Were you there?"

"Yep. Chavis acted weird all night. He kept checking his phone and jumping up to take calls. After one text, he laughed and told everyone that it had been fun, but he needed to take this booty call."

"Did he say who it was?"

"Nope. With him, it usually didn't matter. The next day, the rumor was that Chavis had tied one on and missed filming. Rod was livid."

"Who was the poker player he had words with?" Jules asked.

"Cliff Tipton. Why?"

"Just curious. Anything else you can think of?"

"I went out to smoke at about the same time he left."

"And?"

"Chavis checked his phone. Then I saw him walk over to Tess's trailer," Dez said.

Two women stuck their heads in the trailer before Jules could ask more questions. The taller blond said, "Hey, Dez. You ready for us?"

Jules, disappointed that his work cut into their conversation, rose. "I've got to be heading back. Thanks for the information."

The two women climbed inside the RV and took seats across the table from Dez.

"See ya round," Dez hollered after Jules.

She flew down the stairs and jogged over to the makeup RV. She stopped for a moment on the patio to catch her breath. She'd have to find some time to talk to Dez about the rest of the story. She was dying to know about Tess and Chavis. Could they be linked? And this Tipton guy was someone new to look into.

Someone touched her shoulder, and Jules jumped.

"Girl," Jayden said. "Jumpy. Jumpy. Did you see a ghost? Come on inside, and let me tame those wild locks."

"Thanks. It's been a busy morning," she said, following the stylist in his pink and orange plaid pants, orange turtleneck, and white fuzzy vest.

"Hop right in my chair here, and I'll be right with you. Let me plug in some instruments, and we'll get this party started." Jayden busied himself arranging his station.

Tess leaned over a woman Jules didn't recognize. She applied gel and clumped the woman's hair into random bunches that jutted out of her head from all angles. "I'm going to use a pale whitish-gray foundation on you this morning. That should give Dez a good base to work his magic on, and it'll give you a deathly pallor."

The woman smiled and looked down at her phone while Tess worked.

Jayden hummed as he ran a hot comb through Jules's hair. "You have the best curls."

"Have you heard any updates on Chavis's condition?" Jules asked.

A frown crossed Tess's face. Jules wondered if her question caused that. She wanted to ask Tess about what Dez had said about the night he was attacked.

"Just that he may be released soon. Poor baby has amnesia. I guess we'll never find out what happened to him. He's been boring everyone with his memory loss tale," Jayden said.

"He probably owed somebody money, and he couldn't pay it back," Kat said, stepping through the door. She dropped two mesh bags in her chair and wiggled out of her long, leather coat. She slung her coat over one of the guest chairs and busied herself with unpacking her bags.

"I heard it was a jealous boyfriend who wanted him to stay away from his woman," Jayden said with wide eyes. "Either way, he's going to be in pain for a while, and he won't remember why. There. Your hair looks fabulous. Now I'm going to give you some sultry, smokey eyes. Look up," he commanded.

"I don't know if amnesia is good or bad," Kat muttered.

The gal getting the zombie hairdo rose. "Thanks, Tess. You do a great warmed-over-death look."

Tess smiled faintly.

"Just what all stylists want to hear," Kat said.

Tess ignored her and straightened her station.

When Jayden moved on to Jules's foundation and blush, she said, "Hey,

Tess. I heard Chavis stopped by to see you the night he disappeared. How was he when you saw him?"

A look that Jules couldn't quite identify flashed across Tess's face. "It was nothing. He knocked on the door to see Ashe, but he had taken one of his pills, and he was fast asleep. I told Chavis to come back later."

"How did he seem?" Jules persisted.

"Close," Jayden commanded. He used a rose-colored pen to outline Jules's lips. "Like Chavis, probably."

Tess added, "Loud and pushy. He wanted me to wake up Ashe. I told him to come back later and shut the door."

"Did you see where he went?" Jayden pushed for more information.

"No. It was dark. And why would I care?" Tess slammed one of her barrel brushes on the table.

"Alrighty then," Jayden said. He capped a tube of lipstick and spun Jules's chair around toward the mirror. "Tah-dah. Looking good, sweetie."

Jules checked out her reflection in the mirror. It reminded her of the sultry looks of the fifties Hollywood starlets. "Oh, Jayden. Thanks so much."

"Hope you have a date tonight. If not, get one." Jayden laughed. "Let's take a picture." Jayden grabbed her phone and snapped several. "Come on, girls, get in the picture."

Kat stepped behind the chair and said, "Tess?"

"Oh, sure." She slid in beside Jayden for a few photos.

"Go and break hearts," Jayden said.

Jules wished, but Jake was busy with his tiny house project. It would be fun to go to town with this new look. She texted him a picture with a heart emoji.

Chapter Twenty-Six

Tuesday

Swatches of red, yellow, and orange covered the trees as far as the eye could see. It was nice to enjoy the beauty of nature for a few minutes. The tranquil feeling didn't last long. Thoughts of the murders quickly invaded her sense of bliss. The night before, Jules updated her notes about the murders and stared at the diagram until her head hurt. Jules's thoughts flitted back to the murders. Sorbonne and Chavis had a thing. Poppy and Chavis were together. Poppy was also with Rod. Rod had dated Tess, who was now with Ashe, who Chavis accidentally shot. And Tess may have been one of the last people to see Chavis before he was attacked. And if that wasn't enough, Chavis had had countless flings with others. Everything seemed to revolve around Chavis.

A black SUV caravanned through the main gate behind a police cruiser. The vehicles didn't slow down at the parking lot. They turned and headed down the maintenance road.

Jules jogged toward the vehicles to see what was going on.

Titus, from security, waited in a monster golf cart with three rows of seats near where Deputy Dempsey stopped his patrol car.

Kat shot out of the passenger side of the SUV, and Drake moved from the driver's seat at a slower pace. He slammed his door, and Kat jerked open the back door behind her. She helped Chavis out of his seat belt.

Drake grabbed several bags and tossed them in the golf cart next to Titus.

Kat eased Chavis into the cart and patted his arm like a mother hen. Jules watched her rub his shoulders as Deputy Dempsey climbed out of his car and hiked up his pants. He circled the golf cart and stopped to talk to Drake. Jules moved closer.

"We'll make sure he takes it easy. And the doc will be by later today to check on him," Drake said, looking at the subdued Chavis, who leaned on Kat's arm.

"Call if you need anything." The pear-shaped deputy turned and made his way back to the cruiser.

"Chavis, it's good to see you back." Jules approached the cart.

He nodded. "I'm glad to be out of the hospital."

"He needs his rest. We're going to make sure he gets tucked in and cared for. He'll be back to his old self in no time," Kat said.

As soon as the police cruiser turned and made its way to the resort entrance, Drake drove the SUV across the grass to a spot near the RVs.

Jules followed on foot and arrived at the 1964 Beatles' Airstream as Titus and Kat were helping Chavis out of the cart. The actor looked around and gingerly made his way up the metal steps.

Kat followed him inside and shut the door firmly. Then she closed all the blinds.

"It's good he's back," Jules said.

"The doctors wanted to keep him for a few more days, but he insisted on being on set. He wants to get back to work," Titus said.

"I couldn't tell that he was injured by looking at him," Jules mused.

"He's got some bruises. Whoever attacked him whacked him a couple of times in the head and on his legs. And he doesn't have any memory of what happened. Drake wants one of us to be with him at all times until the police get this sorted out."

"Let me know if he needs anything or if we can make his stay more comfortable."

"Will do," the large man said as he entered the trailer.

Rod, Drake, and Paul made their way to the trailer's tiny patio. Chavis wasn't going to get much rest with this parade of visitors.

Jules waved to the men and hustled to the office to put together a basket for Chavis from her stash of gourmet items for special occasion rentals. She pulled open all the cabinets and filled a basket with glittery paper stuffing.

"What's shaking?" Roxanne asked as she stepped over the items Jules had pulled from the cabinets.

"Chavis is out of the hospital, and I wanted to put something together for him."

"That's nice." Her aunt peered at her with one eye closed. "And if I know you, it's your ticket to get closer to our sweet Chavis to interrogate him."

Jules gave her best "who me" look and smiled. "Speaking of that, has your best source provided any new tidbits of information?"

Roxanne made herself a mug of tea. "No. Our dear sheriff is playing this one pretty close to his bulletproof vest. I didn't know they were releasing Chavis. That's probably a good sign."

"The security guy said Chavis had insisted. He was subdued when I talked to him. I'll take this over to Chavis's trailer later when all his other visitors have cleared out."

Jules pulled out Virginia peanuts, a variety of chocolates, two resort mugs, tea, and hot chocolate. She arranged the contents in the basket, including a book about the history of the Blue Ridge Mountains and a magnet. She wrapped the outside with cellophane and added a huge red bow and a tag with a note from the staff at the Fern Valley Luxury Camping Resort.

"That looks good. Flattery will get you everywhere with that one," Roxanne said, taking her steaming mug to her desk. "Oh, the weather looks like it's going to be rough by the end of this week. Lester came by earlier and gave me a play-by-play of the possible paths of that hurricane in the Caribbean. The weather guys don't expect it to be a full-blown storm by the time it gets to us, but they're calling for some winds and a lot of rain for a couple of days if it stays on its current path."

"I haven't paid much attention to the news or weather lately." Jules checked some local sites and emailed a link to Sherri to make sure her team was aware that it could affect outdoor activities for a couple of days. For good measure, she sent it to Jake, too. She wasn't sure if the tiny house construction needed to be battened down.

Around three-thirty, Jules shut down her laptop, pleased that lots of things had been crossed off her to-do list. She had updated her social media sites, drafted her next newsletter, and plowed through a bunch of business council emails.

"Hey, Roxanne. I'm going to head over to see Chavis and then call it a day. Do you need anything before I leave?"

Her aunt stuck her head through the door. "Nope. I'll lock up here. Matt promised he'd come over for dinner tonight. I need to run into town and pick up food from the Good Thyme Bistro."

Jules winked at her aunt.

"What? I put it on my plates. He knows the culinary arts are not one of my many talents. He's fine with takeout. I can wow him in other ways."

Jules picked up the basket and her keys.

"Have fun. And let me know if he has any information to share," her aunt said.

Jules winked and hustled out the door.

She retraced her steps to Chavis's trailer. The weather was perfect for this time of year. No clouds in the sky and no indication of impending rain.

Titus sat in one of the patio chairs outside the trailer. The chair looked child's seat with him atop it.

"How goes it?" Jules asked.

"All's well in Chavis-land. Nice basket."

"We thought we'd give him a welcome-back gift. Is it okay to pop in?"

"Might be a little crowded. Kat and Derek are in there with him now. It's been a steady stream of visitors since you left."

"Mind if I wait a bit?"

The security guard shook his head, and Jules put her basket on the table and sat in the other chair. By the time she had checked the weather on all the local sites, the trailer door opened, and Derek Stone stepped into the sunlight. He blinked several times and pulled out a pair of Oakley sunglasses.

"See ya around," Titus said.

"Yup. Our guy's doing much better. I'll be back tomorrow." Derek turned and made his way through the row of trailers.

"Next," Titus said with a grin.

Jules picked up her basket and opened the trailer door.

Chavis sat propped up with pillows behind him on the fold-out couch. He tried to stand. "I need something to drink. And I don't mean water."

"You trying to kill yourself? You're on pain meds. You can have water or OJ," Kat snapped as she pushed him back on the couch.

Chavis scowled at her. She stepped into the tiny kitchen and retrieved a bottle of water. "Here, pretend like it's something stronger."

Jules cleared her throat and stepped inside. The pair looked at her. "I'm sorry to interrupt. I wanted to drop this off from my staff. We're glad you're back."

"And he needs his rest." Kat glared at Jules.

"Thanks for the gift. Here give it to me," Chavis said, reaching for it. He ripped off the bow and tore into the plastic. "Good stuff. Perfect for the afternoon munchies." He tossed the book on the couch.

"Let me know if you need anything." Jules backed down the steps. Before she could say goodbye to Titus, she heard a hissing sound.

She and Titus turned toward the door.

"I told you to stay put. You are the worst patient ever," Kat ranted.

"I better go see if I need to relieve her. Babysitting can be tiresome, especially with that one. See you around." Titus climbed the steps and disappeared inside.

Chapter Twenty-Seven

Wednesday

The rain poured sideways. Jules hadn't seen this much rain in years. The cabin walls creaked from the whistling wind. After waiting for it to slack off for about an hour with no avail, she grabbed her raincoat, stuffed several towels in a bag, and picked up Bijou. "Come on. We'll make a run for it. I don't think an umbrella is going to help today."

Flipping off lights, they made their way to the garage. Today's torrent called for the Jeep. When they got to the parking lot with the windshield wipers and defroster on full blast, Jules drove around the curb and parked partially under the carport behind the golf cart. "Okay, let's do this." She hugged Bijou close and pulled her raincoat around the little dog. Bijou looked at her with her best soulful eyes, which Jules took as a thank you.

"I know. We probably should have stayed in our jammies today and watched BritBox. But we've got some things to do. It's now or never."

Once inside, Bijou gave a good shake, and Jules wiggled out of her raincoat. She toweled them both off and wiped up the drips and puddles.

She put a mug under the coffee maker and made hot cocoa. Jules settled in at her desk to catch up on work. From the business council email chains, the Christmas parade had acquired four more floats, a band, a marching dance troupe, a clown car, and a horse club. Jules looked forward to the holidays.

Stomping interrupted her reminiscing. Lester and Jake trudged through the back door and shook off onto the towels at the door.

"I'd say good afternoon, but it's a frog choker out there," Lester said.

"Hey, Boss. Why'd you venture in?" Jake asked.

"I left my laptop here, and I wanted to keep up with what's going on. Plus, I was getting cabin fever. What brings you two out?"

"Doing rounds to see how things were faring. Any maintenance calls?" Jake asked, heading for the coffee maker.

"Nope. So far, so good," she replied.

"Lester, do you want coffee?" Jake asked.

The older man shook his head. "Nope, I'm good. I had two cups with breakfast. If I drink too much caffeine, I won't be able to sleep tonight."

Jules smiled. "Everything else okay on your rounds?"

"Uh, huh. The water's doing its normal runoff down the hill. The meadow area is soggy, but that's expected," Lester replied. "It's the leftover rain from that storm. Hopefully, it'll blow through here pretty quickly."

"No issues with the tiny houses or the trailers." Jake stirred his drink.

Jules's phone interrupted. She didn't recognize the California number. "Good morning. This is Jules."

"Hey, Jules. This is Drake. You in the office? I see the lights on."

"Yes. Anything I can help you with?"

"Maybe. I'll be right over."

"What's up?" Jake asked.

"Drake's on his way over." Jules rose and opened the back door. The din of the rain drowned out any conversation.

A few minutes later, Drake stomped on the cement pad of the carport. He took off his rain poncho and shook it. After draping it on the golf cart, he stomped some more and made his way inside. "Lovely day."

"Want some coffee?" Jake asked.

Bijou went from napping to security mode in three seconds. She yipped and ran around the office.

"No, thanks," the burly man replied, leaning on the counter. "Have you heard anything from Chavis lately?" He leaned over and petted Bijou.

"No, why?" Jules asked.

Lester and Jake shook their heads.

"I saw him yesterday when I dropped off the basket. He was with Kat and your guard," Jules said.

"Not sure what's up. C. J. went to relieve the night guard this morning, and no one was at the trailer. Kat was in her trailer. She said she left before it started raining. The guard wasn't anywhere to be found. I finally got in touch with the security company. He decided to leave when the weather hit. I'll deal with that later, but for now, there's no Chavis. Normally, I wouldn't care, but with his recent injury, there's no telling whether he's okay or not."

"We made the rounds this morning to check on the property. We didn't see anyone out," Jake said.

"We can help you look if you need us," Lester said.

"I don't want to create too much excitement. He's probably visiting one of his friends. If you all happen to see or hear from him, let me know."

"Will do," Jules said.

"Thanks. It's probably nothing," Drake said.

"We're going to make one more loop around and head back home. Call us if you need us," Jake said. He and Lester followed Drake out the back door.

Jules felt like she needed to alert the sheriff, but she didn't want to waste his time if Chavis was just being Chavis. Sheriff Hobbs's team had enough to do today with the weather and the flooded roads.

To kill time, she checked the actor's social media sites. He hadn't posted anything since his hospital exodus yesterday morning. Before that, there were lots of pictures of him posing with EMTs and hospital staff.

Jules fidgeted in her chair. Sitting in the office wasn't helping. Plus, it was almost lunchtime.

"Come on, Bijou. Let's blow this popsicle stand and get some lunch."

The dog's ears perked up, and she danced at the back door.

Jules walked through the office and store and made sure that everything was turned off. She draped her raincoat over her shoulders and picked up Bijou.

The pair dashed for the Jeep as the rain poured.

After tomato soup and a grilled cheese sandwich, Jules loaded the dishwasher. Household chores were perfect opportunities to think things through. *Where could Chavis have gone? Probably visiting an old or new girlfriend. And what's up with Kat? She fluctuates from nursemaid to angry harpy within a matter of minutes.*

Jules pulled out her iPad and searched social media sites. Still no postings from Chavis. Then she checked the local weather sites. It looked like the rain would move across the mountains and taper off in the early evening.

She stood and stretched and found her folder with all her notes. Staring at it didn't seem to help her deduce anything new. She grabbed a pen and doodled around Chavis's entry. The list of people who could be angry with him was endless. And the weather wasn't helping her mood either, or was it? Maybe it was the perfect time to check on some of her visitors. They'd all be holed up today. Jules changed her leather boots for her dark blue duck boots and grabbed a couple of towels.

"Guard the house for me." Bijou, happy to be inside, snuggled on the couch under her fuzzy blanket.

The Jeep was her best friend today. She drove slowly down the maintenance road. The windshield wipers were not much help with the sheeting rain. She turned off the paved road and pulled as close to the first row of vintage trailers as possible. Pulling her hood up, she dodged puddles unsuccessfully and banged on the door of Chavis's trailer. When there was no answer, she hopped back in the Jeep and drove a few rows down. Tess and Kat's trailers were side by side.

She knocked first on Tess's 1950 Airfloat. This larger camper had four portal windows on each side. It reminded Jules of a spaceship, so she themed this one in honor of Area 51 and its aliens. On her second knock, Ashe Lyons opened the door.

"Hey, Jules, what are you doing out in this mess? We didn't even hoof it over for breakfast. Come on in."

"We've been eating candy and popcorn and watching movies," Tess piped up from the couch.

Jules climbed the steps and stayed on the vinyl near the door and the kitchen.

"I was checking to make sure folks were okay. Also, have you seen or heard from Chavis today?"

The pair shook their heads. "It's been a couple of days since I've heard from him. I thought he was recovering from his ordeal." Turning toward Tess, Ashe asked, "You heard from him?"

The petite stylist looked puzzled. She checked her phone. "Nope. Nothing. He must be feeling better if he's out and about in this weather."

"Do y'all need anything?" Jules asked.

"Nope. We're fine. We'll brave the weather later for dinner. It's nice to have a day off and do nothing," Ashe said.

"See ya." Jules let herself out and trekked over to Kat's trailer next door, a 1955 Terry. This red one was built the same year as *Rebel Without a Cause*, one of her mother's favorite movies. Jules had fun decorating this one in memory of James Dean.

Jules knocked as rain dripped down her back.

Kat pulled open the door in mid-knock. "What are you doing here in this deluge?"

Jules took that as an invitation to come in and stepped across the threshold as Kat backed up.

"Just checking on folks. You okay?" Jules dripped in the foyer.

"I'm fine. Glad to have the day off to chill," Kat looked over her shoulder. The taller woman blocked Jules's entrance to the rest of the trailer.

Curiosity got the better of her, and Jules strained to peek around Kat, who spread her arms out like she was going to physically block Jules if she tried to step farther into the trailer. Dishes were piled in the sink and on the counter, and the trash can in the little red and white 1950s kitchen overflowed.

Jules pasted on her best smile. "I'm glad you're enjoying your day off. How is Chavis doing?"

"Sleeping like a baby, I hope. I left last night when the rain started to come down. I needed some downtime. Hopefully, he's using his free day to rest and heal."

"It was so nice of you to help him out. You're awesome." Jules hoped none of the sarcasm she felt seeped out.

"Uh, thanks. Don't stay out in this weather too long. You'll get sick." Kat inched toward the door.

Jules glanced around the trailer. "Okay. See you around."

Jules heard a muffled sound and a noise that sounded like someone dropped something.

Kat coughed.

"Did you hear that?" Jules asked as she turned toward the door.

"No. Sorry. I got choked. I hope I'm not coming down with anything. I think I need to lie down."

"I hope you feel better." Jules pulled up her hood and stepped outside. The wind had died down. At least the rain no longer blew horizontally.

Jules didn't buy Kat's attempt at a coverup. It sounded like a middle schooler trying to mask what she said with a fake cough or sneeze. She walked around the perimeter of the tiny camper, trying to peek in the windows, but all the shades were drawn. She rounded the corner at the end of the bedroom, ducked under the shaded window, and knocked with her fist. A few seconds later, someone inside echoed the knock. Jules repeated her knock, and someone inside answered.

Standing on her tiptoes, she tried to steal a glance in the window, but the shades covered every inch of space.

Jules turned and slogged through the mud back to her Jeep. Once inside, she locked the doors. She texted Drake, **Meet me at the office? I have a hunch.**

B There in a few, he responded.

Jules started the Wrangler and bounced through the mud and puddles to the carport behind the office. She slid out of her rain jacket and kicked off her muddy boots before going inside.

Jules had enough time to find the strongest coffee pod and start the machine before she heard a knock at the back door. Drake had removed his jacket and motorcycle boots, too.

"Coffee?" Jules pointed to her mug.

"Sure. What's up?" Drake pulled out one of the vinyl chairs and sat at the kitchen table.

"I was playing Nancy Drew this afternoon. Ashe and Tess haven't seen Chavis. Then I popped in on Kat. She was surprised, and she did everything but body-block me from the inside of her trailer. I got as far as the entryway."

"Go on," he said while the coffee maker chugged.

"She acted really odd. She was Miss Nursemaid yesterday, and today, she needed her space. I heard a noise in the trailer, and she shooed me out the door. Then I circled the trailer. Near the bedroom wall, I knocked, and someone knocked back. I think it's Chavis," she whispered.

"Why are we whispering?"

"I don't know. It felt all spy versus spy. I think Kat is hiding something."

"She was supposed to stay with him last night, and so was the guard. When I called the company, the supervisor said the guard told him he was sent home by the lady in charge."

Jules raised her eyebrows. "What lady in charge? And why would she dismiss the guard?"

Drake shrugged his shoulders. "Something's definitely up."

"So, what do we do about it?"

It was Drake's turn to raise his eyebrows. "We?"

"I'm the one who thinks she found Chavis, and he might be in danger."

"Or having some kind of fling. We can't bust in there," he said as Jules rose to get his drink. "Black is fine," he said, and she put the mug in front of him. Drake made the mug look like part of a child's tea set when he enveloped it with one hand. "Okay, I guess it's we. You did a better job sleuthing than my guys did."

"I had a hunch. Kat's behavior was odd. She definitely didn't want me to see something. Chavis seems to be the hub among all the other things that have been going on around here lately. I'm not sure how Kat fits in, but I'm going to find out," Jules said. "When we first met, she was super friendly and chatty. Then her attitude chilled."

"She's like that. Kat seems to have one friend at a time. She'll move from person to person. She flips loyalties in the blink of an eye."

"So, what's the plan?" Jules asked.

Drake pulled out his phone and tapped in a message. "Let's wait for it to get dark. For now, I've got Titus watching Chavis's trailer. I told him to check out Kat's place." He tapped furiously on his phone.

"This time of year, it's dark a little after six."

"That's not that far off. We need some excuse to get in to see her."

"Can't you text her and say you have some changes in the schedule because of today's weather?" Jules asked.

"I guess. Sherri usually does all of that via text. I could say I have a message from Rod. She might buy that."

Drake pulled out his phone again and tapped another message. "It's almost six now. Titus has the front door covered, and C. J.'s around back. Let's head over there."

It took the pair a few minutes to put on boots and raincoats. Although the rain had slacked off considerably, the temperature had dropped. Jules flipped up her hood while Drake took out a black watch cap from his pocket and pulled it on.

The pair walked across the field and down the rows of vintage trailers. Jules huffed and puffed to keep up with Drake's stride.

Two rows before Kat's trailer, he stopped suddenly, and Jules almost ran into the back of him. "Let's go that way and walk around the back first." He checked his phone. "Titus said the lights are on, and no one's left since he's been there. Follow me."

The mountain of a man wended his way through the vintage trailers on a path far from Kat's trailer. Then he turned and circled back. Drake signaled for Jules to be silent. They crept closer to the red and white trailer. C. J. popped his head around a neighboring blue trailer and saluted. Drake nodded and moved closer.

He tried to see in the window, too, but the shades were still drawn. Not even a sliver of light was visible. Jules moved to where she heard the knocking earlier. She tapped a rhythm that sounded like Woody Woodpecker's laugh. The pair waited, and the knock repeated from inside the trailer. Jules paused and knocked again. After a few seconds, the pattern echoed.

Drake motioned for her to follow him as C. J. moved closer to the red trailer.

At the corner of the trailer, Drake pointed for her to stay. Jules hunched down under the front window as Drake made his way to the door.

Jules heard him pound on the door. Kat said something that she couldn't hear, and then she heard Drake say, "Sorry to bother you, but Rod wanted you to know."

Jules heard the aluminum door shut. She counted to ten and poked her head around the trailer. She tiptoed closer to eavesdrop.

Jules heard a crash and then another loud thump. She jumped and then panicked because there was nowhere to hide on the patio. Before she could decide which way to run, the trailer door flew open, and Kat dashed out the door in three-inch boots.

Fight or flight. Jules turned and put up her arms. She slammed into the taller woman, who wobbled and fell to the ground, clawing at Jules. Before Jules could step back, Kat yanked on her leg and pulled Jules down on the cement pad. Wrestlemania was on! The two tussled on the ground. Kat grabbed Jules's ponytail while. Jules stuck her thumb between Kat's ribs, and the woman recoiled and let go.

Kat moaned and rolled over. She crawled toward Jules, grabbing at her ankle. Jules slammed her muddy boot down in the middle of Kat's forehead. The woman froze for a minute. Then she crawled a few feet away. *Where were Drake's guys? Where was Drake?*

Kat stood and leaned over, holding her head. Then Jules pounced on Kat like she was a beanbag chair. She knocked the taller woman over and landed with a whumph on her back, pinning the stylist to the ground. The air seemed to leak out of Kat like a punctured balloon.

Jules hung on tightly until a pair of hands lifted her off the other woman. Titus moved her to the edge of the patio. Then he zip-tied the prone woman's hands. "That should hold her for a while. I think you knocked the wind out of her."

Kat looked like she was hog-tied. Her wild hair and the mud spatters on her clothes and forehead added to the imagery.

Jules wondered if she looked like she had been wrestling a pig. She was pretty sure she looked as bad as Kat.

The aluminum door swung open, and Drake half-dragged Chavis out of the trailer. "I found him tied up beside the bed."

"I'm fine," Chavis said weakly. "I need a drink and a chance to talk to the sheriff before she does." He pointed to Kat, who hadn't moved since Titus secured her.

"Let's go back to your office. There's plenty of room there. Jules, can you get hold of your sheriff?" Drake asked.

Jules nodded and whipped out her phone. She tapped Sheriff Hobbs's contact. After two rings, she heard "What's up, Jules?"

"We have a situation here. Can you swing by the resort? Kat took Chavis hostage. He's fine. I'm with Drake and his crew. We're taking Chavis and Kat to the office. Can you meet us there?"

"Not a problem. Everyone okay?"

"Seems to be, but you may want to bring someone to check Chavis out. I'm not sure how long Kat had him tied up. And Kat and I had a little wrestling match. She'll probably have something to say to you about that. We'll see you at the office."

She thought she heard Sheriff Hobbs snicker as he disconnected.

The posse trudged through the mud and puddles. Drake held onto Chavis, who stumbled as he walked. C. J. and Titus bookended Kat. The pair half-led, half-dragged the stylist across the grass.

Jules punched in the security code, and the motley crew stepped inside. Drake put Chavis in a chair at the table, and C. J. stood by Kat, who stood behind Roxanne's guest chair.

"Anybody want coffee?"

The men shook their heads.

"Do you have a Coke or something?" Chavis asked.

Jules pulled a soft drink from the fridge and handed it to him. The pop and fizzle echoed through the quiet office.

Jules heard tapping on the front door, and she rushed through the store. She held the wooden screen door, and Sheriff Hobbs and Deputy Caswell stepped inside, removing their hats almost simultaneously.

"They're back here." Jules pointed to the office.

"Take the stylist to the front and shut the door," Sheriff Hobbs said to his deputy.

When the door closed, the sheriff pulled out his black notebook. "What's going on here?"

The men looked at each other. Chavis stood and waved his arms wide. "Kat and I got into an argument last night, and she tripped me. Then she tied me up and made me go to her trailer in the middle of that monsoon."

"Why?" Sheriff Hobbs asked.

"I'm getting to that part. We were eating dinner and having some wine. I know. I know I probably shouldn't have with my meds, but I was so sick of being out of action. I wanted things to get back to normal. And I also had an epiphany after my life-changing incident in the storage trailer. I decided that since I lived through that attack and kidnapping, I was going to come clean and be a better person."

"And how does that involve Kat?" the sheriff asked.

"Kat kept asking me if I knew who attacked me after the poker game. I honestly don't remember, but she wouldn't let it go. She kept getting more and more agitated."

"Then what happened?" Sheriff Hobbs asked.

"I wanted to call you and confess that I killed Sorbonne. I needed to come clean. But Kat flew into a rage and wouldn't hear of it. She went cuckoo on me and told me to keep my mouth shut. Or she'd see to it that I stayed quiet."

"Okay, explain the Sorbonne part to me." Sheriff Hobbs stared at Chavis, who leaned on one of the chairs.

"I need to sit down."

"Go ahead. Take your time," the sheriff said.

"I found out that Sorbonne was mad at me for dating Kat and a few other people, and she was going to write me out of the script. I couldn't have that. This is a lucrative job, and I play a popular character. Anyway, I told Kat, and she hatched the plan that we get rid of Sorbonne. One night after a lot of tequila, she coaxed her outside, and I waited in the shadows." He paused and coughed.

"You okay?" the sheriff asked.

Chavis nodded and continued, "Kat and Sorbonne fought, but not like the fight that Jules and Kat had today. That was epic. Anyway, back to Sorbonne. It was kind of dark that night. I couldn't tell what was going on, and then Kat called for me to help drag Sorbonne to one of those tiny houses. She handed me a pair of scissors and said that Sorbonne hated me enough to get me fired." He took a deep breath. "It was my turn to fly into a rage. I stabbed her. I think in the neck. You see, I killed Sorbonne." His voice trailed off to a whisper.

Everyone fell silent. Sheriff Hobbs stared at Chavis. "You killed her?"

"Yep. I don't know what came over me. It was like I was blinded by rage. I stabbed her."

"You were definitely involved, but you didn't kill her," Sheriff Hobbs said.

Chavis frowned and glared at the sheriff. "What? Of course, I did. I've been consumed by guilt for days. When Kat found out I was seeing Poppy again, she wanted money to keep quiet about Sorbonne. I knew I loved Poppy. We were going to try to make it work. She was going to dump Rod and everything. Poppy and I were even talking about moving in together. I think it sent Kat over the edge."

"Captain America," Jules said quietly.

Chavis turned his head and looked at her. A faint smile almost crossed his face. "That's what Poppy called me. I thought we had something."

The sheriff cleared his throat. "Kat blackmailed you?"

Chavis nodded. "She said she would tell that I killed Sorbonne."

"The autopsy came back. Sorbonne was choked to death. The stab wounds happened after she was already dead." The sheriff pursed his lips and paused.

The blood drained from Chavis's face. Jules thought he was going to pass out.

Jules ran a dish towel under the faucet, twisted it out, and handed it to the actor. He wiped his face and sobbed slowly into the towel. "It can't be. She said I killed her. She threatened to ruin me. She made it out to be all my fault."

The actor put his head in his arms and sobbed. Jules patted him on the back.

Then almost as suddenly as the crying started, it stopped. Chavis sat up, ran the towel over his splotchy face, and then fluffed his hair with his fingers. "Well, that's a shock and a relief," he said.

"How did the rest of you get involved in this?" Sheriff Hobbs asked.

Drake cleared his throat. "Chavis wasn't in his trailer when my guy went to relieve the contracted guard. We couldn't find him. Kat sent the guard home when the storm started. We looked all over the place but couldn't find Chavis. I told Jules, and she figured out he was in Kat's trailer."

"Of course, she did," Sheriff Hobbs said. Jules frowned, and he cracked a smile. "What happened?"

"I knew Chavis couldn't have gone far in the storm. I first went to see Tess and Ashe. They hadn't seen him. Then I went to see Kat. She wouldn't let me in the trailer, and she tried to rush me out. Then I heard a noise. I walked around the outside of the trailer and knocked on the walls. I heard knocking back. I knew something wasn't right, so I texted Drake."

"And my guys watched the trailer," Drake added. C. J. and Titus nodded.

"Do you have paper?" the sheriff asked Jules.

She nodded and pulled several legal pads out of a drawer.

"Y'all write down everything you remember while I go up front with Deputy Caswell." Sheriff Hobbs closed the Dutch door.

About a half hour later, the sheriff returned and collected the group's statements. "Chavis, I'm going to take you to the station. I need you to answer some more questions. And I'm going to get an EMT to check you out."

"Am I being charged? I'm the victim here. She framed me," Chavis whined. "You said I had nothing to do with Sorbonne's murder."

"I said you didn't kill her. I'm not arresting you. It'll be up to the Commonwealth's Attorney whether or not you'll be charged with anything."

Chavis let out a heavy sigh and rose. "I hope that's good news. Where's Kat?"

"Deputy Caswell arrested her for the murders of Sorbonne and Poppy

Carlson. And for kidnapping you. I'm sure there will be more charges."

A thin smile crossed Chavis's face. He followed the sheriff out the front door.

Drake turned and looked at Jules. "Good job. If you ever want a job in security, call me."

Jules smiled. All she wanted at the moment was a hot shower.

Chapter Twenty-Eight

Thursday

The rain from what was left of Hurricane Jocelyn blew over the mountains, and the morning was the exact opposite of the day before. Jules and Bijou enjoyed the sun, puffy clouds, and the crisp air on their walk to the office.

When she opened the door, the terrier bounded through the store and followed the sounds of voices to the office. Jake leaned against the counter, and Roxanne tapped her foot on the floor next to the coffee maker.

"Hey, Boss. What's new?" Jake said. His face lit up with a smile when she walked in. He picked up Bijou and rubbed behind her ears.

"Not much. It looks like things have settled down here. What a difference a day makes."

"The sheriff said they're charging Kat with a list of crimes as long as my arm," Roxanne added as the machine sputtered and sent a flow of hot liquid in her mug.

The front door creaked and opened. Bijou barked and raced to see who the new person was. Sheriff Hobbs walked into the office with a furry shadow in tow. "Morning, all."

"I thought you were going to be tied up for days with all the paperwork," Roxanne said, smiling at her beau.

"Just wanted to check on things here. I need to talk with the producer and director. We're having a press conference this afternoon at the station, and they wanted an update."

"Coffee?" she asked.

"I'm good. I stopped in to see how you all were doing. Jules, you okay after your smackdown with that Hollywood gal?"

"Hey, a girl's gotta do what a girl's gotta do." Jules cracked a wry smile. "I'm fine." She plopped down in her office chair and rubbed both of her knees. "Nothing that a couple of aspirin won't cure."

"Kat's admitted to kidnapping Chavis and fighting with Sorbonne. But she said Sorbonne's death was an accident. Then, in a flash of anger, she blamed Chavis for it. She also denies having anything to do with Poppy's murder. But my guys say otherwise. They have her phone records, and they found Poppy's cell phone in Kat's suitcase. She's got a lot of explaining to do. Right now, she's blaming everyone else. And it turns out her prints match the one you found on the doorjamb. She wasn't in the system previously."

Jules raised both eyebrows. "What about Chavis?"

"If he gets charged with anything, it will be minor. He looks more like a victim as we flesh out the details. Kat was vindictive, and she took her anger out on anyone with an interest in Chavis."

"Was that the reason for Poppy's death?" Roxanne asked.

The sheriff nodded. "She admitted in one of the interviews that Chavis was going to leave her for Poppy."

"A woman scorned," Jake muttered.

A slight smile crossed the sheriff's face. "She's lawyered up, so we'll see what happens. I've got to go over and talk to the producer."

"I'm sure they'll figure out a way to spin it to help the show," Roxanne added. "And Chavis will be the center of attention. I don't know about y'all, but I won't miss all the Hollywood drama when they leave town. I could use some small-town peace and quiet for a while."

Jules smiled. "I don't want the murders to leave a stain on the resort or the town."

"Don't worry about it too much," Sheriff Hobbs said. "People have short memories. They'll be on to the next big thing in a few days. I think you're doing a good job, and the town benefited from all the dollars that poured in from the filming."

"Y'all look so serious," Roxanne interjected. "Relax. How 'bout we all go to town for dinner tonight to celebrate Nancy Drew and Dick Tracy here and truth, justice, and the American way? I think Pop's burgers and apple pie would be what we all need."

"And milkshakes," Sheriff Hobbs said. "The presser is at three. I'll text you when I'm done, and we can settle on a time. Dinner away from the station or my car sounds nice for a change. Thanks, Jules, for all of your help. You definitely have a knack for finding information." He winked. "But what are you going to do with no more murderers to track down?"

"We've got a whole lot of planning for the holiday lights festival still left to do, and I'm pretty sure that I'm going to recruit all of you to help." Jules winked back and pulled out green and red folders with the business council logo on the front. "Sheriff, you're in charge of the parade."

Roxanne laughed. "I thought you were going to make him play Santa."

"That would be more fun." Sheriff Hobbs plopped his Smokey Bear hat on and strode out the front door.

Jules's Easy Peanut Butter and Honey Fudge

Jules loves peanut butter and honey sandwiches, and this is one of her favorite candy recipes.

Ingredients

- 1 cup of creamy peanut butter
- 1 cup of granulated sugar
- ¼ cup of milk
- 3 tablespoons of honey
- 1 ½ teaspoons of vanilla extract

Instructions

Grease an 8 x 8 baking pan. Mix sugar and milk in a small pot and bring to a boil. Boil the mixture for about 3 minutes. Add the honey and peanut butter. Stir well. Add the vanilla extract and continue to stir the mixture.

Pour the fudge mixture into the baking pan. Refrigerate for at least 5 hours. It will be firmer if you can refrigerate it overnight. Cut and serve.

Crockpot Chicken and Dumplings

Ingredients

- 1 chopped onion
- 1 ¼ pound skinless chicken breasts
- 1 teaspoon dried oregano
- 2 (10.5 ounce) cans of cream of chicken soup
- 2 cups of chicken broth (low sodium is best)
- 2 stalks of celery (chopped)
- 2 large carrots (chopped)
- 1 cup of peas (frozen works well)
- 3 cloves of garlic, minced
- 1 (16 ounce) can of refrigerated biscuits (plain)
- Pinch of Kosher salt
- Freshly ground black pepper to taste
- Fresh thyme to taste
- 1 bay leaf

Instructions

Put the onions, chicken, oregano, salt, and pepper in the slow cooker. Pour in soup and broth. Add the thyme and bay leaf. Cover and cook on high for 3 hours.

Discard the bay leaf and thyme. Shred the chicken with a fork. Add celery, carrots, peas, and garlic.

Cut the biscuits into small pieces and mix into the chicken mixture.

Cook on high until the vegetables are tender. The biscuits need about an hour to cook completely.

Jules's Fabulous Honey Butter

Ingredients

- ¾ cup of butter (salted and sweet cream)
- ¼ cup of honey

Instructions

In a bowl, mix the honey and butter until smooth. Store covered in the fridge. This is good for spreading on toast, biscuits, and bagels.

Baked Spaghetti Pie

Ingredients

- 6 ounces of spaghetti, cooked and drained
- 2 large eggs (beat well)
- 1 cup of spaghetti sauce
- 1 cup shredded parmesan cheese
- 1 cup shredded mozzarella cheese
- 2 tablespoons of olive oil (or melted butter)
- 1 cup of ricotta cheese (or cottage cheese)

Instructions

Preheat the oven to 350 degrees F. Lightly grease a 10-inch pie pan or glass baking dish.

Toss the hot spaghetti with olive oil or butter. Combine eggs and half of the parmesan and mozzarella. Stir the mixture. Add the ricotta and spaghetti sauce. Mix well. Then stir in the remaining cheeses.

Bake uncovered for 25 minutes. Add a garnish of cheese, if desired, and bake for 5 more minutes. Cool for 10 minutes and cut into wedges or squares. This makes about six servings.

Lula Bell's Famous Strawberry Lemonade

Ingredients

- 2 cups of fresh (or frozen) strawberries
- 7 cups of water
- 1 cup of sugar
- 2 cups of lemon juice

Instructions

Combine the sugar and 2 cups of water. Microwave for 2 minutes or until all the sugar has dissolved.

Blend 1 cup of water and the strawberries until the mixture is smooth.

Combine the strawberry mixture, sugar water, lemon juice, and remaining water in a pitcher.

Stir thoroughly. Chill the drink until it's time to serve.

If you want to garnish the drinks, slice lemons, mint, and strawberries and stir into the drink before serving.

Acknowledgements

I want to thank my family and friends who provided all the wonderful support for me and this book: Stan Weidner, thanks for being the key part of my writing life, my parents who instilled in me a lifelong love of reading, Cortney Cain for being my texting buddy at five a.m., Meagan and Jocelyn Cain, my social media gurus, and Bill Cain for always keeping everyone entertained.

I appreciate all the encouragement, love, and support from my Bethia UMC family.

Many thanks to Matt Heath for answering all my film, TV, and crew questions. Thank you to Joy Pfister and her wonderful crew at Studio FBJ for making me look good.

I am so grateful for my talented Sisters in Crime, Guppy, and James River Writer friends. Your support is invaluable! Jayne Ormerod, Mary Burton, Lane Stone, Sherry Harris, Susan Van Kirk – You all are so gracious with your support and advice.

I have the best critique group on the planet: Susan Campbell, Catherine Brennan, K. L. Murphy, Amy Lilly, Sandie Warwick, and Marjorie Bagby. These ladies provide the most interesting feedback.

Many, many thanks to my fabulous agent, Dawn Dowdle and her team for all the help and hard work. And a huge thank you to Shawn Reilly Simmons and the infamous Dames of Detection, and everyone at Level Best Books for letting me share what goes on in Fern Valley.

I am so grateful for my readers who follow Jules, Jake, Roxanne, and Bijou's adventures.

About the Author

Through the years, Heather Weidner has been a cop's kid, technical writer, editor, college professor, software tester, and IT manager. *Film Crews and Rendezvous* is the second in her cozy mystery series, the Jules Keene Glamping Mysteries. She also writes the Delanie Fitzgerald mystery series and the Mermaid Bay Christmas Shoppe Mysteries (2023).

Her short stories appear in the *Virginia is for Mysteries* series, *50 Shades of Cabernet, Deadly Southern Charm,* and *Murder by the* Glass, and her novellas appear in The Mutt Mysteries series.

She is a member of Sisters in Crime and active in Central Virginia, Chessie, and Guppies Chapters, International Thriller Writers, and James River Writers.

Originally from Virginia Beach, Heather has been a mystery fan since Scooby-Doo and Nancy Drew. She lives in Central Virginia with her husband and a pair of Jack Russell terriers.

SOCIAL MEDIA HANDLES:
 Twitter: https://twitter.com/HeatherWeidner1
 Facebook: https://www.facebook.com/HeatherWeidnerAuthor
 Instagram: https://www.instagram.com/heather_mystery_writer/

Goodreads: https://www.goodreads.com/author/show/8121854.Heather_Weidner

Amazon Authors: http://www.amazon.com/-/e/B00HOYR0MQ

Pinterest: https://www.pinterest.com/HeatherBWeidner/

LinkedIn: https://www.linkedin.com/in/heather-weidner-0064b233?trk=hp-identity-name

BookBub: https://www.bookbub.com/authors/heather-weidner-d6430278-c5c9-4b10-b911-340828fc7003

TikTok: https://www.tiktok.com/@heather_weidner_author

YouTube: https://www.youtube.com/channel/UCyBjyB0zz-M1DaM-rU1bXGA?view_as=subscriber

AUTHOR WEBSITE:

http://HeatherWeidner.com

Also by Heather Weidner

The Delanie Fitzgerald Mysteries: *Secret Lives and Private Eyes; The Tulip Shirt Murders; Glitter, Glam, and Contraband;* and *Male Revues and Subterfuge*

The Jules Keene Mysteries: *Vintage Trailers and Blackmailers* and *Film Crews and Rendezvous*

The Mutt Mysteries: *To Fetch a Thief, To Fetch a Scoundrel, To Fetch a Villain,* and *To Fetch a Killer*

Short Stories: *Virginia is for Mysteries, Virginia is for Mysteries II, Virginia is for Mysteries III, Deadly Southern Charm, 50 Shades of Cabernet,* and *Murder by the Glass*

Nonfiction: *The Secret Ingredient – The Mystery Writers' Cookbook*

www.ingramcontent.com/pod-product-compliance
Lightning Source LLC
Chambersburg PA
CBHW020617110726
47899CB00002B/545